DEVIL IN DISGUISE

QUENTIN SECURITY SERIES #4

MORGAN JAMES

CHAPTER
ONE

KATE

The receptionist sitting beneath the Walker and Raines placard smiled at me, and I returned it despite the turmoil swirling in my stomach. I hated coming in here. God willing, this would be the last time I ever had to see the inside of this office and the people in it.

Not that I had anything against my lawyer—the guy was a total shark, not to mention incredibly easy on the eyes. Gavin Price was both a welcome and unsettling distraction from the reason for my visit.

I pulled open the door and strode into the welcoming air-conditioning, then pushed my sunglasses to the top of my head. The receptionist sitting beneath the Walker and Raines placard smiled at me, and I returned it despite the turmoil swirling in my stomach.

I stepped up to the desk and signed in. "I have a ten o'clock with Mr. Price."

The older woman nodded and clicked away at the keyboard. "I'll let him know you're here."

The appreciative smile melted from my face as a familiar voice spoke from behind me, and I automatically stiffened.

"Hey, Katie."

I closed my eyes for a moment before turning to face my soon-to-be-ex-husband. "Steve."

His eyes flicked over me before zeroing in on my forehead. "How are you feeling?"

"Fine, thanks." Self-consciously, I lifted one hand and arranged my bangs to cover the wound as best I could. I'd been in my office at the healthplex a little over a week ago, getting ready to head out for a girls' night with my friend Victoria, when a man seemingly came out of nowhere. Something had sliced through the air, and pain exploded across my forehead. The next thing I was aware of was waking in the hospital a day later.

Thank God, Victoria had let herself in and scared him away, then run for help. Her boyfriend, Blake, had come to my rescue and kept me stable until the medics arrived. The man had escaped, but the ordeal had cost me seventeen stitches and one hell of a bruise. The wound was still an angry red line against my face. "Stitches came out yesterday, but..."

Steve nodded. He knew the drill. Like me, he was a licensed medical professional, and we shared a practice in the healthplex downtown. Though for how long, I didn't know. Steve had proposed during college, and I'd happily agreed to marry him, a youthful, rash decision that seemed to make sense at the time. We'd had everything all planned out—we would graduate, start a practice together, then, once it was established, we'd start a family. Except it hadn't quite worked out that way.

"How's Libby?"

Steve's gaze cut away before meeting mine again. "She's good."

"And the baby?"

His face relaxed, taking on an expression of elation. "Healthy. It's a girl."

His words were like a knife to my heart, and I offered a small smile, then dropped my gaze to the travertine tile floor. Up until just a few months ago, I thought everything was fine. Not perfect, certainly, but it was... okay. We were both busy with work, and I hadn't seen the signs until it was too late.

From the information I'd gleaned from friends, the affair had started a little over eight months ago. Steve had gone on a health kick and joined a new gym. It was there that he'd met the perky little blonde and fallen head over heels for her. The fact that he had a wife was apparently little more than a blip on his radar. Within a couple months, Libby was pregnant, and he'd presented me with divorce papers.

Thank God we hadn't rushed into starting a family. I would never want to drag kids through this. It was bad enough that we were fighting over the business. The house, I didn't care about. I hadn't stepped inside since the day I'd learned about the affair. It had taken just under ten hours for me and two friends to pack up my belongings and my fur baby, Peanut, and move me into a condo across town.

"Mr. and Mrs. Gerber? You can come back now." The receptionist gestured to the long hallway, and I breathed a sigh of relief, grateful that I didn't have to stand there any longer and feign interest in the man who had left me for another woman.

Steve gestured for me to precede him into the room, and I slipped by, careful not to brush against him. After his infidelity, I could barely stand to be in the same room with him, let alone touch him. I couldn't help the resentment I felt toward him. He'd chosen to cheat instead of work things out or even address the issue, and I could never forgive him for that. I knew I was better off without someone like Steve in my life, but his betrayal still hurt.

I'd known for a while that things were... off. But after six years of marriage, wasn't that to be expected? The potent sexual desire we'd experienced at twenty-two had gradually declined, and the last time we'd had sex was more than a year ago. It had felt stiff and awkward, like a necessary evil performed out of obligation. Although I'd blamed Steve for his cheating, I couldn't help but wonder if I'd been partially responsible for driving him away.

In the process of building our careers, there had been so many long nights, so much to do. And I was acutely aware that I'd changed since college, too. I'd put on a few pounds and rarely wore makeup. Was Steve more physically attracted to Libby or was it purely chemistry, a connection between them that had never existed between Steve and me? Maybe if I'd tried harder...

I stepped into the conference room, my gaze automatically drawn to the man standing by the coffee service. His broad shoulders stretched the fabric of his dark suit, and his pants were perfectly tailored, skimming his muscular thighs and breaking perfectly over his polished shoes. Gavin Price was the kind of man who had been put on this earth purely for women's pleasure. His dark eyes caught mine as he turned, and I blushed furiously, quickly averting my eyes as I sank into a chair.

"Would you like some coffee, Ms. Winfield? Water?" I reluctantly lifted my eyes to meet Gavin's intense gaze. He was the only person outside of my patients who called me by my maiden name. Though I had taken Steve's last name for personal use as per tradition, I'd chosen to maintain my maiden name professionally. I was damn proud of what I'd accomplished, and I wanted my name—and my name alone—on that degree.

Those deep brown eyes continued to bore into me, and I shifted under the scrutiny. As lawyers went, I couldn't have chosen better. Gavin Price was a shark. Better than that, though, he was gorgeous. Not just attractive, more than handsome, the man was model material.

The lines of his face were sharp, almost angular, with high cheekbones and the tiniest hint of a cleft in his chin. Coffee-colored eyes stood out from his lightly tanned skin, and his thick, dark brown hair was cropped short. He left just enough at the top for a woman to run her hands through, to play with the silky-looking strands. At a couple inches over six feet, he was every fantasy come to life.

Heat raced through my blood and I forced myself to swallow and respond. "No, thank you."

He studied me for another moment before turning away to pour himself a glass of water. He made his way around the table then unbuttoned his suit jacket before sliding into the seat next to me. I glanced at him out of the corner of my eye. This close to him, I could smell the unmistakable scent of his aftershave, or maybe his cologne. It was musky and masculine, an apt fit for the man sitting only inches away.

I glanced over my shoulder as Richard Patterson entered the room, thankful for the distraction. He slipped into the seat next to Steve and flashed a smile in my direction. He was a nice enough guy, but since he was Steve's lawyer, I kind of disliked him on principle. "Good morning, Kate."

I nodded politely, eager to start the proceedings. I was tired of this dragging out. All I wanted was an expeditious resolution so I could get on with my life. Whatever the hell that meant. Ever since the incident at the healthplex, I'd been seriously contemplating my future. Maybe it was time to leave the past where it belonged and start something new.

Gavin spoke up. "All right, are we ready to begin?" After a quick check around the table, he launched into his discourse. "So, we've decided that Mr. Gerber will retain the house and my client will receive compensation for her portion upon completion. Now we have the matter of the office at the healthplex. In light of Mr. Gerber's infidelity, I feel that Kate should be awarded the business and—"

"Actually..." His head snapped toward me as I laid a gentle hand on his arm. "I'm strongly considering selling out. Would you mind if Steve and I spoke alone for a moment?"

Gavin's eyes blazed with fury. "Kate, that's not—"

"I think that's a great idea," Steve spoke up from the opposite side of the table.

Gavin threw a glare his way, then swiveled toward me once more. "As your lawyer, I strongly advise—"

I curled my fingertips into the fabric of his suit jacket and felt the muscles of his forearm tense beneath my touch. "Just give us a minute. Please."

He searched my eyes for a long moment, then finally seemed to accept my need for privacy. He didn't look at all happy about it, but he shoved his chair back from the table and stood, nodding to Richard as he did so. "We'll give you two a moment—but we'll be right outside."

I couldn't decide if it was a warning or... something more. There was something in his tone that I'd never quite heard before. As soon as it flitted through my mind, I shook the thought away. It wasn't like I knew the man well enough to make any assumptions about his behavior. He was my lawyer —he was paid to act in my best interest. And right now, this sudden change of plans was like a train derailing that he couldn't stop.

I waited until the door latch clicked into place, then I met Steve's gaze. For a long moment, we just stared at each other, separated by the table between us and a mountain of lies. How had we gotten to this point? I'd loved him once; now there was far too much to overcome.

I cleared my throat. "As I'm sure you can imagine, I have no desire to work at the healthplex."

He dipped his chin, and his eyes swept over my face again. "I'm glad you're okay."

I offered a tight smile. "Thank you."

"Libby and I are getting married."

The words exploded from his throat, and my heart seized in my chest. All of a sudden, I knew exactly how a deer felt in its final seconds before being splattered all over the highway. Steve looked uncomfortable, his gaze fixed on the table, and I forced myself to draw air into my lungs. Our divorce wasn't even finalized, and he was ready to sprint to the altar with her the second the ink was dry? It wasn't totally unexpected considering the circumstances, but... *damn*. Hearing those words *hurt*.

"Congratulations." Hot tears stung my eyes, and I quickly blinked them away.

Silence fell again before he finally let out a harsh sigh. "Look. I'm sorry." I quirked a brow, and he continued. "I want to do what's right. You deserve better. I should have done things... differently."

No shit. I almost snorted a laugh but managed to smother it before it could escape. I didn't trust myself to speak, so I just nodded.

Steve studied me. "What are you going to do?"

I shrugged. "I haven't decided yet. But I think it's better for both of us if I bow out."

"What about your patients?"

"I'll finish out the month, if that works for you. That'll give you some time to bring in another physician, or... whatever you want to do."

"So, you've really thought about this?"

I nodded. "I have. Ever since..." I trailed off, and he nodded sympathetically.

"I understand." He took a deep breath. "If you truly want out, I'd be more than happy to buy you out. At a premium."

His mouth quirked into a small smile at my look of skepticism. "I don't want to fight over this anymore. When you got hurt..." His eyes darted to my forehead, and I barely resisted the urge to lift my hand to cover the wound from his inspection. "I was so worried about you. It got me thinking about old times. We had fun together."

My throat tightened, and I closed my eyes. How could he say that to me? If we'd had fun together, then how the hell had we ended up here? If he'd loved me, why had he cheated on me? The pain was still too fresh for me to look back on the fond memories of our times together. I wanted to lash out, to scream at him for his unfaithfulness, but what was the point?

He's not worth it. Repeating my new mantra in my mind, I swallowed down every acrid word on my tongue and met his gaze.

"I really am sorry, Kate. I should have been up-front with you. Let me make it up to you."

Trying to come up with something other than the words that started with *f* and ended with *u,* I bit my lip and swallowed down my contempt. "That's... generous of you."

"It's not nearly enough, I know. I'm sorry I hurt you." His gaze cut toward the window as he spoke. "I know you don't want to hear it, but I really do love Libby."

And, just like that, my heart broke a little more. There was nothing quite like sitting across from the person you thought you'd spend the rest of your life with only to have him tell you how much he loved another woman.

"You're wonderful, Kate. Some guy will be lucky to have you."

But not you, I thought bitterly. I clearly hadn't been wonderful enough, otherwise he wouldn't have left me for the blonde bimbo with more boobs than brains. It was uncharitable, but I couldn't give a damn at the moment. I'd never actually met the woman—nor did I ever intend to—but alcohol and the internet were a deadly combination.

After a couple glasses of wine one night—oh, who the hell was I kidding? I'd drunk the entire bottle—I'd dug up everything I could find on the young woman. Barely twenty-two, she'd just graduated college with a degree in Liberal Arts and was working as a trainer at Steve's new gym. How fucking clichéd.

The door opened, and Gavin entered first, his gaze immediately zeroing in on me. He must not have liked the expression on my face, because he strode toward me and leaned close, one hand resting on the back of my chair.

"Are you okay?"

Those intense brown eyes seared into mine, and I offered a small smile. "Everything's fine."

The corners of his mouth dipped into a frown, like he didn't believe a word. I lifted a brow and nodded to the chair beside me. If possible, his expression darkened further, but he sat anyway. I let out a soft sigh of relief and leaned back in my chair. From my vantage point, I watched Gavin's leg bounce anxiously under the table.

I knew he was just doing his job. He hated to lose, and I was just one more case to him. But the way he looked at me sometimes, I couldn't help but feel... more. It spoke of a sort of protectiveness, and the thought filled me with warmth.

"So, have we come to an agreement?" Richard asked, dispelling the discomfort in the atmosphere.

My gaze slowly lifted from Gavin's leg, up and over the table to Steve. I curled my hand into a fist. "Yes. He'll buy me out."

Gavin spun in his chair to look at me, fury evident in those dark eyes. "We haven't discussed this at all. I thought—"

"Just give him the practice."

He leaned even closer, practically caging me in with his

body as he propped one elbow on the table and rested the other hand on the back of my chair. His tone was hushed but severe. "Are you certain this is what you want?"

"Yes."

"Kate, you deserve—"

"I don't even care about the money; I just want out." I was surprised to realize that the words I spoke were the truth. I couldn't stand to be held back any longer—not by a job I liked but didn't love, and certainly not by a man.

"Please," I said softly so only he could hear me. "Just... I want to move on with my life. Help me do that."

His expression softened a bit. "All right. Okay."

I listened with half an ear as the lawyers bartered back and forth for the next hour. Since we'd already had a realtor run comps on the business in case we couldn't come to an agreement, it was fairly easy to determine the value of the business and the cost of the buyout. Gavin watched me warily as I glanced at the figure presented to me, then nodded. He looked as if he wanted to say more, but I turned away, studiously avoiding him.

The meeting finally came to an end, and after exchanging polite handshakes, we began to filter from the room. Gavin waylaid me just as I approached the door.

"Are you sure this is what you want?"

I closed my eyes for a moment, steeling myself before meeting his gaze. I'd given Steve years of my life only to be betrayed, my life ripped to shreds. But this was the key to my freedom. He might not approve of my choice, but now I'd have plenty of money for a fresh start. I could do whatever I wanted—and now it was time to do something for me.

"I already gave you my answer. I just—"

He cut me off, his eyes angry, his tone harsh. "Tell me, Kate, because I really need to know."

Something flickered in the dark depths. Disapproval?

Disappointment, maybe? My lips flattened into a straight line, and I drew myself up to my fullest height. Who the hell was he to judge me?

I lifted my chin defiantly. "Excuse me, Mr. Price. I believe we're done here."

I strode down the hall and through the lobby, acutely aware of his penetrating glare on my back as I pushed open the door with more force than necessary and stepped into the bright sunlight. No more. Today was the start of something new. I strode forward with purpose, shoulders straight, ready to start the next chapter in my life.

CHAPTER
TWO

GAVIN

I silently fumed, somehow managing to curse her even as I appreciated the way her hips swayed purposefully toward the door.. Rob moved to stand beside me in the hallway.

"Kind of a spitfire, isn't she?"

I growled low in my throat, then spun on a heel and stormed into my office. "Stubborn-ass woman. Should've gotten the practice." I threw myself into my chair and glared at the ceiling. "That tool bag doesn't deserve a penny, and she's giving him everything. Goddamn it!"

Rob lifted a brow. "Maybe she needs the money."

I snorted. "She doesn't need the goddamn money. Her finances are in way better shape than his."

I had a feeling it was exactly as she'd told me: she just wanted out. But, damn it, she deserved so much more. She needed more than a husband who cheated on her and knocked up some tramp. She'd get a nice chunk of money out of the deal, sure, but it wasn't nearly enough.

"Why does it bother you so much?"

I dipped my head just enough to glare at him. Kate was why. Because she was the smartest, most amazing, sexiest woman who had ever stepped foot in my office, and I wanted to help her. I wanted to do a hell of a lot more, but she was also my client. It wasn't as if it never happened, but it was the biggest cliché in the book.

"It just... does."

I stared at my best friend, debating whether to open up or not. Rob and I met in first grade when Dad had picked up our family and moved us south. Back then, I'd been scrawny and nerdy, an undersized young boy with glasses who'd been teased relentlessly. Rob had intervened one day on the playground when Jeff Sutton, the class bully, had knocked me down and stolen my lunch money. One punch to the jaw had sent Jeff to the ground—and forged our friendship in stone.

A growth spurt in high school put me two inches taller than Rob, but we remained friends all through school. After graduation, we'd enlisted in the military—he in the Army and me in the Marines. After our tours were up, we'd returned home and chosen to go to law school.

We'd each had several offers from different firms, but when Walker and Raines had two open slots to fill, we jumped at the chance to work together there as well. The internships turned into full-time positions, and we'd been side by side for the last three years.

I steepled my fingers and rested them against my lips, mind racing. Why the hell was she being so difficult? I could've gotten her a good deal, a hell of a lot better than what she was settling for. That asshole should be handing everything over to her, not the other way around. I commended her for wanting to move on with her life and leave the asshat behind, but... why wouldn't she let me help her?

Rob lifted an eyebrow. "You've done this hundreds of times. What's the big deal with this chick?"

I growled. "She deserves better."

He shrugged nonchalantly. "So do a lot of the women that come in here."

True, but Kate Winfield was different. I'd never—not since the moment she walked through these doors—been able to call her by her married name. Wishful thinking on my part, maybe, but I'd known within seconds of meeting her that I wanted her.

More than that, ridiculous as it was, I adamantly refused to accept that she in any way belonged to another man. There'd been a spark between us the first time we spoke, and when she smiled at me... my reaction to her was like grabbing an electric fence.

Despite trying to talk myself out of it, I couldn't get her off my mind. I wanted her to see me in a different light—as a flesh-and-blood male instead of just her lawyer. Right now, I meant literally nothing to her other than the fact that I had the power to grant her freedom from the idiot she'd called her husband for the past several years.

"That dickhead treated her like shit." I could hear the derision in my voice, and I quickly cleared my throat. "I'm just trying to get her what she deserves."

"Sounds like you're trying to get something else."

I met Rob's pointed stare with one of my own. "Not sure what you're implying."

His friend snorted a laugh. "Don't gimme that shit. I've known you too long. You got something going on with this broad?"

"Not yet, but..." My gaze darted toward the door where a curvy blonde lounged against the doorjamb, clearly eavesdropping, and I stifled a groan.

Shannon Raines—as in my boss, Larry's, daughter—wore a pleased expression, as if my words were meant for her. Twenty-one if she was a day, she was pretty enough, but *damn* she was about as dumb as a brick wall. And unfortunately, it wasn't a learning curve. She'd been here for nearly a year, yet she continued to make the same stupid mistakes every day. Knowing she was a partner's daughter, everyone here had tried to be polite, but their patience was wearing thin—and so was mine.

Shannon had spent the past few months doing her best to fall on my dick. She'd started by making small talk, pulling me aside from time to time to ask questions. At first, I hadn't minded helping her—until I realized it was a ruse. I'd almost given in one night when she'd invited me back to her place, but thank God I'd had the presence of mind to decline. She'd become increasingly aggressive in her pursuit, and I almost snorted out loud as my eyes swept over her.

The clothes themselves would have been acceptable for any office job, but the way she wore them was far from it. The red button-down shirt matched her vibrant lipstick and pulled tightly across her breasts, unbuttoned so far that I could see the lacy material of her bra in the open V of the neckline. Her demeanor screamed for attention. Too bad she wouldn't be getting it from me.

Despite her best attempts to win my favor, I had no intention of going there—ever. Especially not now. Not when I was so close to getting what I really wanted, which was a fiery redheaded doctor with a temper to match. I lifted my chin at the blonde still draped against my doorway. "Yes, Shannon?"

She sashayed into the office, hips fluid with the movement, and practically laid herself over my desk as she passed me a sheaf of papers. "Here's your deposition for the Lyle-Mills case, Mr. Price."

I watched Rob's eyes drop to her ass as she leaned over right in front of him, and I barely refrained from rolling my eyes.

"Thank you." I accepted the file and dropped it into the

tray at the corner of my desk. When she made no move to leave the room, I met her gaze with a frosty glare of my own. "That will be all. Please close the door on your way out."

Shannon's lips tightened into a firm line of displeasure, but she flounced out of the office, slamming the door in her wake. I flinched at the sound and met Rob's amused eyes.

"Looks like she was less than impressed with your handling of the situation."

I shook my head. "I'll never be desperate enough to stoop that low."

"Aw, come on. She's not that bad."

"Yeah, I noticed you were enjoying the show." I leveled a stare at my best friend, wondering how the man could be so naïve sometimes. "The chick's a succubus. Go near that and you'll pay for it."

Rob chuckled. "I'll keep that in mind. So what is it about this broad?"

"Did you not see that?" I pointed toward the door. "She'd been trying to nail me down since she walked in the door, like she singled me out."

"Not Shannon." He tapped a finger on Kate's file. "Ms. Winfield."

I hesitated. Besides the fact that she was drop-dead gorgeous, I wanted her—had to have her. I couldn't explain it, but from the very moment I'd laid eyes on her, I'd known she was different. She was a game changer.

I lifted one shoulder. "There's nothing going on."

"Yet." Rob met my hard glare with one of his own. "Spill it. You've been pushing to get this resolved for weeks. You want her that bad?"

I blew out an exasperated breath. Why the hell couldn't Rob just leave it alone? Ever since that time on the playground nearly twenty-five years ago, Rob had considered himself my protector. And if that meant dragging the information out of me, I had no doubt he'd find a way to accomplish it.

"Honestly? I don't know what it is about her, but I want her. I need to get this shit wrapped up so I can finally go talk to her. That's why I needed to get that asshole on board. He cheated on her, for Christ's sake. The least he could do was give her the damn practice she's worked all her life for."

"Can't make her take something she doesn't want," Rob chided.

No, I couldn't, but that didn't make me want to throttle the asshole any less. "Regardless, she deserves better."

"And that's you?" Rob lifted a brow, and I flipped him the bird.

"I just want a chance with her. That's all."

He nodded. "Maybe that'll get the message across to Shannon loud and clear."

I seriously doubted it. All I could do was avoid her and hope she eventually turned her attention elsewhere. "How quickly do you think we can get Howard to sign off on the decree?"

Rob lifted a shoulder. "He owes me. I'll request he get it approved ASAP. I'll just add that tally to your list of favors, too."

I reached over and fist-bumped him. "You're the best."

CHAPTER
THREE

KATE

I flopped to my back and threw one arm over my eyes to block out the light as I slowly came awake. I felt exhausted, emotionally drained, like the last six months had leached all of the energy from my body.

I was definitely in a funk, one I wasn't quite sure how to get out of. I knew moving on was for the best—new house, new job. Outwardly, it was all coming together. Inside, I felt like I was falling apart. It didn't make sense; I'd finally decided on a course of action for my life, so why did I feel so... broken?

I knew part of it was Steve and our marriage, or lack thereof. What had been a constant in my life for so long was... gone. No matter how badly he'd hurt me, I couldn't bring myself to hate him. I really did wish him the best. I just wished that I was happy, too.

For several long minutes, I just lay there, eyes closed, trying not to think at all. Finally, I rolled my head to the left and glared at the chair next to the bed. A stack of clothes and a pair of running shoes taunted me with their presence. I had to put them there where I would see them as soon as I got out of bed, otherwise I would put it off.

I'd promised myself I was going to start being healthy again, and I wasn't going to give up now, damn it. Forcing myself to move, I sat up and swung my legs over the edge of the mattress, then reluctantly dressed and laced up the shoes before I could change my mind.

The routine had been the same for the last four days. It was time for me to move on, to take back control of my life, and working out was just one element to that. After I used the bathroom, I bounded downstairs and whipped up a quick protein shake to drink before I headed out. Peanut danced around my feet, and I let him out into the backyard to relieve himself as I sipped at my strawberry shake.

The morning was clear and bright, still a little cool but carrying the promise of heat later in the afternoon. It was the perfect time for a run, and I found myself looking forward to it. Peanut darted back inside, and I locked up, then poured some food and water into his bowls before snatching up my phone and earbuds. Pulling up my favorite playlist, I popped the wireless headphones into my ears, then made my way out the front door.

I took a minute to stretch in my driveway as I looked around, enjoying the calm morning. The condo complex was located just out of town before the landscape transitioned into farmland. I'd seen a few kids out and about in the afternoons, but the residents seemed to be mostly middle-aged nine-to-fivers.

The last few days, I'd run through the neighboring allotment back toward town. Today I wanted to try something new. Turning left out of my driveway, I walked for a couple of blocks before easing into a slow jog. My muscles ached with the familiar burn, but it felt good. As I warmed up, my muscles became looser, my steps longer and more graceful.

It was amazing how quickly I'd gotten my stride back, even after being stagnant for so many years. I couldn't remember exactly when or why I stopped running. I loved it once, so much so that I'd run cross country in both high school and college.

I settled in, listening to the soft music playing in my ears, the familiar rhythm of my feet slapping the pavement with every step. Though I kept a watchful eye on my surroundings, checking constantly for cars or other people, I allowed my mind to drift. I had a phone preliminary interview with a small local branch of the VA coming up tomorrow, and I was incredibly nervous.

Mentally preparing responses for my interview, I crested a small knoll, then turned right and broke away from the main road. An older-style farmhouse sat back from the road a little bit, and I waved to the woman puttering around a small garden in the front yard.

I continued another mile or so down the road, where corn rose up along both sides. *Knee-high by the Fourth of July.* I smiled as the old adage came back to me from my youth. According to farmers, if corn was knee-high by July, it would be a prosperous year. Judging from the size of the stalks, it looked like this year was going to be a good one.

Suddenly, something came crashing through the leafy green stalks, and a small yelp left my throat as I reared back in surprise. I quickly looked around, thankful that no cars were coming, before turning my attention back to the mangy-looking dog in front of me. His brown fur was matted and muddy in places, and he clutched a large bone in his mouth.

I couldn't help the laugh that bubbled up. The dog wasn't small, maybe seventy pounds or so, but the bone protruding from either side of his mouth looked abnormally huge. He eyed me warily and let out a little growl as if warning me away from his treasure.

Smiling at the dog, I slipped the headphones from my ears and tucked them into the waistband of my shorts. "Whatcha got there?" I crooned to him. "Looks yummy."

The dog eyed me but didn't move, and the smile slipped from my face as I inspected the bone more closely. Unease spread through my gut as I took in the ball joint on one end, then down to the familiar nubs at the opposite end. I'd taken too many anatomy classes to not know exactly what I was looking at. It was a femur—a human one by the looks of it.

"Where did you get that?" I asked softly. The dog tipped his head slightly to one side, almost as if he could understand what I was saying.

"Show me," I encouraged him. "Where is it?"

The dog turned and started back through the cornfield, and I hesitated for a long moment before hopping over the ditch and following him. I briefly acknowledged this was one of the stupidest things I'd ever done. Not only was I venturing away from the road where I could get lost, but I'd also potentially find a crime scene at the end of this trek.

I mentally crossed my fingers that I wouldn't meet any ill-meaning humans wherever the dog was taking me. Thank God I at least had my cell phone in case anything happened.

Leaves slapped at my legs, slowing my progress, but I brushed them away as I hurried to catch up with the dog. What felt like an interminably long time later, the cornfield came to an abrupt end, opening up to a large grassy field. The dog tossed a look over his shoulder without breaking stride as he trotted through the weeds brushing at his shoulders.

I grimaced and carefully picked my way through the field, keeping one eye peeled as my sneakers squished into the wet ground. I prayed to God that the dog made enough noise to scare off any critters hanging around before I stumbled upon them. The last thing I needed was to be out here all alone and fall victim to a startled rattlesnake.

About thirty yards in front of me, two birds took flight, startled by the dog as it loped a little too close. The dog stopped right where the birds had been, his tail beating the air enthusiastically. A faint buzzing noise filled the air, unmistakably flies that had already settled in to feast. I smelled it before I saw it, and dread curdled in my stomach as the body came into view. Though most of the body was intact, the flesh and bone of one leg had been stripped away, presumably by the dog.

This close, the scent was overpowering, and I turned away, covering my nose, willing the nausea to subside before pulling my phone out and dialing 911.

"This is Dr. Kate Winfield," I introduced myself when the dispatcher answered the call. "I've found a deceased person in a field somewhere off Hartwell Road."

She assured me that police had been dispatched but asked me to remain on the line until they arrived. Meanwhile, I watched the dog out of the corner of my eye, still reluctant to relinquish his treasure.

"By the way," I told the woman almost as an afterthought, "there's a dog here who appears to have one of the person's bones. You might want to have them bring something, see if we can get the dog to give it up."

The dispatcher occasionally commented, both letting me know that she was still there and checking to make sure that I hadn't hung up. I moved away from the overwhelming smell, but not far enough to let the dog out of my sight. At least half an hour had passed before the sound of voices reached my ears.

"The police are here," I said to the woman on the other end of the phone before hanging up. I shoved the phone into my pocket, then lifted both arms high in the air and waved to get their attention. It took them several minutes to reach me, at least a dozen men and women spread out, carefully picking their way across the field.

A man in khakis and a white button-down shirt stuck his hand out in greeting as he approached. "Detective Mayfield. You're the one who found the victim?"

"Dr. Kate Winfield," I said by way of greeting, then shook his hand before gesturing over my shoulder. "He's just a few yards over this way. And the dog is over there." I pointed toward the edge of the tree line.

His face remained impassive as his dark eyes swept over the scene. "Have you touched anything?"

"No." I shook my head. "I was going to try to get the bone away from the dog, but he didn't like that idea."

Mayfield's lips quirked into a tiny smile. "I imagine not. We'll see what we can do about that."

I explained how I'd recognized the structure of the bone and followed the dog to the scene. A small commotion drew our attention back to the edge of the field closest to the road, and we watched the medical examiner and her team approach.

The detective turned back to me. "We'll let Dr. Pratt take a look at the body first, then we'll look around, see if we can find anything."

Her stride brisk and sure, Dr. Pratt crossed the bumpy field, a serious expression clouding her pretty features. "Mayfield." She tipped her head at him, then turned to me. "Are you on the investigation as well?"

"No, I called it in."

Her eyes cleared. "You're the doctor."

"Family medicine," I clarified. "You can call me Kate. I actually found the dog first, then he led me back here to the man."

She lifted a brow. "You're sure he's male?"

Mayfield and I fell into step beside her as she strode toward the body. "Judging from his facial features, which seem to be mostly intact."

Dr. Pratt nodded but stayed silent, and I stayed several feet behind, watching as she kneeled carefully next to the man's remains. I wasn't terribly familiar with necrotic tissue, because I'd always preferred living patients over dead ones, but if I had to guess, this guy hadn't been out here all that long. Even in the early morning heat, his flesh was only in the beginning stages of decomposition.

Mayfield turned to me. "Aside from the dog, did you see anything out of the ordinary?"

I shook my head. "No. I almost brushed him off until I noticed the femur."

I quickly walked Dr. Pratt through what had happened, and she nodded along, asking questions intermittently as she inspected the man's body. She pointed at one hand lying on the ground. "Fingers have been amputated at the second knuckle."

Truth be told, I hadn't paid that much attention initially, but her assessment piqued my curiosity. "Interesting."

She lifted one shoulder. "Probably to eliminate fingerprints if he was found immediately," she replied.

The thought turned my stomach, but it made sense. She opened the bag at her feet, then put on a pair of nitrile gloves and gently probed at the man's mouth. Inside, his gums gaped wide, completely devoid of teeth.

"Won't be pulling any dental records either," Mayfield remarked dryly.

Despite the heat of the day, I wrapped my arms around my waist to ward off the chill that had settled over me. "Who the hell would do something like that?"

"Unfortunately, it's not all that uncommon." Flies buzzed around, and Dr. Pratt batted them away as she peeled back the ragged layer of flesh covering his torso. "What the...?"

Not really wanting to get any closer, but unable to curb my curiosity, I peered over her shoulder. "Everything okay?"

"Look."

I covered my mouth to block the smell and leaned forward to get a better look. "Holy shit."

"What?" Mayfield looked between us, and Dr. Pratt and I exchanged a look.

I glanced up at Mayfield. "Every single organ is missing."

"Not just missing," Dr. Pratt corrected. "Removed."

CHAPTER
FOUR

GAVIN

I lifted my free hand and rapped my knuckles on the door, three short beats that seemed to linger in the stillness of the quiet afternoon. The main road was empty, the small neighborhood seemingly lifeless. I suspected most people were still at work, their kids at daycare or in school.

I shifted anxiously, praying she was here. The driveway was empty, but the little condo had a one-car garage, so I could only hope her car was parked inside. I'd called the healthplex to see if she was at work today but was told she'd taken the rest of this week off. I was still furious about how our last meeting had gone.

She'd looked fine on the surface, resolute in her decision to completely cut ties with her past. It bothered me, because I wanted to know how she was doing mentally, emotionally. Kate was an enigma, and I had a feeling she buried her true self way down deep where no one would see it.

I knew I wanted Kate the first time I laid eyes on her

beautiful face, the fiery red of her hair rivaled only by the flames in her eyes. My fingers clenched the handle of my briefcase, reassuring myself with a squeeze that it—and, more importantly, the information I was about to deliver—was still there.

Tucked under my arm was a bottle of Dom that I'd picked up on the way, because, well… I still hadn't figured that part out yet. Maybe I was an idiot for thinking she'd welcome my presence, but I wouldn't know unless I tried.

My patience was rewarded when, moments later, muffled footsteps approached the door and hesitated on the other side. I sucked in a breath as the pause elongated. I could feel her eyes on me through the peephole, wondering why the hell I was here. That made two of us. I fought the doubt slowly creeping up inside and struggled to school my expression into one of calm aloofness. Finally, the snick of the lock turning in its case reached my ears, and I let out the breath I'd been holding.

Kate's face peered around the door, brow furrowed. "Mr. Price?"

I smiled charmingly despite the churning in my gut. "Please, Kate, call me Gavin."

The corners of her lips turned down even as she opened the door wider and allowed me to enter. "What can I do for you?"

I strolled into the entryway and turned to watch Kate as she diligently closed and locked the door, then turned toward me, wary eyes fixed on mine. "Actually, I'm here on your behalf. I couldn't show up empty-handed."

I extended the bottle of champagne to her, and her eyes swept over me, one sardonic eyebrow cocked upward. "Oh? I guess four hundred dollars an hour buys me a bottle of Dom Perignon. Maybe I should get divorced more often."

My smile dimmed a bit, irritation overriding the giddy anticipation I'd felt. Still, I bared my teeth at her in a semblance of a smile. "This is a congratulatory gift."

Kate crossed her arms over her chest. "I thought the gift was that you're going to relieve me of my scumbag ex-husband so he's free to marry that little blonde tramp?"

My heart went out to her. I saw it all the time, but it had never affected me before, not the way it did with Kate. Her husband had treated her like shit, and she deserved better than that.

My gaze swept over her. Clearly she'd been relaxing or taking a nap, judging from her laid-back outfit. I'd only ever seen her in beautifully cut suits or dresses, but even in yoga pants and an oversized T-shirt, the woman was beautiful. Beyond beautiful. Gorgeous. Why in the hell would that stupid shit leave her for another woman? Didn't matter. Steve Gerber's loss was going to be my gain.

I lowered the bottle of champagne that she still hadn't accepted. I hadn't come here with any real plans, but the longer I stood here staring at her, the more I itched to have her. The gift was her freedom—she could be with whomever she wanted. And I was damn sure going to make certain she wanted me.

"That, too," I admitted. "I have something for you."

"Fantastic."

My lips compressed at her sarcasm. I set the briefcase on a side table and extracted the folder within. "Here."

Her eyes met mine, her body immediately tensing. "What does he want now?"

"Nothing." I shook my head. "Steve was approved for the loan to buy out your portion of the practice, so all I need is your signature to make it happen, and we'll get it all finalized."

I passed the sheaf of papers to her, and she stared at them, dumbfounded. "It's... Really?"

Shit. Was that disappointment I saw there?

She closed her eyes for a moment and breathed out a heavy sigh, her voice low. "Thank God. I was worried he wouldn't come up with the money."

I lifted one shoulder. "I know the loan officer at the bank who approved him." Her head tipped to one side in question, and I continued. "If it makes you feel any better, he's getting raped on interest."

A slow smile spread over her face, lighting her eyes, and my chest constricted at the sight. "Actually, it does."

I grinned back. "I thought it might."

She flipped through the papers, found the correct tab, then hastily scrawled her name and the date on the lines. I filed it away, then snatched up the bottle of champagne. "Come on. After all this, you deserve a drink."

Leaving the briefcase behind, I pushed past her in search of the kitchen, leaving her to follow at her will. As soon as I entered the kitchen, I stumbled to a stop as a streak of white blew past my feet. A tiny, curly white-haired dog eagerly circled me, and I knelt down to scratch the dog behind the ears. "Hey, there."

Kate's footsteps stopped just behind me, and I glanced at her over my shoulder. "What is he?" I glanced back at the dog. "Or is it a she?"

"He. His name is Peanut."

She watched me with a strange sort of expression, and I tipped my head at her. "What's wrong?"

"Nothing." She shook her head bemusedly. "He's usually not a big fan of men. He hated Steve."

I grinned and gave the dog one more good scratch before rising to my feet. I set the bottle of Dom on the counter and turned toward Kate. "You know what they say, dogs are an excellent judge of character."

She made a derisive sound in her throat before directing

her next words to the dog. "Looks like your instincts are broken, Peanut. He's a *lawyer*."

She said it like it was a dirty word, and I couldn't help the laugh that rumbled up out of my throat. Dramatically, I slapped a hand over my heart. "Dr. Winfield, you wound me."

A mischievous smile broke over her face. "Not yet."

Goddamn, I loved that smile. She didn't do it nearly enough, but the curve of her mouth completely transformed her face. She was still out of my league, but the smile made her softer, more human... more approachable.

"You didn't dislike me so much a few minutes ago," I teased.

She rolled her eyes playfully. "You do have your uses, I guess."

I loved this side of her—the one that was open and unguarded. Though I knew almost every detail of her life, I hadn't really had a chance yet to meet the real Kate and learn what made her tick. It was something I planned to rectify immediately.

"Let's break this sucker open. Where are your glasses?" She gestured to a cabinet, and I pulled two flutes down. "Would you like to do the honors, or should I?"

She shook her head. "I've never been good at that kind of thing."

"All right." I peeled the foil off. "I guess it's my turn, then."

"Just don't break anything," she warned. "I've seen videos where those things ricochet and shatter windows. I wouldn't want to have to sue you for damages."

I grinned at her. "I'd find a loophole."

She rolled her eyes but couldn't contain the smile that overtook her pretty mouth. "No doubt you would."

I extracted the cork with little difficulty, but she still

jumped at the loud pop that resounded in the room. The liquid fizzed as I poured it into the glasses, the potent smell reaching up and tickling my nose. I recorked it, then extended one to her and picked up my own. "To new beginnings."

She lifted her glass and touched it to mine. "To cheating husbands."

I rolled my eyes. "You're horrible at this. You can't toast to that."

"I certainly can," she retorted. "That's why we're here today."

I let out a beleaguered sigh. "Fine, keep your toast. I'll just have to come up with another one. To..." I threw a flirtatious smile her way. "To beautiful, intelligent company."

She nodded thoughtfully. "To a great pair of boots."

The smile slipped from my face as my eyebrows drew together in confusion. What the hell was she talking about?

"For when the shit gets too deep," she clarified, her lips twitching with humor.

I studied her for a moment before slowly shaking my head. "You're something else, you know that?"

"I'll take that as a compliment," she snapped back.

"Good. I meant it as one."

Her gaze met mine over the rim of the glass as she took her first sip. I could tell the precise moment the bubbles hit her tongue, because her eyes closed in pleasure. I watched, mesmerized, as she drained the glass, then twirled the stem of the flute between her fingers for a moment before glancing up at me.

"So you came all this way to bring me a bottle of champagne?" She lifted the bottle and refilled her glass. "It's good, don't get me wrong, and I appreciate the gesture, but I don't believe you for a second."

"Fair enough, and true. I was driving past the store when it caught my eye, and it sounded like a good idea at the time." I shrugged one shoulder. "I actually just wanted to see how you're doing."

Surprise flashed in her eyes before she quickly blinked the emotion away, replacing it instead with a cool detachedness. "I'll be okay. The cut is healing fine, and I've been putting cream on it to help with the scarring."

Her hand automatically lifted to her face, fingertips tenderly brushing the cut. My gaze drifted to the pink line that cut across her forehead and into her hairline. The stitches had come out, but the scar itself was still an angry pink. Ironically, it didn't detract from her beauty. If anything, it almost brought her down to my level. Not quite, but almost.

She skirted my real question—how she was doing emotionally. I watched her gaze flit around the kitchen, landing on everything but me, and I debated just how far to push her. To Kate, I was just her lawyer; I wasn't even a friend she could confide in—yet. Winning her over would be one hell of a journey, and I was going to enjoy the hell out of it.

I cleared my throat. "I also wanted to bring you the paperwork."

She snorted, and her hand dropped back to her side as she threw a dubious look my way. "Which you could have mailed."

"I could have, but I didn't want to."

"You came all the way out here just so you could hand-deliver these? Why?"

I took a predatory step toward her, and her eyes widened as she retreated until her back was pressed against the edge of the counter. "Because I couldn't wait one more minute."

"For... what?" Her voice was breathless, and the fire in her eyes melted away, revealing a mixture of confusion and... was that desire? I sure as hell hoped so.

"You want to know why I'm here?"

She nodded, eyes hooded and sultry as she watched my every step. I set my glass down with a hard clink and wrapped an arm around her waist, pulling her close. My gaze dropped to her lips.

"This."

CHAPTER
FIVE

KATE

His lips were warm and firm as he captured my mouth with an almost bruising force. Momentarily caught off guard, I hesitated, the feeling strangely new yet erotic.

I hadn't kissed another man in years. I'd been with Steve since undergrad, almost nine years ago now, and to have another man's lips on mine felt foreign but oh, so welcome. Kissing Gavin was nothing like kissing Steve. The perfunctory pecks I'd received sporadically from my ex-husband couldn't compare to the passion flowing between Gavin's lips and mine.

My attention turned back to the man whose mouth hovered just millimeters from mine. Gavin had pulled back the barest fraction at my lack of response, and I slowly lifted my gaze to his. Eyes the color of the richest coffee stared deep into mine as if he was looking through me, straight into my soul. My nipples tightened under his intent perusal, and heat curled through my body, pooling in my core. For the first time in years I felt... desired. Wanted. I needed more—I needed him.

Curling one hand into his hair, I yanked his head back down, and our teeth clashed under the raw force of the kiss. His large palms stroked up my back, down over my bottom, lighting every inch of my skin on fire. I shifted, trying to get closer, needing to alleviate the ache between my legs.

I opened my mouth to him, and his tongue swept inside, curling over mine. He tasted of the sparkling, smooth champagne, and I melted against him. His hands cupped my ass, and I sucked in a breath as he lifted me, then settled me on the counter. Pushing my legs wider, he stepped between them, pressing as close as he could get.

His fingertips caught the hem of my shirt, and I lifted my arms, breaking the kiss just long enough for him to pull it over my head and toss it to the floor. I curled my fingers in the fabric of his dress shirt and pulled him back to me once more, needing to taste him again, unable to get enough. It'd been so long since I'd felt this way—so long I couldn't remember anything even remotely comparable.

Warm hands slid over the curve of my hip and around my back. He expertly popped the clasp on my bra, then slid the straps off my shoulders, gently coaxing it down until my breasts were exposed to his view. A shuddering breath left me as he cupped them in his huge palms, testing their weight, a reverent look on his face.

Suddenly, my head felt too heavy for my neck, and it lolled to the side as his thumbs flicked over the sensitive peaks thrusting toward him. I let out a sigh as he rolled one tip between his thumb and forefinger, and I arched my back to get closer.

His hands dropped away as his head drooped against the space where my shoulder met my neck. "God, I want you so bad. But if you're not ready..." He trailed off, then pulled back to look at me.

I knew it was wrong. I was still technically married, even

though things had been over between Steve and me for months—years, even. Whatever was happening with Gavin was different, stronger... more potent. He did something to me that I didn't understand, and I wanted... I didn't know what the hell I wanted. I wanted his addictive kisses. I wanted him to keep touching me. I wanted him to never stop.

Unable to speak, I met his dark gaze and nodded my permission to continue. The air left my lungs in a rush of excitement as he yanked me against him, and I wound my legs around his waist. Although he was only a few inches taller than my own five-nine frame, he carried me from the room like I weighed nothing at all.

Wrapping my arms around his shoulders, I clutched at the back of his head and pulled him to me. His lips fused with mine as he made his way down the hallway toward my bedroom like he'd done this hundreds of times before.

The thought froze me for a moment. He probably had done this very same thing, more times than he could count. He was successful and gorgeous; what woman would turn him down?

But I had no claim on him. Shoving the irrational jealousy and disappointment away, I fell into the kiss and allowed the pleasure to pull me under.

I didn't realize we'd reached my room until his arms loosened around me and the cool fabric of the sheets grazed my back. Propping a knee between my legs, he levered himself over me, caging me in his arms. I curled my fingers around the lapels of his shirt and nipped at his bottom lip as he started to pull away.

He returned the favor, capturing my lower lip between perfect white teeth. I arched upward, needing to feel every hard inch of him against me. He obliged by settling his heavy weight in the cradle of my hips, the hard ridge of his arousal pressing against my stomach. My hands wandered down his spine and beneath the hem of his shirt, exploring the hot flesh of his lower back.

A low whimper left my mouth when he lifted away from me again, and he let out a strained chuckle. "Right here, babe. I'm not going anywhere."

His fingers skimmed over the outside of my thighs then slipped beneath the waistband of my pants. Thank God for yoga pants. The stretchy black material gave way as he yanked it downward, and I shimmied my hips free. They landed on the floor with a whisper, but his eyes never left me.

Clad only in my underwear, I shifted under the scrutiny. "What?"

His intense stare was broken by a single blink. "You're so beautiful."

My cheeks heated, the compliment warming me to the tips of my toes. I'd never been considered beautiful. As tall as most men, I was lean and willowy, resembling a teenage boy more than the mature woman I was. I lacked the curves other women seemed to have in abundance, and I'd agonized over my nonexistent breasts for years.

Steve had told me more than once it didn't matter to him, but I'd caught him ogling women with huge boobs more than once when we were out at bars and restaurants. Turned out it had mattered more than he'd let on. Libby had a perfect pair of lab-manufactured double Ds, something I was sure he very much appreciated.

Gavin didn't seem to suffer from the same affliction, though, and my hips bucked off the bed as he fastened his mouth over one rosy peak. Any memory of my ex-husband dissolved under the pressure of Gavin's mouth as he used his lips and tongue to tease the tip to a firm point.

Hooking one finger in the waistband of my thong, he began to inch the silky material downward. I lifted my hips in offering, and he coasted down my body, trailing gentle kisses over my stomach as the material slowly slipped down my legs. As soon as my feet were free of the garment, I sat up and reached for the fly on his slacks. I freed the clasp, and he stepped from the material as it pooled around his feet.

He leaned over me, pressing me into the bed with the weight of his body. "You ready for me?"

"Why don't you find out for yourself?" I lifted my chin at Gavin, daring him.

I didn't have to wait long. One thick finger moved to the tiny nub at the apex of my thighs, and I bit my lip at the sharp bolt of pleasure that streaked through me. He rubbed in a tiny circular motion, pressing ever so gently before slipping inside.

More surprised than anything, I gasped at the sensation. My legs fell open, and my breath came in pants as he dipped in and out, sliding a second finger inside. He lubricated the folds with my arousal, gently rubbing my clit in a circular motion. I lifted my hips, moving with him, the friction pushing me closer to the edge with every stroke.

A soft cry ripped from my throat as he sank his fingers deep.

"Come for me, baby."

His thumb pressed down on my clit, and another hard thrust of his fingers sent me spiraling upward in a shower of stars.

"Oh, God... Holy..." I couldn't even string together a coherent sentence, my mind was so jumbled with pleasure.

Gavin chuckled. "Well, that was fast." I lifted a hand to flip him off but promptly let my arm drop back to the bed, exhaustion pulling at my limbs.

He kissed my stomach. "Don't worry, red, it's great for my ego."

Cocky asshole. "Like you need that," I scoffed as I twisted away from him.

Shame turned my skin hot, and I fought to sit up, to put

distance between us. I should have known this whole thing was a huge mistake. I was nothing more than another conquest for him, an emotionless sexual attachment. This would be the last time I ever laid eyes on him. I wouldn't even have to see him in the office anymore; they would mail the final paperwork to me, and it would be like we'd never known one another.

He caught my hips as I tried to scoot out of his grasp. "Where you're concerned? Hell yeah, I do."

I lifted a brow, irritation causing me to lash out at him. "Why would my opinion matter? Don't get the reinforcement you need from your other women?"

His eyes narrowed. "I don't give a damn about other women. The only one I care about is you."

My heart lurched in my chest at his words. He seemed so earnest, and I immediately felt contrite. "I'm sorry. I just…"

"Forget about it." One hand slipped beneath my hair and cupped the back of my neck. "Let me make you feel good."

His lips came down on mine, soft at first, then more forcefully as he rolled his tongue over mine. Tension drained from my muscles, and my head dropped back as he kissed his way over my jaw, scraping his teeth along my throat, sending tingles of pleasure to the tips of my toes.

The fingers curled around my hip slid downward, caressing the flesh of my inner thigh before once again moving upward. I jumped when he found the moist folds of my center and slipped one finger deep inside.

He let out a little chuckle, and the rumbling vibration shot straight to my core. He pulled his hand free, then straightened. Still suspended on my elbows, I watched through lowered lids as he stripped out of his underwear and socks, then scooped up his pants and pulled a gold foil packet from a pocket.

I lifted a brow, and an unrepentant grin split his face. "Wishful thinking."

I wasn't going to complain. I hadn't been with a man since Steve and I had last shared a bed. I sure as hell didn't have any condoms lying around, and I appreciated the gesture. We were both adults here; we knew what we wanted. And, right now, that was each other.

He rolled the condom over his stiff erection and placed a knee on the bed between both of mine. His intense gaze met mine, silently asking if I was ready. If I told him no, he would walk away right now. I gave a jerky nod and hooked my feet behind his thighs to pull him closer.

He happily obliged with a low chuckle. "Patience, gorgeous."

He braced his hands on the mattress beside my shoulders, and I felt his arousal brush my sensitive folds as he lowered himself over me. My hips lifted of their own accord, inviting him in. His lips covered mine, and he swallowed my gasp as he thrust hard, seating himself deeply inside me. The sensation was almost overwhelming, bordering on painful as he stretched every inch of me.

He didn't give me time to adjust, just pulled out and slammed back in again, stealing my breath. My already heightened awareness tipped me over the edge, and the sensation within me boiled over, rocketing toward another orgasm. I clutched his shoulders as heat raced through my body, and I let go on a silent scream. Gavin pumped into me several more times before emptying his seed into the condom with a ragged groan and slumping over me.

He lay heavily on my chest, covering me from head to toe, and I absorbed the heat from his body. His lips brushed over my collarbone, and I shivered as the tingles of pleasure fanned outward, down to the deepest recess of my body, spurring me on. He was still inside me, and I couldn't bear to break that connection with him just yet. I needed more time—I needed him.

I protested with a low cry as he rolled us so I lay sprawled over him, and he chuckled at my expression.

"You good?"

I was so much better than good. I hadn't felt this wonderful in... hell, maybe ever. It was a sobering thought.

I lifted my head to look at him. "I'm kind of on the fence. Maybe we should do it one more time?"

CHAPTER
SIX

GAVIN

I couldn't help the grin that spread over my face as I took in her expression, a mixture of hope and apprehension, like she was worried I might turn her down. Like there was even a chance in hell of that. I'd barely just pulled out of her body, and all I could think about was sinking right back in. Everything about her felt so good, so right. I wanted to bury myself inside her and stay there indefinitely.

I'd known it would be good between us, but this? Holy Christ. She turned my blood to fire, made me so damn hard I was ready to go again. I'd spent the past six months digging around in her personal life, yet I didn't truly know her. All that was about to change, though. Kate and I were about to get as well acquainted as two people ever could, because I wasn't anywhere near ready to let her go.

"Your wish is my command." With a low growl, I rolled her to her stomach—and froze. "Damn, red."

She threw a look over her shoulder, her teeth cutting into

her bottom lip, her eyes filled with something akin to discomfort. "Is that a good 'damn'?"

"Definitely good. I just never expected anything like it. Pandora's box?" She nodded, and her eyes fell closed as I swept my fingers over her skin, tracing the intricate image that covered the delicate flesh of her back. "It's beautiful."

"Thanks."

My fingers glided over a particularly gruesome-looking specter. "Does it have some sentimental meaning for you?"

"I'd like to say yes but would be lying if I did." She lifted one shoulder. "I always liked the myth, and... I don't know. I like the idea that, despite everything bad, there's still a spark of hope out there, no matter how small."

The only color in the image was the small, glowing kernel of hope nestled at the bottom of Pandora's box. Whoever had designed it had done an amazing job. It looked like the spirits were preparing to lift into flight right off her skin, ready to wreak havoc on the world. It seemed so totally uncharacteristic from the staid, quiet doctor I knew her to be, yet at the same time, it just... fit. "I love it."

"I'm glad." She glanced over her shoulder at me, and our gazes met, then held. Her lids lowered slightly, her irises darkening, and her tongue darted out to sweep across her bottom lip. Heat shot through me, spurring me into motion. Tunneling my hand into those long auburn locks, I claimed her mouth. Her lips parted under the pressure, and I swept my tongue inside, tasting every inch, drawing her very breath into my lungs.

With a sigh, I ripped my mouth from hers. Still holding the back of her head, I met her gaze and searched those pretty blue eyes. "Don't move. I'll be right back."

Pushing off the bed, I jogged out of the bedroom toward the front door. Grabbing up the briefcase I'd dropped on the floor on my way in, I fished inside for the string of condoms

I'd stashed inside. I felt the telltale coolness of the folded packets, and I snatched them up before racing back to the bedroom. Vindication filled my chest when I hit the doorway and saw she hadn't moved a single inch.

Hearing my footsteps, Kate threw a curious look my way. I ripped one off the roll and let the others fall to the floor, already tearing the foil open with my teeth.

She flicked a glance at the floor. "Exactly how many times do you plan on doing this tonight?"

"Making love to you?" I clarified.

Her cheeks burned bright pink, and I grinned as she dropped her chin to the pillow.

Fitting the condom over my erection, I clambered over her on the bed and leaned down close to her ear. "I've been looking forward to this longer than you'll ever know. I plan on keeping you very busy for the next several hours." Her body jerked in surprise as I nipped her earlobe. "Until you're so exhausted you can't move or until we run out of protection, whichever comes first."

Her hips wiggled, lifting slightly toward mine, and I slipped one hand beneath her belly. My shaft nudged her folds, and she arched her back as I pressed forward. Kate tried to push to her hands and knees, but I roughly pressed her shoulders down. "Right here, baby. Ass in the air where I can see it."

She let out an indignant little huff, and I grinned. Her flesh was so pale, so perfectly flawless, and I couldn't help the overwhelming urge to mark it. Pulling my arm back, I delivered a stinging slap to her right cheek, then slammed into her.

Kate let out a little shriek, hands fisting in the covers as she glared over her shoulder at me. "What the hell was that for?"

I caressed the pink spot blooming over her pale skin. "Just marking what's mine, baby."

"Fuck you."

Straightening, I pulled out almost to the tip, anticipation singing through my veins. I slapped her left cheek—hard— then drove deep. Kate's hips bucked under the pressure, and another cry ripped from her throat.

I leaned forward, pressing deeper into her. "I should fuck that sass right out of you."

"Good luck with that," she snapped.

Sounded like a challenge to me. Palming her ass in both hands, I swept my fingers over the soft skin before curling them into her hips for better leverage. Heat enveloped me as I slid all the way in, and I bit back an oath as her flesh tightened around me. Over and over, I pulled out and thrust back in, hard and fast. She let out a strangled cry as her flesh tightened around me, trying to hold me in. I dug my fingers into her hips and pounded into her, reveling in her body's response to me.

"Fuck, baby, you feel so good."

I could feel every inch of her as her pussy clenched around me, grasping me tight. I didn't know what it was about her, but no woman had ever made me feel the way Kate did. It wasn't just the sex—it was everything. The fiery attitude, the streak of witty humor, the explosive chemistry... I loved it all. She was everything I could've dreamed of and more.

Her fingers grasped at the comforter as if to ground herself, and I plunged deeper, harder. A feral grin split my face as she cried out, the expression on her face somewhere between pleasure and pain. That look mirrored exactly how I felt. Pleasure, because she was so soft and perfect, and being inside her felt like heaven. Painful, because I felt like I would explode, and I wasn't nearly ready for it to be over.

"Gavin!"

I leaned forward and bit her shoulder. "Tell me, baby. Tell me what you need."

"I... Oh, God... Harder!"

Surprise caused me to lose my rhythm, and I discarded it completely in favor of driving into her over and over as hard and fast as I could, intent only on making her come. Her inner walls pulsed around my shaft, and I knew she was close. Heat licked through my balls, and my stomach tightened as I tried to stave off my orgasm. Two more deep strokes later, she shattered with a keening cry, and I let the fire overtake me as I came harder than I ever had.

Kate collapsed limply on her belly as I pulled out, and I had to steel my shaky muscles as I climbed from the bed to dispose of the condom. I tossed it in the trash, then returned to the bed and slid in next to her. Kate turned onto her side as I gathered her close and tucked her against my chest.

"You good?"

"Mmm..." Eyes closed, she let out a little hum of pleasure. "Amazing."

I dropped a kiss on her forehead. "Me, too."

I lay there next to her, our limbs tangled together, hearts beating next to each other, and I wondered when I'd ever tire of having her here like this. The only answer I could come up with was... never.

CHAPTER
SEVEN

KATE

I blinked my eyes open and stretched as the morning sun slid over the windowsill, spilling its golden glow over the dark wood floor. My muscles were deliciously sore and well-used, courtesy of the man whose body heat was radiating off him in waves next to me.

I tossed a glance over my shoulder and grinned at the image of him sprawled out. One arm tossed over the pillow above his head, face relaxed while he slept, he was so beautiful it made my heart hurt to look at him. His eyes were closed, but the brown irises like strong, dark coffee had the ability to warm me from the inside out. A faint dark stubble had sprouted over his jaw, and I ached to trace the chiseled contour.

Over the last—I glanced at the clock on the nightstand—fourteen hours, we'd alternated between having sex and talking about everything and nothing. Sometime in the middle of the night I'd woken up to find him between my legs, his mouth on my most intimate place. It was a shame I couldn't wake up that way more often.

My smile slipped away, and longing and regret pulled at me as I stared at him. I'd truly enjoyed our time together last night—but that's all it could ever be. Technically, I was still married—even if it was only for another few weeks. I knew Steve had moved on long ago, but I couldn't do the same. No way would I throw myself back into that fire. This one moment, this one delicious indiscretion, would have to be enough.

Sliding from the bed, I picked my way around the clothes that Gavin had so shamelessly ripped off yesterday afternoon and over the pizza box that lay discarded by the chair. We'd left the bed yesterday evening just long enough to answer the door, then made a picnic of sorts on top of the sheets before he'd tossed the box aside and pulled me beneath him once more.

He'd made good on his promise, too—we'd used every single condom he brought with him. My skin heated at the thought of the things he'd done, the things we'd done. Jesus. I pressed my palms to my cheeks and closed my eyes as my chest rose on a rapid inhale. He'd touched literally every inch of me, places that even Steve had never dared.

God, how could I even look at him in the light of day? Completely naked, I hastily pulled on the robe draped over the chair in the corner, then snatched up the discarded clothing from the floor and made my way to the bathroom. I dumped my stuff in the hamper, then folded Gavin's clothes and left them on the counter where he'd be sure to find them.

It was better this way. I'd had my night of fun, but now it was time to get back to the real world. I didn't need—or want —anything serious. In fact, it was the very last thing I needed in my life after the whole debacle with Steve. Thank God that was almost over, at least. Now I could put him from my mind forever.

It still stung that he'd moved on so easily while I'd spent so much time feeling hurt. But now it was my turn to be happy. It was time I did something for myself—and last night with Gavin was the first step in that direction. I had no intention of ever repeating it, so I'd have to make a clean break as soon as he woke up.

He'd probably be relieved. After all, what man would complain about a night of meaningless sex? The corner of my mouth lifted in a cynical smile. Oh, yes, he'd be more than happy to go on his way with no commitment. I quickly splashed some water on my face, then brushed my teeth and ran a brush through my unruly waves. Peeking into the bedroom, I saw that Gavin was still asleep, so I snuck out, closing the door behind me, and made my way to the kitchen.

After letting Peanut out, I leaned on the counter while I waited for the coffeepot to spit out the fragrant, warm brew and stared out the small window over the sink. The tiny condo was a far cry from where I'd lived with Steve in one of the wealthier areas of the city. Still, it was mine alone, and although it was further from the healthplex, that fact alone made it worth it.

Besides, I wouldn't have to worry about that in just a couple weeks. The condo wasn't tainted by bad memories; here I could start fresh. I could decorate the way I wanted, without anyone to question or overrule my choices. Nine years ago, I'd been young and naïve, blindly in love with a fellow medical student. I'd wanted so badly to impress him, to impress my family and make them proud of me.

I'd followed everyone's dreams but my own. I loved being a doctor, but family medicine had been Steve's dream—a husband and wife team that everyone could come to for whatever ailed them. All I'd ever wanted was to help people—

to really make a difference in the world. I wanted to give back. Maybe it was time for a radical change.

Carrying the mug of coffee into the living room, I scooped up the remote and flicked on the TV in the corner. I rolled my eyes as a commercial immediately filled the screen. Figured. Didn't matter what the program was, at least fifty percent of it was filled with ads for hemorrhoid cream or some sleazy law firm trying to "make them pay." I bit the inside of my lip at the thought of Gavin still passed out in my bed. I had to admit—for a lawyer, he really wasn't a bad guy.

The news finally came back on, snagging my attention as the reporter launched into her description of the victim I'd found just over a week ago down the road, and a composite sketch filled the screen.

"Police are asking for any help in identifying a man found off Hartwell Road last week. If you have any information, please call..." The number flashed on the screen, and I shook my head. Hopefully someone would recognize him and give the family some closure.

The composite sketch disappeared, replaced with video footage of police spread around on a riverbank, combing through weeds and mud. "Police are also investigating a second set of remains that was found yesterday in Twin Oaks. The person has yet to be identified, and there is no connection between the victims at this time."

I glanced out the window, and a shiver stole down my spine. That was a little too coincidental, wasn't it? That made two bodies, found only a few miles from one another. Was the person male or female?

The reporter hadn't mentioned anything, nor had the policeman who'd been interviewed. It was an interesting omission, and I wondered if the decomposition was too bad to determine on site. Though the police hadn't mentioned anything, I wondered if the second victim exhibited the same signs of surgical removal.

"In other news, a local woman, Dr. Victoria Carr, was abducted early yesterday morning from her home, and..."

I didn't wait to hear the rest. My fingers were already flying over the phone, waiting for the call to connect. I was on my feet and halfway to the kitchen before Victoria's voice came on the line.

"Hey, how—"

"Are you freaking kidding me? That's all you have to say? Are you okay?"

"I'm fine, I just—"

"Why in the hell are you so calm?" I demanded. "God, Vic. I just saw the news. What the hell happened yesterday?"

Victoria let out a soft chuckle. "Really, everything is okay now. It's a really long story."

I couldn't believe Victoria was laughing about this. I knew her better than almost anyone on this planet, and I knew how badly the events of the previous night must have affected her. "Are you sure you're okay?"

"I'm fine, really," she assured me. "I'll tell you all about it later."

"Damn right you will. Can I come over?" I dumped my coffee down the drain and set the cup in the sink. "I'm coming over."

Victoria laughed. "All right. Blake's here, too."

I let out a relieved sigh. Thank God. That made me feel better, at least. I hadn't spoken much with Victoria since Wednesday, and I was relieved to hear that they'd made up. The fact that he was with her now spoke volumes.

After the murder of a local woman a few weeks ago, the killer had reached out to Victoria—either as a taunt or a plea for help, the police couldn't quite decide. She'd been plagued by the same person for the last several weeks, and Blake had been hired to work security at the healthplex where Victoria and I worked.

She'd turned a disgruntled patient away just before the murder, and I wondered if it really was him. Greg Andrews had a bad temper, but as far as I knew, the police hadn't been able to dig anything up on the man. A shudder rolled through me. The police suspected it was the same man who'd assaulted me in my office. I definitely wouldn't miss going back there.

I glanced down at my robe and bit my lip. I couldn't very well go out like this. On silent feet, I crept back down the hallway and into my room. Flicking a glance at Gavin, I saw he'd shifted positions but his breathing was still deep and even, a good indication that he was still asleep. Tiptoeing over to the dresser, I pulled out a bra and T-shirt, then snuck into the bathroom to change. I quickly dressed and washed my face before opening the door and peeking out.

Gavin had one arm thrown over his face, and I pushed the door open just wide enough to slip out. The hinges squeaked, and I froze, holding my breath, eyes glued to Gavin to make sure he hadn't heard. I remained that way for several long moments before slinking out of the bedroom and down the hall into the kitchen.

Anxious to get out of the house before he woke up, I scooped my keys off the counter and slung my purse over my shoulder just as a floorboard creaked behind me.

CHAPTER
EIGHT

GAVIN

I stifled a smile as Kate inched the bathroom door open and tried to contort her body through the narrow space. She froze when I shifted slightly, as if holding her breath to make sure she'd hadn't awoken me, then released a soft sigh and slipped out of the room when I didn't stir. As soon as the door closed behind her, I dropped the arm covering my eyes and let loose the grin threatening to split my face.

She was truly something else. So open and passionate last night, she scurried around this morning like a nervous little mouse, afraid to wake me. I'd bet any money that she was terrified to come face-to-face with me, instead trying to usher me out the door like a dirty little secret.

Kate was strong and independent, but she wasn't one to act rashly, and I had a feeling that's exactly how she would see our night together: as a mistake. It would be up to me to soothe her fears, show her how good we could be together. Because after last night, I wasn't done with her. Not by a long shot.

Eager to ease her misconceptions, I swung my legs over the bed and went in search of some clothes. I had no idea what time we'd finally fallen asleep, but I estimated it to be somewhere around dawn, judging from the faint glow lighting the sky as I'd fallen asleep with Kate tucked in close to my chest.

She'd felt so perfect there, the perfect fit with her head tucked beneath my chin, her body so warm and content. A quick glance at the floor told me Kate had already picked up my clothes from last night.

A peek into the bathroom confirmed my suspicions. My clothes were folded neatly on the counter, a silent message that it was time for me to gather my things and get the hell out. If that's what Kate thought, she was in for a rude awakening, because I wasn't going down without a fight. I was going to take that fiery little redheaded temper of hers and wrestle it into submission. And I was going to enjoy every second of it.

A feral grin lit my face at the thought, and I quickly tugged on my boxers and dress slacks from yesterday. I refused to greet her naked, but there was no way I was going to put all of my clothes on, either. If I did, that would mean that my time with her was over—and that was the very last thing I wanted. My plan was to get out there and find her before she had more time to second-guess herself, then take her back to bed and show her how good we were together.

I padded down the hallway to the kitchen, toward the smell of freshly brewed coffee. Kate stood by the counter, purse over her shoulder and keys in hand, and I immediately tensed. What the hell? She was running out on me?

A floorboard creaked under my heavy tread, and she whipped toward me, eyes wide. Guilt shone brightly in the blue orbs, and anger flared around my heart. How dare she? She'd really planned to just cut me out of her life without any explanation at all—just disappear like our night together had meant nothing. Fuck that.

Back rigid, I stopped several feet in front of her and crossed my arms over my chest as I glared at her. Her eyes flicked over the broad surface of my chest, but I couldn't find it in me to be pleased by her obvious reaction to my nearness. I was still too pissed. "Going somewhere?"

Her eyes darted back up to mine, and she licked her lips. "My friend... I've got to go."

"Running away already?"

"No, of course not. I—"

"No? Because that's exactly what this looks like."

She shifted uncomfortably. "Well, it's... Fine," she huffed as she threw her hands in the air. "You're right. Kind of. But I really do need—"

"I can't believe you were just going to run out. Seriously?" I swept my arm toward her in an agitated motion. "Goddamn, Kate. You're such a coward."

"I am not." She stepped forward so she was almost toe-to-toe with me.

"You're afraid," I taunted. "You loved what happened between us last night, and now you're running scared because you're afraid."

"What the hell do you think I'm afraid of?" She propped her hands on her hips and stared me down, fire in her eyes. Perfect. She was almost where I wanted her. Just another little nudge and she'd be mine.

I'd push her until that redheaded temper of hers snapped, then once she was all good and riled up, I'd take the little wildcat back to bed and settle her the best way I knew how. I had a feeling that, with a little love and reassurance, she'd turn from a ferocious tigress into the cuddly kitten she'd been last night.

"I think you're afraid of me. Of us." I gestured between us. "Tell me you didn't enjoy last night."

"I didn't—"

"Liar."

She rolled her eyes. "That's not what I was going to say. I was going to say"—she punctuated her words with a hard poke to my chest—"it's not that I didn't enjoy it, but I can't do this right now. I'm not in a good place in my life."

"We haven't even talked about what this is!" I exploded.

"Then what is it?"

The question stumped me for a second as she turned the argument around. "I... I don't know. What if it could be something? You were just planning to run away before you even found out?"

"It doesn't matter," she said airily, waving one hand in the air as if it meant less than nothing.

"Is this how it's going to be? You pretend nothing happened between us?"

"I don't know what you want from me!"

"I don't either. I just want the opportunity to find out."

"I don't want... I can't do this again."

"Why not?"

"We shouldn't have done this. I have to go." She spun around but froze as the next words left my mouth.

"Really? Because you were more than willing to drop your panties for me last night."

She turned slowly back to me, her fiery eyes meeting mine. Satisfaction at getting a rise out of her flared deep within me. Good. She was as pissed as I was.

"What did you just say?"

The corner of my mouth lifted in a cocky smile. "I said, you stood right here," I laid a hand on the counter where we'd made out like teenagers, "and dropped your panties around your ankles."

"God, you're such an asshole."

"Yeah?" I sneered. "And you're an easy lay who used me for sex."

I didn't have time to duck or weave or even breathe as her fist collided with my jaw and blackness seeped into the edges of my vision.

"Okay, spill."

I glanced at Rob, whose mouth had curled into a mischievous smile. I shook my head adamantly. "Oh, no. I told you before," I jerked a thumb toward the doorway that Shannon had just sashayed through. "There's not a snowball's chance in hell of that happening."

"Not that. This." He slashed his hand in front of his face, indicating the bruise on my jaw.

I felt my cheeks heat, but I should have expected the question. I had, actually, but it didn't make telling the story any easier. And I never could lie to my friend. "You know Ms. Winfield?"

Rob's eyes widened. "Jesus, you didn't get into a fight with the ex, did you?"

"Um, no." I shifted uncomfortably in my chair, intensely aware of his scrutiny. I relayed the events of the past weekend, and Rob's raucous guffaw echoed through the room.

"She really... You... That's fucking hilarious." He panted the words between laughs, and I sank lower in my seat.

"Thanks for the support, asshole."

Rob finally got his laughter under control. "You've gotta admit, this is new."

I rolled my eyes. No shit. I could honestly admit that, during my almost thirty-five years on this earth, not once had a woman turned me down, much less hauled off and punched me in the face. Not that I hadn't deserved it—I'd immediately regretted the words as soon as they'd left my mouth. I'd been trying to get her attention, to get a rise out of her.

Well, I'd certainly done that. I was so certain she was just nervous and worried about falling into bed with me the night before that I hadn't paid attention to the little red flags she was throwing up all over the place. I was too blinded by my feelings for her to see that something wasn't right.

In truth, I had no idea what I wanted from Kate—but I sure as hell wanted more than the one night we'd spent together. Things might fizzle out quickly enough, but I at least wanted the chance to find out. In hindsight, I now saw that her face had showed signs of distress, but at the time I'd chalked it up to nerves at our confrontation.

Then I'd seen the news. A local woman, one of Kate's friends, had been attacked around the same time I'd been with Kate at her house. It was no wonder she'd tried to run out on me. I'd completely misread the worry on her face, mistaking it for shame instead of the true anxiety of a woman fearing for her friend.

I'd felt like a complete and utter ass as soon as I saw the news and recognized the woman's name. I'd called Kate yesterday and again this morning, but I'd yet to hear anything from her. After the way we parted, I suspected she'd go out of her way to avoid me at any cost right now. Which just meant that I'd have to go to her, even if it meant putting my face in harm's way again.

I resisted the urge to smile as I tested my jaw. The woman's killer right hook was proof of her perfection in my eyes. God, I'd almost be willing to go through that all over again just to see that fire in her icy blue eyes—almost. I didn't have a death wish.

A smile curved Rob's face. "Well, I guess that was over before it even started."

"No." I shook my head. "No, this is just beginning."

He shot me a skeptical look. "Sure you don't want to just quit while you're ahead?"

"Not a chance."

"Must be good."

I leaned back in my chair and glanced at the open doorway before turning back to Rob. I pursed my lips in thought. I'd known Rob for decades, and I knew I could trust him implicitly. Despite the fact that Rob insisted he'd stay a bachelor forever, he was always good to bounce thoughts off.

Right now, I needed to voice my thoughts out loud. Maybe I really was crazy and overthinking things. But saying it out loud, weighing the pros and cons of a situation always helped. I prepped for hours, sometimes days, before making an appearance in court, and the habit was so deeply ingrained in me that I couldn't help it.

"You have no idea. She's incredible." My tone dropped several octaves in sincerity. "Not just the sex—though it was fucking fantastic. But she's smart and funny, the whole package. I could really like this woman."

Truth was, I already liked her. I'd liked her from the moment she walked into my office months ago.

"Then I guess you've gotta suck it up and go apologize."

I would, but the damn stubborn woman wouldn't answer her phone. Not that I blamed her. I was an asshole, just as she'd accused me. She obviously wasn't going to come to me anytime soon, so that meant I'd just have to track her ass down.

I glanced at my watch. I had a meeting in an hour across town, which would put me in the vicinity of the healthplex. If all went according to plan, I'd catch her just as she was leaving for the day and convince her to go to dinner. I wasn't stupid enough to think she'd fall into bed with me so soon after what had happened last Friday, but all I needed was a chance.

Kate was the kind of woman who needed to come to a decision on her own; trying to rush her would do no good. I just needed a few minutes of her time to convince her that I wasn't a complete asshole—most of the time, anyway. She'd only really seen the business side of me, except for those few hours we'd spent together. If I could just plant that seed, make her see that I wasn't as terrible as she'd decided I was, then I could slowly begin to move in.

I pushed out of my chair and nodded to Rob. "Come on. Let's head over to meet with Gallagher."

"Driving separately?"

"Yep." I grabbed my briefcase and shoved the files inside before snapping it closed with a decisive click. "I've got business on that side of town."

A knowing grin lit Rob's face, and he extracted his wallet before pulling out a small square and tossing it in my direction. The foil packet bounced off my chest before I caught it one-handed. "You'll need that."

"Nah." I tossed it back to him. "Thanks anyway, man."

Rob lifted a brow. "You skipping the makeup sex?"

"Hell, no." I grinned and nodded toward the prophylactic. "It's too small."

"What the fuck ever." Rob let out a snort, and I laughed.

"Seriously, though. Long game, man."

He rolled his eyes. "Why bother? There's not a pussy in this world worth that kind of torture."

Could I seduce her back into bed? Probably. Was it tempting? Hell, yeah. But I wanted more from Kate than just sex. I wanted it all—and I'd do whatever it took, however long it took, to get it.

CHAPTER
NINE

KATE

"I still can't believe it." I paused in the act of packing up the last of my books and glanced across the room at Victoria, who was in the process of taking framed photos and diplomas off the wall.

"I know." Moisture sprang to Victoria's eyes, and I immediately regretted bringing it up. She was still covered in bruises, scrapes torn into the flesh of her neck and wrists. Shadows filled her eyes, but she was determined to push through, to move forward.

I'd spent most of Saturday at Victoria's house and, though I'd heard the story from both Victoria and Blake, I still hadn't come to grips with everything that had happened. After surviving a harrowing kidnapping as a teen, Victoria had recently been targeted by the same killer who'd returned after almost a decade. He'd killed two local women and attacked me in the healthplex because I had interfered.

Victoria had been lured out of her home by someone she trusted—the man who'd planned to carry out the murder he'd been denied years ago. Thankfully, Blake and his guys from QSG had shown up in time to rescue Victoria. The man had been killed that night, finally ending the horrific nightmare.

Looking back now, it all seemed so obvious. I shook my head, wondering why I hadn't seen it before. Hell, maybe deep down we'd all known and hadn't wanted to believe it. Just went to show that people were capable of all kinds of unspeakable evil, even those you thought you knew best.

I moved around the desk and pulled Victoria into a tight embrace. "I'm sorry."

"Me, too."

I knew it would be hard for her to move on. I wondered if she'd stay here in the healthplex or if she'd go somewhere else, too, leave the bad memories behind. I wouldn't blame her one bit. I glanced around the office I'd used for the past seven years. The walls were now almost bare, packed into the boxes we had brought in. It was the first step in moving on, starting fresh myself.

Pulling away from Victoria, I rested my hands on her shoulders. "What can I do to help?"

Victoria shook her head. "It'll just take time, I think. Blake's been amazing. Having him around has been really helpful."

"You look happy," I offered, studying her.

Victoria smiled back, her features lit up bright by the joy shining within. "I am. I love him so much. Thank you for your advice."

I waved away her thanks and propped a hip against the edge of the desk. "You guys are meant to be together. I'm just glad things worked out."

"Oh, it's incredible. He's..." Victoria trailed off and bit her lip.

I suddenly realized why she'd veered from her train of thought, and I shook my head adamantly. "Hey, don't you worry about me. You don't have to hold back just because of my divorce with Steve. I'm better off without him, and you're better with Blake. I want to hear everything."

She shot me a shy smile. "He's taking another job close to home so he can commute."

"Home?" I lifted a brow and smirked at Victoria, who blushed profusely.

"We're staying at my place right now since it's a little bigger. But the plan is to fix up Blake's little house and flip it. We'll see how everything's going by that point." She lifted a shoulder. "Maybe then we'll get a place together."

I smiled. "I think that's a great idea."

God only knew where Blake's job would take them. Ex-military, he now worked for a local security company that he and a friend had started, doing basic security coverage and private investigation work.

Quentin Security Group was based out of Dallas for now, but the plan was to put an office on each coast in the near future. In the meantime, Blake and the other ops would travel if needed. He could be away for days or weeks, depending on the job, but I had no doubts that he and Victoria would make it work. They both deserved happiness, and I thanked God they'd both come to their senses and found what was right in front of them.

I tipped my head toward the door. "Come on, let's get outta here so you can get home to your man."

Victoria sent a blazingly bright smile my way before turning back to the box in front of her and loading the last few picture frames. I grabbed my purse out of the closet and slung it over my shoulder.

"Seriously, Kate?"

I turned to meet Victoria's wry gaze as she held up the small bromeliad that had taken up residence on the window ledge. "What?"

"When was the last time you watered this poor thing?"

"Um..." My lips twitched in humor, and I bit back a smile. "Maybe it's just sleeping."

"It's dead." Victoria rolled her eyes and held the pathetic-looking, brown withered stalk over the trash can. "It's a good thing you take care of people and not plants."

The potted plant hit the bottom of the can with a solid thunk, and I couldn't help but compare it to my marriage: dull and lifeless. The only time I'd felt the smallest spark of anything lately was when I was with Gavin. He'd made me feel... incredible. He'd been an attentive lover, treating me as if I was beautiful and perfect.

Maybe if I'd gotten out of the house before he'd woken, I could have tried to contact him later. Despite my initial discomfort, I really had enjoyed being with him. I didn't want a boyfriend, but maybe we could have dated casually, seen each other occasionally. I almost felt bad for leaving the way I had—almost—but not after the things he'd said.

The memory came flooding back, and anger infused me all over again. No, I was done with that arrogant asshole who thought the whole world revolved around him. I'd had that once with Steve, and there was no way in hell I'd ever put myself in that same position ever again.

If I ever married again—and that was a huge if—it was going to be right. The right man, the right time. I wasn't going to rush into anything ever again, no matter how good a man made me feel. An hour of sex—or several, in Gavin's case—wasn't worth a lifetime of heartache.

I took another glance around the nearly bare office. This was what my life had been reduced to. It was easy to look at the space and see only an empty shell, but a spark of anticipation lit within, and I now saw a whole new set of possibilities. Though I was leaving this life behind, there were so many opportunities ahead of me. I could go wherever I wanted, do whatever I wanted.

With a small smile, I shook my head and gathered the box on the desk. "All right, all right. No more plants. Now let's go."

Victoria followed me to the elevator, and we rode the car down to the lobby. She glanced over as the door whooshed open. "When's your last day?"

"I'm planning on staying through..." My words trailed off as Victoria let out a squeal of glee and practically skipped across the tile floor to where Blake reclined in one of the visitor's chairs. I watched with mild envy as he stood and opened his arms to her, accepting the box of memorabilia in one arm and his girlfriend in the other, pulling her tightly against him.

I approached the duo, and Blake met my gaze over Victoria's small frame, sending me a small nod. I never would have paired my petite friend with this giant of a man, but they were just so freaking cute together, I couldn't help but smile.

Victoria stepped away, her hands on Blake's chest. "I completely forgot my purse in my office. Can you please carry that out to Kate's car for her? I'll meet you out there."

"You sure?" Blake's eyes clouded with concern.

Generally speaking, walking to the parking garage next door wouldn't have been a big deal, but with everything Victoria had been through in the past few weeks, I doubted he wanted to let her out of his sight for even a second. How she'd managed to convince him to let her go to work without him watching over her was beyond me. He took his duties very seriously and would do everything in his power to keep Victoria safe. For that, I was extremely grateful.

"It's no problem," I cut in. "I'll just carry this one out and come back for that one."

"No, no. Blake can take care of it. I'll only be a minute

anyway." Victoria stretched up on her toes and planted a soft kiss on Blake's mouth. "Everything will be fine, I promise."

"If you're sure." He still looked uncertain, but he let her go, and together we watched Victoria stride back toward the elevators.

I turned to Blake. "She's happy. Thank you for taking care of her."

Blake watched the elevator door close behind Victoria before turning to me, his voice low and sincere when he spoke. "Thank you for bringing her back to me."

I waved it away, just as I had when Victoria had thanked me earlier. They deserved to be together, and I was just happy that everything had worked out. "I didn't do anything."

He shook his head. "I thought I'd lost her. I don't know what you said to her, but... I owe you. Anything you need, it's yours."

I studied him for a minute. "You saved my life, Blake. I would say we're more than even."

My gaze was drawn toward the glass front doors, to a dark figure striding purposefully toward the building, and I swore silently. Blake went rigid at my side, and I realized I hadn't been so quiet after all.

"What's wrong?"

"It's nothing. Just a guy." I kept one eye on the door as it was yanked open, and Gavin strode across the brightly lit lobby.

His gaze seemed to zero in on me, and he immediately amended his stride, steadily closing the distance between us. The faint fluttering of butterfly wings battered my ribs as I watched him approach. Damn, the man looked good—even with his battle scar.

The dark bruise stood out along the line of his jaw, and I guiltily bit down on my lip. I was a doctor, for God's sake—I'd taken an oath to help people, and never in my life had I harmed another person. But the man was so damn aggravating and conceited, I hadn't been able to control my reaction when I'd popped him in the jaw.

"Looks like he pissed someone off pretty good."

A small smile curved my mouth before I could stop it. Don't get me wrong—I felt bad for busting up his jaw, but the jerk had definitely deserved it. "That was me."

Blake snorted a laugh from where he stood next to me, and I shifted the box in my arms just as Gavin stopped in front of us.

"Kate."

The butterflies inside my stomach broke into full flight as the smooth honeyed sound of his voice wrapped around me like the sweetest caress. Steeling my spine, I lifted a brow at him, forcing myself to maintain his intense stare instead of allowing my gaze to stray lower, over the sculpted muscles I'd perused at length just days ago. Heat flared within me, but I tamped it down, focusing instead on the ire I was trying so desperately to hold on to. "Gavin."

He studied me for a moment. "You haven't answered any of my calls."

"I didn't know I was supposed to."

His eyes narrowed, and his tone took on the slightest hint of aggravation. "I've been trying to get a hold of you."

"Why? Did you need a recommendation for that?" I tipped my chin toward his jaw and pointed over my shoulder to the elevator bank behind me. "Dr. Harbaugh's on the third floor."

"Who?"

"Dr. Harbaugh. Maxillofacial surgery."

He stared at me blankly for a moment, then blinked hard, his frustration quickly rising to the surface. "I don't even know what that hell that means, but I don't need a damn doctor."

"Do you have paperwork for me?" I wanted to put our time together behind us and move on. I'd purposely ignored all of his calls, hoping he'd do the same. Didn't look like that was the case.

"Not yet. I—" He gave a little shake of his head, like he was trying to get back on track. "Listen, I wanted to apologize."

I stared at him for a long moment. "Was that your pathetic excuse for an apology?"

He looked completely taken aback. "No, I—"

"Apology accepted," I said brusquely, cutting him off with a little toss of my head. I didn't want to dwell on him being nice. Just having him nearby brought back all the memories from last week, short-circuiting my brain. I needed to get the hell away from him before I did something stupid, like ask for a repeat. I couldn't afford for that to happen.

"Now, if you'll excuse us, we have to go."

With a head tilt to Blake, I started toward the front door. Within seconds, Gavin was beside me once more and placed a hand on my upper arm. Blake, who up until this point had remained blissfully silent, let out a low growl. Gavin's hand immediately fell away, and his eyes darted to Blake as if just realizing that the giant man was, in fact, with me.

That familiar chocolate gaze slid again to me and hardened slightly. "Are you with him?"

"That's none of your business," I snapped.

He looked absolutely furious, and I couldn't help but needle him further. Maybe he'd finally get the picture and leave me alone. "But if you absolutely have to know, then yes, he's—"

"Who's this?"

My shoulders tensed as Victoria's soft voice floated over my shoulder. Damn Victoria. She had the worst timing ever. I briefly closed my eyes before spinning around and trying to capture her gaze, praying that she would get the hint and play along.

"No one," I said loudly, just as Gavin stuck out a hand for her to shake.

"Hello, I'm Gavin."

I cleared my throat and tried once again without success to meet my friend's gaze.

"Nice to meet you. I'm Victoria." Victoria smiled and released his hand, then stepped into Blake's embrace and slipped her arm through his.

Seriously? I glared at Victoria, but her eyes were focused solely on Blake. Damn her guileless, naïve self for not picking up on the signal I'd so blatantly thrown up. Gavin watched the proceedings with interest, and the tiniest glimmer of a smile lifted the corner of his lips as he met my gaze, clearly calling my bluff. I glared back, and the smug expression slipped from his face.

Victoria glanced between the two of us. "Blake and I are heading to dinner. Would you two care to join us?"

Gavin turned his attention to me, his brows lifted in question. Or maybe it was challenge. The damn man was impossible. Trying to get through to him was like shoving at a brick wall. The last thing I wanted to do was be stuck in a restaurant with him for the next two hours, let alone a vehicle. I was seventeen once; I knew very well what happened in back seats, and I didn't need the temptation.

"You guys go ahead. I'm not hungry."

Gavin pried the box from my hands. "At least let me carry this out for you, then."

Without another word, he turned and started for the front door.

"But... Gavin!" I threw my hands in the air in exasperation before feeling Victoria's bemused gaze on my back. I swiveled toward her. "Can you believe the gall of that man?"

"I think it's sweet." Her head tipped to the side as we fell into step behind him. "He's very handsome." She ignored Blake's low hum of disapproval. "Who is he?"

"No one."

"Please." Victoria pulled me to a stop and propped her hands on her hips. "How do you know him?"

"It's not important." I tried to propel Victoria toward the exit, but she remained frozen in place, face tipped up in defiant expectation. I knew she wouldn't give in until I told her something. I shifted restlessly on my feet. "We kind of..."

Victoria's eyes lit up. "Did you finally go on a date?"

Good Lord, she made it sound like I'd been in a convent. Though, to be fair, that wasn't far off the mark. Still, I grimaced and bit my lip. "Not a date."

Victoria tipped her head to the side as she contemplated what I'd said—and what I hadn't. "So... oh!"

I smirked. Oh, indeed. There'd been quite a few of those during my night with Gavin. I stared across the lobby at the man who sent a curious look my way as he got ready to hold the door open for us. The black suit accentuated his sleek form, and I couldn't help but be drawn to him.

My eyes skated over him one more time, and I was transported back to Friday when I'd skimmed my fingers over every inch of him. It was a shame the man was such a jackass, because he was definitely worth going back for seconds.

Victoria squealed beside me, tearing me from my reverie. "I'm so happy for you!"

"No, no," I warned her. "Don't get your hopes up. It was just a one-time thing."

"I don't know," Victoria sang as she started again toward the door. "He looks pretty determined to me."

"Yeah, well..." I didn't have a response for that. Still, I had my life to figure out before I could even begin to think about inviting a man into it. "I can't."

"Why not?" Victoria asked as we continued on. "I know the whole thing with Steve has made you wary, but..." She lifted her hands in a little shrugging motion. "It doesn't have to be serious, not yet. You deserve to find someone who cares about you."

"Maybe." It was all the response I could muster at the moment. Gavin had taken my reserve and turned it upside down, then shaken it like a snow globe. I'd never felt more comfortable with a man than I did with him.

The rational part of me screamed to give him a chance, to let him prove he was as serious as he seemed. My heart, on the other hand, was locked up tighter than a vault. I couldn't bear to endure that kind of hurt again, and I wasn't sure I'd ever let someone fully inside ever again.

Our small group reached the front door, and Gavin held it wide, then followed us to the parking garage. I was hyperaware of his presence as he strode beside me, doing his best to make small talk. When I failed to respond, he finally grew quiet, and we passed the last portion of the trip into the parking garage in an awkward silence. The four of us stopped beside my car, and I took the boxes from Gavin and Blake, then set them in the back seat.

"You good from here?"

I met Blake's intense gaze before turning to Gavin. He looked so sincere, I figured he deserved at least a couple minutes of my time. With a sigh, I turned to Blake.

"Yeah, we'll be fine. Thank you."

I hugged Victoria, who looked like she might burst with happiness. I rolled my eyes and gave Blake a lopsided smile. He studied Gavin, the corners of his mouth tugging down in a frown like he still wasn't quite sure what to make of the other man.

He finally met my eyes and gave me a meaningful look. I clearly read the message in his hazel eyes that he'd gladly tear the man apart if he made a wrong move. With a surreptitious wink to Blake, I leaned against the car and turned my attention to Gavin with a raised brow.

He waved to the others as they walked away, Victoria comically craning her neck to watch us. Blake finally managed to corral her and guided her around the corner to where her car was parked. I tipped my head at Gavin. "That bruise looks like hell."

His lips pulled up in a grin. "I'll bet you can kiss it and make it all better."

My mouth kicked up in a smirk before I could stop it. Not wanting him to see how appealing I found the suggestion, I let out a little scoff. "There's too much wrong with you to fix with just a kiss."

His expression turned serious, and he stared at me imploringly. "I really need to apologize. What I said was..." He shook his head. "I was a dick."

I nodded once. "You were."

"I didn't know about..." He raked a hand through his hair before gesturing after Victoria. "That was her, right?"

"It was."

"I'm sorry."

I met his solemn gaze. If he could own up to his actions, then so could I. "Me, too. I was a coward. I was going to leave you a note."

He raised a brow in my direction, and I felt my cheeks heat. I knew I'd taken the easy way out, running out of my own home without a word to escape a one-night stand. "I think I was, anyway. To be honest, I wasn't totally thinking clearly. I saw the news, and I had to go see for myself that she was okay."

"I understand." He reached out and took my hand. "I don't blame you for that. I thought you were running away from me because you were embarrassed."

I gave a little nod but remained silent. What could I say to that? Admit that it was partially true? I'd been terribly ashamed of my behavior that night; part of me still was. My husband and I had been separated for only months, and my divorce hadn't even been finalized before I'd thrown myself at Gavin like a sex-starved lunatic. I almost cringed just thinking of the things we'd done that night, things I'd never done with another person, including my husband of six years.

"I really hope you'll let me take you out on a date sometime."

It was tempting, I couldn't deny that. But the insecurities of my failed marriage came rushing back. I didn't want or need a man in my life at the moment. I needed to get my head on straight and fix my life. I needed a job, something positive to focus on. Maybe down the road Gavin and I could be friends or... more. But today was not that day.

I shook my head and reluctantly pulled my hand from his. "I'm sorry. I just... I can't."

"Can't or won't?"

I met his gaze. "Both, I think. I just... With everything that's happened recently, I have a lot of things to sort through, and I need to do something for myself for once, not what someone else wants, and—"

I caught myself rambling and immediately jerked to a stop. He stared deep into my eyes as if trying to read what lay in my soul, and I shifted under the scrutiny.

Finally, he took a step back. "Okay."

Okay? My brows drew together. A mixture of relief and disappointment swirled in my gut at his immediate acquiescence. Maybe everything he'd said was a lie; maybe he didn't want me as badly as he'd tried to convince me.

I swallowed hard and forced myself to speak. "Okay, then."

After all, what more was there to say?

Eyes still locked on mine, Gavin took several slow steps backward, each one putting more and more distance between us. Panic suddenly seized me. I'd only felt truly happy lately when I'd spent time with him. Granted, it was only one night, but still... What if I was letting a truly good thing slip through my fingers?

Part of me wanted to lunge after him and apologize, beg him to go out on that date he'd offered. My fingers twitched at my side, and I curled them into a fist to keep from reaching for him and drawing him back to me.

I didn't need his kind of complication in my life. If I said it a hundred more times—maybe a thousand—I'd start to believe it. I shook off the thought. No, this was definitely for the best.

With a slow nod, Gavin winked at me. "I'll see you soon, red."

Before I could utter a response, he'd spun on a heel and was already striding away. I'd turned him down. Why did he look so upbeat? Then his words sank in.

"I meant what I said!" My words lacked conviction, even to my own ears, and I resisted the urge to stamp my foot.

He didn't respond, didn't even turn around, just waved a hand over his head to acknowledge my statement. With a harrumph, I yanked open the car door and slid inside. I slammed the door on the thought of him and started the car, heading toward home and a whole future of possibilities— hopefully one lacking arrogant, overbearing men.

CHAPTER
TEN

GAVIN

Playing with fire had never been so much fun. I sat back in my chair and linked my fingers behind my head, the scene from the healthplex playing through my mind once more. I loved the way Kate got all fired up. I'd had to bite my cheek to keep from smiling when she tried to pass the huge guy off as her boyfriend. Yeah, right. I saw the appeal, but he wasn't her type—not like I was.

Her cheeks had gotten bright red, and I swore she was tempted to smack her friend—Victoria—when she'd refused to play along. I should send the woman flowers or something for doing me a favor. Then I'd heard them talking about me as I strode away. Victoria was solidly Team Gavin. I grinned. Winning over the best friend was step one.

My desk phone rang, and I picked it up, tossing a quick look at the clock in the lower right-hand corner of the computer screen.

"Yes?"

The elderly receptionist's warm voice flowed through the speaker. "Your two o'clock is here."

"I'll meet them in the lobby. Thank you, Mrs. Hodges."

Dropping my feet to the floor, I shrugged into my jacket, then straightened my tie before heading out of my office to meet my next clients. I flipped on the light for the conference room as I passed, then continued toward the lobby, following the childish peals of laughter that drifted my way.

I rounded the corner and paused midstride at the sight that greeted me. A tall man stood in the middle of the small lobby, making airplane sounds as he held a baby suspended high over his head. The toddler waved her arms and legs, clearly delighted with the activity. Next to them, seated on the couch, a pretty brunette watched on, her lips curled into a soft smile.

As soon as they saw me, the woman stood and the man lowered the baby to his chest, a huge grin on his face. "Sorry about that."

I waved away his apology. "No need. She seemed to be enjoying it." I held out a hand, first to the woman. "Gavin Price."

She tipped her head in acknowledgement and slipped her hand into mine. "Lydia McLean."

I turned next to the man, who returned my handshake. "Xander McLean, and this"—he bounced the baby on his hip —"is Alexia."

"Hey, beautiful." The baby turned her head into her father's shoulder, peeking at me with one eye, and I grinned as I gestured down the hallway. "You can follow me."

I watched with interest as the man wrapped his arm around his wife's waist, then fell into step behind me. As soon as they were seated along one side of the table, I closed the door and sat opposite them.

While Lydia extracted a sippy cup and some snacks from a

large bag, I took a moment to study them. She wore a wide head wrap to hide a portion of hair that had been shaved away, and the white square of a bandage was visible over her temple. The baby sat on the table in front of Xander, her curious gaze flitting around the room.

It suddenly struck me, seeing the baby's face next to his, how much they looked alike. From her pale blonde locks and bright eyes, she seemed to be spitting image of her father. They were a beautiful family, which made me all the more curious about their appointment today.

I'd looked over the paperwork just a few days ago, and it seemed like a pretty cut-and-dried case to me—Mrs. McLean had requested to annul the marriage nearly a year ago, and all we were missing was a signature from each party in order to prepare the final paperwork. From the looks of things, though, the annulment no longer seemed to be required.

Finally all settled, Mr. and Mrs. McLean gazed across the table at me expectantly, and I jumped right in. "First of all, I'd like to apologize for not following up sooner. It was an oversight that should never have happened."

"Don't worry about it," Xander said. "Actually, I'm glad it worked out this way—we both are."

He and his wife shared a warm look, and I sat back in my chair with a little smile. It wasn't often that I dealt with happy clients like this. "So," I began slowly, "should I assume that we can disregard the paperwork?"

"We..." Lydia faltered for a second, her cheeks pink with embarrassment. "It was kind of an impetuous mistake on my part."

Her husband draped one arm over the back of her chair and lightly grazed his knuckles across her shoulder. "On both our parts," he said before turning his icy blue gaze to me. "We met in Vegas a couple years ago. One thing led to another, and..."

My brows rose, and I lifted my chin in understanding as my gaze bounced between them. "Got it."

As a lawyer, this was precisely the type of situation that I typically advised clients to be extremely wary of. Seemingly aware of the same thing, Lydia dropped her eyes away, blushing furiously, and Xander pulled her closer.

I couldn't help but wonder how many people had said the exact same thing—that eloping in Vegas was rash and would never work out. Neither tried to defend themselves; they didn't have to. It was obvious to anyone with eyes that they'd found something special.

Lydia leaned into her husband, and he dropped a kiss on her forehead. The baby squirmed on the table, one of Xander's arms curled loosely around her, ready to catch her in case anything happened. The man in question turned back to me. "We've decided to give things a second chance."

"Good. I hope it works out for you," I said sincerely. They truly looked happy, and I wished them the best—but I still couldn't figure out exactly why they were here. "Well, then, you can disregard the paperwork you've received, and I'll make the changes on my side."

"I appreciate that," Xander replied, "but there's actually something I was hoping you could help us with."

I tipped my head in question, and he continued. "The woman I spoke with told me you could help us with our wills."

I nodded. "I can do that. Do you have an existing will, or are you starting from scratch?"

They exchanged a quick look. "From scratch," Lydia said.

"I work security," Xander spoke up, "and I want to make sure the girls are taken care of in case anything happens."

My eyes moved to the insignia on his chest displaying the letters QSG in white thread, and I nodded thoughtfully. It looked so familiar, but I couldn't place where I'd last seen it. I tipped my chin toward the logo embroidered into the shirt. "Is that where you work?"

His head dipped, his eyes following my gaze before meeting mine again. "Quentin Security," he clarified. "I was discharged from the Army a couple months ago, and a buddy of mine invited me to come work for him."

"I've seen that logo before." Focusing intently, I tried to bring the man's face into view. I'd seen him when I visited Kate at the healthplex. What was his name again? I stared across the table at Xander. "Tall guy, broad, beard. I met him at the healthplex not too long ago."

Xander nodded knowingly. "Blake."

I snapped my fingers. "That's it. His girlfriend works with a friend of mine." Calling Kate a friend sounded childish, but I didn't have a better word for our relationship—yet. "Is your group local?"

Xander nodded. "We do a little bit of everything—PI work, personal protection. We're in the process of setting up a gym upstairs to offer self-defense courses."

"Nice. I'll have to keep that in mind."

With that, we transitioned into a discussion of preparing a living will for both of them, listing assets and beneficiaries. Half an hour later, Alexia began to fuss, and I smiled over the table at them. "I can finish this up and send it your way in a couple days to check over."

Lydia gathered her things and stood, holding one hand out to me. "Thank you so much."

"No problem." I shook Xander's hand. "I'll be in touch."

I walked them to the lobby, then returned to my office and closed the door. Pulling my cell from my pocket, I flipped through the messages and emails, noticing that the one name I was looking for remained infuriatingly absent. I set the phone on the blotter on top of my desk and sat back in my chair, pondering my next step. I wanted Kate to reach out to me, but

I had a feeling she never would. I'd have to take that step—but I had to do it carefully. If I came on too soon or too strong again, she'd bolt like a fractious pony.

If there was ever a woman worth waiting for, it was Kate Winfield. I'd never felt this way about a woman, not even as a horny teenager ready to fuck anything with two legs and tits. I knew I wanted her from the moment she walked into my office more than six months ago. I'd spent a grand total of about twenty hours with her, but I knew—just knew—that she was it. Now that I'd touched her, tasted her, felt every curve beneath my hands, there wasn't a chance in hell that I was ever going to let her go.

Everything about her appealed to me—her intelligence, that wicked sense of humor, her fiery hair and temper to match. And then there was her passion, wild and unrestrained, giving as good as she got. God, how I wanted her—all of her—but I knew I needed to keep it slow and steady, acclimate her to my presence.

I knew how badly she'd been hurt by that asshole ex of hers, and I needed to prove to her that I wasn't the same. I couldn't risk moving too fast and spooking her. If I pushed too hard, she would run like hell, and I would lose her forever.

I knew that whatever was between us wasn't love, not yet. But it could be. I just need to convince her to take another chance. I'd be here waiting until she was ready. After all, I'd already waited this long. What was a few more weeks, or even months?

Kate Winfield would be mine. She just didn't know it yet.

CHAPTER
ELEVEN

KATE

I smiled at the receptionist—Stella, according to the name tag on her chest—and introduced myself. "Hi, I'm Dr. Kate Winfield. I just accepted a position here, and I'm supposed to start training today."

The young woman returned my smile. "Of course. I'll let Becky know you're here."

I'd spoken with the woman in the HR department during my initial interview two weeks ago, and she gave me a brief rundown of what to expect. It was strange, working in a practice like this that was government funded. Steve and I had opened our practice in the healthplex right after we graduated, so I'd never had any experience working in a large practice like this.

I took a seat in the lobby and smiled at one of the patients across from me. Becky came out just a few moments later, greeting me with a smile.

"Dr. Winfield, good to see you again."

"You, too." I shook her hand, then fell into step as we

made our way past the reception desk and down a long hallway. Patient exam rooms lined both walls, and I nodded greetings to the nurses as we passed them.

"This will be your office." Becky paused beside a door at the end of the hall and held out a hand, gesturing for me to enter first. "There's a key in the top drawer of the desk if you'd like to leave your things here. I have some paperwork for you to fill out, and I'd like to show you around."

"Of course." I left my purse, and we began the tour of the facility. It was designed in a basic U-shaped, with the receptionist desk front and center. Doors to the exam rooms were located on either side, and the patients would be directed through the doorways to either station A on the left, or station B on the right.

A young male nurse in blue scrubs stood behind the desk, and Becky smiled at him. "Chris, this is Dr. Winfield."

"Nice to meet you." He extended his hand with a smile, and I shook it.

"You as well."

"Are you new to the area?"

I shook my head. "No, my husband and I actually had our own practice over in the healthplex downtown." Something flitted across his features at the mention of my husband—my ex-husband—but I didn't bother to clarify that we were almost divorced. I had no intention of dating a man I worked with, and I saw no reason to give him false hope.

"That's great. I'm sure you'll like it here. Everyone's awesome to work with."

"That's good to hear, thank you."

Becky turned to me. "I'll introduce you to the others later, but if you don't have any questions at the moment, I have some paperwork for you to fill out."

I nodded. "Lead the way."

The remainder of the afternoon was spent filling out

paperwork and studying the requisite training materials. I also met another dozen nurses and another physician, Dr. Elijah Coleman. As good as I was with names, my head felt like it was spinning trying to absorb all of the new information. It was both the same and completely different from the small practice Steve and I had together. I truly felt like it was a good fit for me, though, and I could see myself there for a long time.

By the end of the day, I was exhausted. I stumbled through the front door of my condo and absently petted Peanut on the way to the bedroom. As I passed the kitchen, I checked to make sure that he had food and water, then I proceeded on through to the bedroom.

Kicking off my shoes, I crawled into the middle of the bed and lay down. I'd just barely close my eyes when the vibrating of my phone caught my attention. Digging it from my purse, I glanced at the screen. I didn't recognize the number, and I deliberated for a moment before swiping my thumb across the screen.

"Hello?"

"Hey." My stupid heart leapt at the sound of Gavin's sexy deep voice. Though we'd only shared one night together a week and a half ago, his presence seemed to permeate my bedroom. I could still feel him, smell him next to me, and I closed my eyes as his deep voice washed over me. "How's the new job?"

He knew about that? I fought to modulate my voice as I spoke. "Good. How did you know about that?"

A low chuckle filtered over the line. "You underestimate me, red. I make it my business to know everything about you."

"That's not creepy or anything," I quipped.

"I prefer to think of it as dedicated," he corrected.

Despite myself, a smile tugged at my lips, and I forced my mind to get back on track, needing to take control of the situation. "I see. Whose number is this? I didn't recognize it."

"It's my cell," he responded.

That's why it hadn't looked familiar. When we'd spoken previously, we'd used the office phone number to communicate. We lapsed into silence for a moment before Gavin picked up the thread of conversation.

"So what do you think? Do you like it?"

"I do," I admitted. "I'm actually really excited."

"Good," he responded. "I'm happy for you. This was your first day, right?"

"Is that a question or a statement? I thought you knew all about me," I teased.

"Never know," he responded in that sexy drawl. "I've been known to be wrong once or twice."

My brows shot upward in disbelief. "Did you just admit that you were wrong?"

"Only once in a while," he replied. "But don't tell anyone."

I laughed, and I had the sense that he was smiling on his end, too.

"So, did you get all settled in today?"

"A little bit," I said as I lay back down and stared at the ceiling. "Most of it was training, getting used to the feel of the office. And the computer system—God, that's a nightmare."

His sexy laugh washed over me like a warm caress. "That's always the worst, isn't it?"

"It is," I agreed. I let out a long yawn, and I heard Gavin take a deep breath on his end.

"Well, you sound exhausted. I should let you go relax."

"Okay," I whispered as a pang of disappointment pierced my heart. Silly as it was, I wasn't quite ready to hang up yet. Neither was I able or willing to offer more at the moment, so I kept my mouth shut. Gavin seemed to understand, because he spoke just a moment later.

"I'm glad you're doing well. I'll talk to you soon."

The phone clicked off, and I stared at it for a long moment, a mixture of anticipation and worry settling over me. He'd called... Why, exactly? To wish me luck with my new job? I bit my lip and replayed our conversation in my mind. It'd been brief and friendly, but it lacked the overbearing confidence Gavin normally threw my way. He'd said he would talk to me soon, but not when. Was this just a friendly conversation, or was it more?

I told myself it was stupid, that I was reading too much into things. I wasn't looking for a relationship, but I couldn't help the satisfaction I felt that he'd reached out to me. I truly enjoyed Gavin; I just wasn't sure that I was ready to offer him everything he deserved.

CHAPTER
TWELVE

GAVIN

I sat at my desk, head bent over a case file, completely absorbed in the details when the knock on the door captured my attention. I jerked my head up and met Larry's silvery-blue eyes.

"Mind if I come in for a second?"

I lifted my chin at him. "Sure."

I watched curiously as he stepped inside, then closed the door behind him. His gaze flitted around the room, over the degrees hanging on the wall behind me, then out the window at the perfect summer day.

Hands in his pockets, he prowled slowly toward me and stopped in front of my desk. I leaned back in my chair and crossed my ankle over my knee, adopting a casual pose. He remained standing, taking a position of power, towering over me. I hated feeling at a disadvantage, and I had a feeling that was exactly what he was trying to do. I wiped any trace of expression from my face and stared up at him impassively. I refuse to let him see my ire. For several heartbeats, we remained that way.

Finally, he broke the silence. "You have a great record."

For some reason, it wasn't what I was expecting. "Thank you, sir. I do my best."

My father had always told me I was too stubborn for my own good, so it was probably a good thing that I got paid to argue for a living. Once I decided on a course of action, I rarely, if ever, strayed from it, and more often than not, I got exactly what I wanted. The only contradiction to that recently was Dr. Kate Winfield, but I'd been working on my game plan for her too.

I pushed thoughts of Kate away as Larry spoke again. "How long have you been with us?"

I was sure he knew exactly how long it had been, but I answered regardless. "Three years, sir."

He gave a tight little nod. "I have several other men and women who have been here much longer than you."

"Yes, sir." I wasn't sure where the hell he was going with that.

"You may have heard that Walker is retiring at the end of the year."

I'd heard the rumors, including the speculation that they would be looking for a new partner. I hoped to be the man to fill that spot, but I didn't come out and say so. Instead, I gave a little nod. "I did."

"I'd like you to join me tomorrow night for dinner with a client. I've already had Mrs. Hodges add it to your calendar. I hope that won't be a problem?" He lifted a brow, almost as if he were daring me to decline.

"Of course not. I'll be there."

"Good, good. You're always willing to step up. I appreciate that." Icy blue eyes bored into mine. "Shannon seems quite taken with you. She says you're always nice and helpful when she needs something."

Somehow, I managed to mask my initial reaction. Shannon was a complete space cadet, and she was probably just grateful that I didn't scream at her for her mistakes like some of the other lawyers here. Still, I didn't know what to say, so I went with the first thing that came to mind. "I know how hard it is just starting out. I'm glad to be of service."

Something entered his expression, but he blinked it away as quickly as it came. "I'm glad to hear that. She means the world to me. In fact..." He let out a little laugh. "I think she has a crush on you."

My gut tightened, and I fought to school my expression. The last thing I wanted was for my boss to think I was hung up on his daughter, the apple of his eye. I couldn't defend myself without looking guilty, even though I had zero feelings for Shannon, so I turned it around. "Like you said, I'm sure she's just grateful for the help."

He stared at me for a moment, then—"I'm sure. You know," he said slowly, "you're like a son to me."

It was a rather strange thing to say, considering I knew he had a son of his own. If I remembered correctly, the kid was somewhere in his midtwenties, approximately ten years younger than myself. I vaguely recalled Larry holding a grudge against him because he'd chosen not to follow in his father's footsteps.

"Thank you, sir," I said. "I appreciate the compliment."

His gaze left mine again for a moment before returning. "It would be nice to have family here. Wouldn't it be nice to be a partner, with Shannon to help us?"

Was he implying what I thought he was? I couldn't formulate a suitable response, so I merely nodded and said, "I'm sure everything will work out."

He eyed me for another long moment, then nodded. "Well, I'll let you get back to it."

I watched, confused and more than a little irritated as he left my office. If he thought he was going to pressure me into dating his daughter just for a partnership, he had another thing coming.

CHAPTER
THIRTEEN

KATE

Across from me, Victoria and Blake chattered away, their heads tipped close together, and I eyed them with envy. They were so different, but so damn good together. I almost felt as if we were imposing on some private moment, despite the fact that they'd invited me along tonight.

I adjusted the napkin over my lap, and Clay leaned in close, his breath tickling my ear as he spoke. "You good?"

I lifted my gaze to his. "Yep!"

I almost cringed at the high-pitched voice that left my mouth, and by the way one brown brow ratcheted upward, it hadn't gone unnoticed by Clay, either. I scrambled for something to say before he could read any more into the situation than necessary. "So what are you doing again?"

Beside me, Clay Thompson's eyes roved the room once more. "Working."

"No kidding." I rolled my eyes. "But what does that mean?"

Clay let out a low chuckle. "I'd tell you, but then I'd have to kill you."

"I'm supposed to be your cover tonight, but I don't get to know what you're doing?" Victoria had called me last night and asked me to tag along to dinner with her and Blake as well as his friend and coworker, Clay. Not one to turn down a dinner I didn't have to cook, I readily accepted. She'd mentioned that the guys were doing some recon, but she either chose not to elaborate or didn't know the details. Having met both men now, I was betting on the latter.

His mouth kicked up in a smirk. "Tailing a cheating husband."

"Ooh," I whispered as I glanced around the room. "Which one?"

Knowing exactly how it felt to be on the receiving end of that particular situation, I hoped Clay would catch the bastard in action. An almost unnatural glee filled me at the prospect of the man—whoever he was—getting his comeuppance.

Clay gave a slow shake of his head. "Be a little more obvious, why don't you?"

I bit back a smile. "Sorry. Not really cut out for the cloak-and-dagger type stuff."

He smiled. "Cloak-and-dagger?"

"Whatever." I lifted a shoulder. "You know what I mean."

"Mmm..." He pulled out his phone as if to check something, and I watched from the corner of my eye as he took a few discreet photos, then set it down again.

The curiosity was killing me, and I fought to keep from looking at the man across the room. "Was that him?"

"Maybe."

I turned in my chair to face him fully. "So, what now?"

He shrugged. "We eat."

I stared at him. "But... you only took a few pictures. Couldn't you have done that from outside?"

"I could have, but this was easier. People tend to notice a man hanging around outside a restaurant all alone like a creeper."

I grinned. That was probably true, especially a man like Clay. Trying to miss that man was like trying to overlook a boulder. "Fair enough. So what's with Blake and Victoria?"

The couple across from us didn't even look up. "Just an extra layer of invisibility. Right now, we're just a couple on a double date with friends."

Made sense, I supposed. I nodded and picked up a roll from the basket, then tore it into tiny pieces. Clay turned quiet again, probably surreptitiously watching his mark, and I popped a piece of the bread into my mouth as I looked around the restaurant.

It was beautiful, elegant and intimate, the perfect place for a date—a real date. Though the restaurant was popular, I'd never been here before, and I doubted I would be again. I couldn't help but wish the circumstances were different, that I was here with someone who cared about me.

"In case I didn't tell you earlier, I appreciate you coming out with us. Having a good time?"

I lifted my head and forced a smile. "Fine, thank you."

Clay's tawny eyes studied me for a long moment, then the corners crinkled up in a smile. "You're a terrible liar, red."

"Don't call me that."

His brows lifted, and the smirk on his lips became a full-fledged grin. "I like a woman with some fire." My lips parted to shut him down, but he cut me off. "Too bad you're not my type."

I jerked back slightly at his words, not sure if I should be relieved or offended. He rested one arm over the back of my chair and turned his body to fully face me. "You're beautiful, no doubt about that, but I know a taken woman when I see one."

I dropped my gaze and fiddled with the napkin in my lap. "I'm not taken. I'm not seeing anyone."

"Not even the guy who can't take his eyes off you?"

I snapped my head toward him. "What?"

At the very same moment, the sensation of being watched tickled at the back of my neck, and I turned to survey the restaurant. Abruptly, like a magnet drawn to steel, my gaze collided with a pair of familiar dark brown eyes, smooth and dark as melted chocolate, and a thousand times more tempting. I wanted to drown in the deep depths.

My heart leaped, and my breath caught in my chest as he stared back at me, unblinking. He flicked his eyes toward Clay before returning them to mine, and his brows lowered slightly. Despite our brief interactions, I knew that look. He was *pissed*.

I swallowed hard and picked up a glass of water just to give my hands something to do. I took a tentative sip, but the glass trembled in my grasp, and I quickly set it down again.

"You good?"

I tipped my face up to Clay, whose expression now registered concern. "I'm fine," I assured him.

"You sure? Because if he's bothering you—"

I waved one hand in the air, as if batting the thought away. "No, no, nothing like that. He's not dangerous or anything. He would never hurt me." Just my heart.

Clay's lips pressed into a firm line, and I set a gentle hand on his forearm. "I promise. I appreciate your concern, though. And besides, it was never serious between us."

The charismatic smile returned. "Not sure I believe that. Price looks like he wants to rip my face off right now." Glancing toward Gavin, I snatched my hand away from Clay's arm. If he'd looked angry earlier, now he looked downright thunderous.

Suddenly, his words registered. "Wait—you know him?"

Clay dipped his chin. "Went to school with him."

Oh, Jesus. Just what I needed, for Gavin to think I was dating a friend of his. I didn't owe him a damn thing, but I didn't want to hurt him, either. My stomach twisted, and I felt the sudden need to get away from both of them.

My hands fumbled as I picked up the napkin, then folded it and placed it on the table. "Excuse me." I pushed my chair back and stood. "I need to use the restroom."

"Oh," Victoria started. "I—"

Across the table, I shot her a look, and she immediately fell silent. "I'll be back in just a moment."

Without waiting for a response, I cut across the restaurant, desperately trying to escape the dark brown eyes I could feel burning a hole in my back.

CHAPTER
FOURTEEN

GAVIN

I stared at the sloppy fat fuck in front of me, just barely resisting the urge to choke the life out of him. He was the one who'd been in the wrong, yet here he sat, trying to screw his wife out of what she rightly deserved.

I wasn't one to judge someone on their looks, truly I wasn't, but I wouldn't have blamed the woman one bit if she had cheated on him. Though that was the story he had tried to spin, it was actually the other way around.

His wife had gotten curious at his extended absences and had hired QSG to tail him. Come to find out, the man had a hot little side piece nearly twenty years his junior. Why in God's name the girl was interested in someone like him blew my mind.

Mentally, I rolled my eyes. *Of course*. Money. It was one of life's greatest motivators. I couldn't even bring myself to feel bad for the little gold digger. She deserved whatever happened when he got tired of her ten years from now, too.

"I want full custody, too," Howard Garlington said as he swiped the napkin over his mouth.

I took a drink to cover a snort. That was highly unlikely. The courts almost always sided with the mother, except in situations where they suspected illegal activity or abuse. I seriously doubted the asshole even wanted his kid. It was more than likely just a power play, something to hold over his wife's head to make her more amenable to giving him whatever he wanted. It burned me that he might actually be able to make it happen by bribing whichever judge was assigned to his case.

My lip curled up in a sneer, and I forced myself to look away before I snapped and said something that would jeopardize my job. Tables were spaced evenly around the large room, giving the impression of privacy and intimacy. Couples talked quietly amongst themselves, and I couldn't help the little pang in my chest, wishing that Kate was sitting across from me instead.

Though I'd texted her a few times over the past two weeks, and we'd spoken once, right after she'd begun her new job, she'd been mostly reserved. I didn't know what to make of that. I'd hoped she would begin to open up a little bit, but it hadn't happened yet. I admired her decision to postpone a relationship until after her divorce was finalized, but damn... I'd be lying if I said I hadn't been hoping for a little more from her—some indication that she was open to dating me. Something—anything—other than polite, stiff replies.

I scanned the sea of faces, and my heart stopped as I caught a familiar profile across the room. Soft light overhead made her hair shimmer, turning it even more red, and a soft smile graced her lips. Dressed in a conservative black dress, her hair twisted up into an elegant updo that showed off the sleek column of her neck, she made my mouth water. I wanted to trail my lips over the smooth flesh, nip and kiss until she made that sexy little sound I loved so much.

Across from her was the woman she'd introduced me to at the healthplex—Victoria. A large man sat to Victoria's left, his back to me, and I recognized him as Blake, Victoria's boyfriend. It took me several long moments to notice the fourth member of their party, so caught up was I in my fantasies of Kate.

My stomach clenched, and I ground my molars together as I studied the man sitting to her left. Tall, muscled, and good-looking, there was no doubt in my mind who he was. Kate's date for the evening—and the guy who'd made my high school years a living hell.

Clay Thompson was the biggest prick walking, or at least he had been twenty years ago. I doubted anything had changed. From the wrong side of the tracks, he'd had a huge chip on his shoulder and hated pretty much everyone, and I seemed to be the lucky person at the top of that list.

His twin brother, Cole, wasn't much better, but I'd at least been able to tolerate him. Clay, for whatever reason, seemed to go out of his way to insult me every chance he got. It was petty to still feel distaste for the man after all this time, but I couldn't help it. I had to know if she was really with him.

As if she could feel my eyes on her, her head whipped toward me, and we locked eyes. Our gazes held for a long minute, then Clay dipped his head toward her, and I watched as she laid her hand on his arm. Jealousy and anger reared up, turning my skin hot.

Larry's laughter boomed out, ripping my attention away from Kate, and I forced myself to tune back into the conversation. "Who could blame you for that?"

Garlington stabbed at the table with his forefinger. "Tara's expecting a ring, but I can't propose to her until this shit with Beverly is over. I need to expedite this divorce, but I want to retain all assets."

I blinked hard. "You may want to consider settling."

"Why the hell would I do that?" His lip curled up in a sneer. "She didn't bring anything to this marriage. Why should she get anything out of it?"

Larry shot me a quelling look over the table, and I snapped my mouth shut. I knew for a fact that the asshole had refused to let his wife get a job. Beverly, in fact, was a very intelligent woman. She'd gone to UT for pre-law but had met and married Garlington prior to finishing her degree. Once they'd married, he guilted her into becoming a stay-at-home wife and mother, the perfect image for his political aspirations.

Being a young bride, Beverly had wanted to make her husband happy. She'd done everything expected of her, yet risked leaving the marriage empty-handed if Garlington falsified evidence that showed she'd cheated on him. I fucking hated people like him. I prayed with all my being that Beverly's lawyer would shred whatever evidence he presented and force him to give up half his shit on principle.

The waitress finally deposited the check on the table, and I breathed a sigh of relief. I felt on edge, and I couldn't wait to speak with Kate. It seemed like kismet that she had shown up here tonight, and I wasn't going to let her run away from me again. Larry glanced at the check, then across the table at me and gave a slight lift of his eyebrow. Staring back impassively, I reached for the check. The moment my fingers brush the leather folio, he let out a laugh.

"I'm just messing with you, Gavin. It's on the company tonight. Unless, of course, you want to buy."

I heard the faint thread of challenge in his voice, and I gritted my teeth. I wished the slimy fuck would just make up his mind and spell out what it was he wanted. I was tired of his mind games, tired of dancing around the subject. I wanted to be partner, no doubt about that, but I wasn't going to jump through hoops to get there. I was a damn good lawyer, and that in itself should speak to my credibility.

I smiled blandly back at him. "You know I don't mind."

Next to me, Garlington laughed and slapped a meaty palm on my back. "Gotta work for what you want."

That was ironic as fuck coming from him. His wife had put up with him for years but wouldn't have a damn thing to show for it if Larry had any say in the matter.

Larry's face kicked up in a condescending half smirk I detested. He was the epitome of a scumbag lawyer and precisely the reason the rest of us were stereotyped as such. "Nah, I've got it."

He threw down what I assumed was the company card, then snapped his fingers at the waitress. I bit the inside of my cheeks at the pretentious show of dominance. Dick.

The waitress hurried away, and I listened with half an ear as Raines and Garlington bullshitted over the last of their scotch until she returned with the checkbook. Raines scribbled his signature, then slid his card back into his wallet and stood.

I did the same, noting with fury that he hadn't left her a tip. I tensed as Larry clapped one hand on my shoulder. "Nice job, son."

I forced a smile to my face and pulled away. "Thank you, sir. I need to hit the head. See you Monday."

I glanced back toward Kate's table as I moved across the restaurant, but she was gone. Hell, no. I wasn't about to let her hide away from me. I'd used the bathroom excuse to get the hell away from Larry, but I had a gut feeling that was where Kate had slunk off to, so I headed in that direction. I didn't care if I had to stand here like a stalker for the next twenty minutes, I was going to get an answer, damn it.

The doors to the kitchen were close to the hallway where the bathrooms were located, and I noticed our waitress exit just as I approached. I pulled a couple twenties from my wallet and discreetly passed them to her. "I believe we forgot to add a tip to the bill," I lied.

She nodded her understanding, her expression grateful as she tucked the money into her apron. "Thank you."

I gave a curt nod and turned away. Kate exited the bathroom just as I entered the short hallway, and I froze. Goddamn, she was beautiful. She was busy adjusting her sleeves, and she'd taken several steps in my direction before registering my presence.

Her gaze collided with mine, and she stopped dead in her tracks. I allowed myself a moment to drink her in. She looked more beautiful than ever. The scar on her forehead was still visible against her pale skin, but that too had begun to fade since I'd seen her last.

I finally settled on her piercing blue eyes. "How have you been?"

She remained unnaturally still, like she was barely even breathing. "Fine. What are you doing here?"

My gaze narrowed at her unease. I'd seen the way Thompson touched her at the table. I didn't believe his intentions were friendly in the least. "You on a date?"

Her eyes snapped with fire. "What business is that of yours?"

I shoved my hands in my pockets and leveled her with a stare. "Just asking. Think I have a right to know after what happened between us."

Her eyes darted around as if checking to make sure no one had overheard. "Nothing happened between us," she hissed.

Fury had my spine snapping straight. "Are you kidding me?"

Crystal-blue eyes glared up at me. "No. And what the hell does it matter to you if I'm on a date, anyway?"

"Oh, I don't know," I drawled, sarcasm saturating my

tone. "Maybe the fact that I've told you a dozen goddamn times that I want to be with you."

Something flashed across her face, then just as quickly faded away. She opened her mouth to speak, then closed it again and looked away, pinning her gaze to the wall instead of meeting my eyes.

I shook my head, the heat of anger melted away at her indifference, and an icy coldness took up residence in its place, seeping into my bones. "You know, I shouldn't be surprised. You threw up every red flag, and I ignored them all."

I felt like a fucking fool for having reached out to her repeatedly her over the past couple weeks. I'd been waiting for her to come around, to finally see that I was the one for her. I thought if I gave her the time and space she'd asked for, she'd see how much I respected her and cared for her. Looked like I'd been wrong the whole way around.

"I should've known when you said you weren't ready to date that it was a crock of shit. What you really meant was you didn't want to date me."

Kate's head snapped toward me. "That's—"

"Everything good here?"

I turned slightly, and every muscle in my body stiffened as the man approached. I lifted my chin at him. "Thompson. It's been a while."

Clay Thompson returned the favor, then continued past me—toward Kate. I couldn't rip my eyes away as he stepped up next to her and settled one hand low on her back. "You good?"

"Yeah. I'm fine." Her gaze never wavered as she answered Clay's question, those bright blue eyes fixed on mine.

The heat of jealousy and rejection curled through me, and I forced my gaze away from her. Clay's mouth twisted into an arrogant smirk, and I wanted to wipe it off his face. He acted like he'd one-upped me, like Kate was some fucking prize to be won. Well, he could have her. Thompson was a cocky bastard, and she was a deceptive bitch. They belonged together.

"Just talking business," I said to Clay. "Nothing important."

His brows drew slightly together as I pasted on a fake-ass smile and turned to Kate. "Feel free to contact my office if you need anything else, *Mrs. Gerber*."

Kate stood stiff as a marble statue, and just as pale. Pushing off the wall, I directed my gaze to Clay. "Best of luck to you both."

Fuck you both, I amended in my head as I turned on a heel and stomped toward the bar. A red haze clouding my vision, I slid onto a stool, then motioned for the bartender.

"Dewars, neat," I said when the young woman stopped in front of me. With a concise nod, she turned around and grasped the bottle from the shelf behind the bar. She slashed the liquid into a glass then slid it in front of me. I tossed down my credit card, then curled my fingers toward me. "Leave the bottle, please."

The bite of the fiery liquid would hopefully prevent me from getting too drunk too quickly, but I relished the burn as it slid down my throat. It gave me something to focus on other than Kate. I didn't know how much time had passed, but I glanced up as someone slid onto the stool next to me. The scent of her perfume hit me first, and I followed my nose, swiveling to inspect the pretty brunette next to me.

I let my gaze trail over her, from the top of her perfectly coiffed hair, over her buxom curves, then down to the hem of her too-short skirt that barely covered her ass. I dragged my eyes back to her face, and her lips curled into a sultry smile. She was obviously looking for a good time and a man to give it to her.

"Hi."

Her voice was silky and smooth, and I couldn't help but smile back at her. "Hi, yourself."

"Catalina."

I took her proffered hand. "Gavin. What brings you here?"

She eyed me as her fingers played with mine. "Probably the same thing that brought you here."

I seriously doubted that. I released her hand and picked up my drink. "What's that?"

"Just looking for someone interesting. Fun." The woman rested an elbow on the bar and leaned toward me. My eyes followed her movements as she placed one hand on my knee. Everything in me coiled and tensed as she slid her palm upward. "Would that be you?"

It was impossible to miss her intent. Before I could form a response, I felt the sensation of being watched, and I snapped my head up just in time to meet a pair of familiar blue eyes. Kate's gaze dropped to the woman's hand lingering near my crotch, and her cheeks flushed bright pink. Her eyes met mine again, and I swore I saw a flash of hurt before she blinked it away. Straightening her shoulders, she strode determinedly past the bar, gaze focused in front of her.

My heart dropped to my toes. I felt simultaneously vindicated that I'd managed to get a rise out of her and guilty for hurting her. Son of a bitch.

I turned back to the woman and extricated her hand from my thigh. "I'm sorry. I appreciate the offer, but I can't."

Her eyes clouded with confusion, and I smiled gently. "It's... complicated."

With a resigned nod, she turned back toward the bar, and I slipped off the stool and hustled toward the front door. I was already scanning the sidewalk when I stepped outside, but I was too late.

Kate was gone.

CHAPTER
FIFTEEN

KATE

"Did you see that they found another body?"

I turned a confused glance at Brandi as I closed the door of the fridge and propped one hip against the counter. "What?"

Chris used his fork to point toward the small flat-screen TV hanging on the wall of the break room. "Have you seen this yet?"

Brandi thumbed the button on the remote to turn up the volume. On the screen, a perky blonde reporter relayed details of a police investigation into a body that had been found along the edge of the river.

Chris sat there, riveted to the TV. "Unreal."

I shook my head in commiseration. This made three—and everyone knew what that meant. For the next few moments, we watched the segment. Investigations into all three of the victims' deaths were ongoing, but there was no mention of them being connected.

I pondered that for a moment. Really, how couldn't they

be? Maybe it was my nature to suspect the worst, but bodies weren't just found in the woods every day, especially not so close to one another. And I'd bet my left hand that the other remains would show the same brutality the first victim had—the amputated fingers, the missing teeth.

It could, of course, be a complete coincidence. Maybe they hadn't released the details so as to not spark a panic. That made more sense than anything. I trusted the police to do their job and keep people safe. It was hard to tell, too, just what was happening until they identified the victims and determined an actual cause of death. Was there a connection between them—a similar motive for killing them?

The first victim had been identified only days before as Mr. Robert Tripp. The second body had yet to be identified, as they were still working on a composite for the man. He'd been found only two miles from the cornfield where I'd found Mr. Tripp, but what remained of the corpse was so badly decomposed that the police suspected the person—another male, according to the preliminary investigation—had actually been abducted and killed prior to Mr. Tripp.

Between the heat and the animals, a body wouldn't last too long in nature, but the police had evidently found enough to piece together most of a cadaver. According to the reporter, they had yet to identify the man. Though she didn't say as much, I wondered if that was because, like in the case of Mr. Tripp, all distinguishing characteristics had been removed.

A searing anger shot through me. Whoever it was had medical training, probably a surgeon. Doctors were supposed to help people, protect them—instead, someone was taking it upon themselves to hunt down innocent citizens of Dallas for their own personal gain. Black market organs went for a pretty penny—some sold for hundreds of thousands of dollars.

"Bastard," I murmured. Three sets of eyes swiveled toward

me, and I pointed to the screen. "There is no excuse for something like this. I hope they find the person responsible."

Brandi's eyes turned sad. "You never expect things like this to happen in your hometown, to people you know."

That was an understatement. Bad shit happened everywhere, but this was too much.

"Do you remember Mr. Tripp?" Chris asked.

Brandi shrugged. "Only vaguely. I know he was in here a couple times."

No longer hungry, I tossed my sandwich back in the fridge and headed to my office, where I closed the door and sank down in my chair. The thought of something like this happening so close to home made me sick, and a shiver raced down my spine. Not that it was any consolation, but the victims so far had been male. Hopefully, I wouldn't have anything to worry about, but that didn't mean I would let my guard down at all until they figured out who was behind the killings and why.

I desperately hoped they would ID the second and third victims soon. Maybe the police would get lucky and find a definitive connection and catch the killer. That would at least give the families some closure. I couldn't imagine something like that happening to someone close to me. Victoria's incident was bad enough. It'd been horrible, seeing her story on the news the morning after Gavin and I...

At the mere memory of him, my heart twisted in my chest. He'd tried to call me a couple times, but I'd ignored him each time, unable to bring myself to speak with him. The thought of him with that girl tore my heart to shreds.

He'd startled me by accusing me of being on a date, and I'd immediately gotten defensive. Everything had gone downhill from there. He'd stormed off at the sight of Clay, heading for the bar near the front of the restaurant. After dinner I'd headed in that direction to speak with him. I at least wanted him to hear my side of the story.

As it turned out, he'd already turned his attention elsewhere. Beautiful, big boobs, hand possessively on his thigh. I couldn't get the image of that woman out of my mind. It was just like Steve's indiscretion, but worse somehow. Seeing them together reminded me of why I refused to let another man in.

I knew it was irrational, but I couldn't help it. Though I'd been the one to push him away, subconsciously I wanted him to care about me the same way I was beginning to care about him.

Rising from my chair, I pushed my negative thoughts away and wandered toward the nurses' station. Stella was headed toward me at a fast clip, her brow furrowed with concern.

I lifted my brows in question. "Everything okay?"

"I just got off the phone with Mr. Price a little while ago. He called with chest pains, and I suspected it was a heart attack. I went ahead and called dispatch and had them pick him up, then reached out to his emergency contact."

"Good," I said, relieved. "Thank you."

We walked back to station A side by side, and I leaned my elbows on the counter. "Who do I have next?"

"McPherson, room 104."

"Thanks."

I took care of my next patient, but I couldn't get Mr. Price off my mind. I could call the hospital to check with the attending physician, or... I leaned my elbows on the counter at the nurses' station.

"Stella, what else is scheduled for this afternoon?"

She clicked through the system. "Dr. Coleman has a patient at 4:20, but that's it for the day unless we have any walk-ins."

I chewed on my lower lip. "Still haven't heard anything about Price?"

She shook her head. "Not yet."

I checked the clock hanging over the desk on the wall. "I'm going to head over, see how he's holding up. I assume you already sent a copy of his chart to the hospital?"

She nodded. "Taken care of."

"Awesome, thanks again. I'll see you in the morning." I headed toward the back of the office and shrugged out of my lab coat, then grabbed my purse and locked up before heading toward Dr. Coleman's office. I froze in the hallway as the sound of angry voices met my ears.

"I swear, I never meant for any of that to happen." I recognized Dr. Coleman's voice.

"Like that makes it any better." The second voice sounded bitter and resentful.

"I'm sorry. Believe me when I say I tried—"

"That's not good enough!"

"You'll never know how sorry I am."

"You think you can apologize and make all of this go away?"

Make what go away? I bit my lip and leaned infinitesimally closer.

The man paused, and I imagined him seething, shaking his head. "It's too late for that."

"Please, I—"

"You'll pay for this."

The man's parting words punctuated his exit, and I jumped out of the way as he stormed out of Coleman's office. He seemed taken aback to see me standing right outside, but he gathered himself quickly and continued down the hallway. I peeked my head around the doorway and saw Dr. Coleman with his elbows braced on the desk, head resting in his hands.

He looked more saddened than concerned by the threat, and sympathy tugged at me.

"Everything okay?"

His head jerked up, and his startled eyes met mine. "Yeah, yeah." He waved it off. "Loss is hard. Sometimes people just..."

So, this was a patient they were discussing, someone who hadn't survived. "It never gets easier, does it?"

He shook his head, his expression sad. "No, it doesn't."

Silence descended for a second, and I cleared my throat. "I've got a patient over at Memorial. I'm gonna head out and check on him."

"No problem." He offered me a strained smile.

The drive to Memorial passed slowly as I battled the afternoon traffic, and I let out a little sigh of relief when I finally pulled into the multilevel parking deck. I headed straight for the ER and took my place behind an elderly couple as I waited to speak with the nurse on duty. I offered her a smile when I got to the window, then flashed her my badge. "I'm Dr. Kate Winfield from over at the VA. I believe one of my patients, Philip Price, was just admitted here a couple of hours ago."

She checked the system, then nodded. "They just moved him up to the fourth floor. He's in room 416."

"Thank you." I shot her a smile, then headed toward the metal detector to pass through into the main portion of the hospital. The elevator was just getting ready to close when an older man stuck his hand out and stopped the doors, allowing me to step inside.

"Thank you." I punched the button for the fourth floor, and we rode in silence, the car stopping every few seconds to let people off. I finally stepped out onto the fourth floor and made my way to the nurses' station. A young man was just writing Mr. Price's name on a whiteboard behind the desk when he caught sight of me and lifted his chin. "Can I help you with something?"

"I'm Dr. Kate Winfield, here to see Philip Price."

"Oh," the young nurse said, "he's mine."

"How's he doing?"

"Great, so far," he responded. "Tests show it was pretty mild, but he's had a series of them, spaced pretty close together."

"Do you mind if I check in on him?"

"Go right ahead," the nurse invited. "Let me know if you need anything."

I nodded to him, then headed down the hall toward room 416. Inside, the television played softly, but I was surprised that his family hadn't arrived yet. I rapped my knuckles on the doorjamb before stepping inside.

Mr. Price's head swiveled my direction, and his eyes lit with a combination of surprise and pleasure. "Dr. Winfield. What are you doing here?"

"Stella told me you called into the office, said it sounded like a heart attack, which it was. Just wanted to come check up on you." I lifted his chart from the bin attached to the wall and flipped through it as I approached the bed. "How are you feeling?"

"Old," he quipped.

I chuckled softly, then set the chart on the small wheeled table before pulling a chair up to the side of the bed. "Apparently the tests show that you've had a series of mini heart attacks recently. Have you been stressed out, overexerting yourself?"

He let out a little sigh. "No more than usual."

I studied him for a long moment. "It might be better if you stayed with a family member for a while, just in case anything happens. Do you have anyone close by?"

"My boy is on his way here," he responded less than enthusiastically. "I guess I could ask him."

"That sounds like a great idea," I encouraged.

A scuffle in the doorway dragged my attention to the man there, and my eyes widened. Gavin looked dumbstruck as he paused midstride. I sat riveted, as helpless as a deer caught in the headlights, watching a series of emotions flicker in his dark eyes. Surprise. Pleasure. *Lust.*

I couldn't rip my gaze away from his, and my heart skipped a beat in my chest. God, he looked good. Had he looked this good a week ago? Of course he had. That was precisely why the brunette at the bar had practically climbed into his lap.

A faint buzzing filled my ears, and my mind felt curiously blank as I tried to process the turn of events. Why was he here? Unless...

"Well, don't just stand there," I heard Phil say, completely oblivious to the tension crackling between Gavin and me. "Come on in, son."

Oh, God. Swallowing hard, I dropped my gaze to the floor. I couldn't believe I hadn't figured it out before now. Gavin Price was Philip Price's son.

I watched a pair of shiny leather shoes cross the floor until they were directly in front of me. I glanced up, expecting to find those dark eyes on mine, but Gavin's gaze was instead fixed on Phil. "How are you feeling?"

"Fine, fine," the older man commented, waving one hand toward the extra chair. "Gavin, this is Dr. Winfield. Doc, this is my son, Gavin."

Gavin didn't make a move except to slant a look my way. My breath suspended in my lungs as he stared down at me. "How are you?"

"Good, thanks."

After a painfully long silence, I pushed up from the chair,

careful to avoid brushing against Gavin in the process. "Well, I should be going. Take care of yourself, Phil."

He offered a little wave, and I departed the room like my heels were on fire. I'd just made it to the elevator when a strong hand wrapped around my wrist, halting my progress. Not hard enough to hurt, just enough to get my attention, there was no mistaking who the hand belonged to. Slowly, I turned to face Gavin.

He released my arm and let his own fall to his side. He just stared at me. Why did this man affect me so badly? There never seemed to be any middle ground with him—he made me feel too much. Too much passion. Too much pain.

I steeled my heart as I peered up at him. "Do you need something?"

He opened his mouth like he wanted to say something, then snapped it closed again. "It didn't mean anything."

My heart cracked at his admission. Hearing him say out loud that our time together meant nothing hurt more than I thought it would. I couldn't even muster up the ability to speak over the lump in my throat. I started to turn back toward the elevator when his voice stopped me cold.

"That woman—she meant nothing. I... We didn't..." He let out a harsh sigh. "Nothing happened."

Honestly, I didn't know whether to believe him or not. He looked sincere enough, but I was well aware of how conniving and manipulative people could be when they wanted to be. "Okay."

"I just wanted you to know," he said softly. "There hasn't been another woman since you."

My heart leaped in my chest, and I fought like hell to control my expression as he continued to speak, his voice low, his eyes serious.

"I promised I'd wait for you, and I will."

Damn, I wanted so badly to believe him. I wasn't honestly

sure what scared me more—my intense reaction to him or his avowal to win me over. Either way, it seemed like a losing proposition for me. I'd fall and have my heart shattered once more. I couldn't let that happen.

The elevator arrived with a quiet ding. Without a word, I stepped inside and turned. Gavin's eyes remained locked on mine until the doors closed, just like the walls surrounding my heart.

CHAPTER
SIXTEEN

GAVIN

I slowed to stop in the garage, then shut off the engine and headed around to the passenger side. My father waved me off as I opened the door and held out a steadying hand.

"I'm fine on my own," he groused. "Don't know why they insisted on me coming home with you."

I bit back an exasperated sigh. "Because you just had a heart attack—multiple, actually—and your body is still weak. They wanted to make sure you had someone close by in case you needed help."

He struggled out of the seat, then leaned against the side of the car for a moment, catching his breath. "I've been taking care of myself for sixty years. Nothing's going to change now." He drew in a panting breath and glanced around the garage. "It's too damn hot in here."

I turned away as I rolled my eyes. Of course it was hot in the garage; it was damn near a hundred degrees outside. I was half tempted to give in and take him back to his house, but both Kate and the staff at the hospital had insisted he have someone close by at least for the next few days.

Like it or not, we were stuck together for the foreseeable future. My baby sister Whitney was his favorite, but she lived three states away and had a family of her own. I couldn't make her walk away from that just because Dad was being stubborn.

I let out a sigh. "Let's just go inside."

I turned and headed toward the house, leaving him to follow. God forbid should he think I was doting on him. I opened the door and stepped into the kitchen, then made my way to the fridge for a bottle of water. I cracked the lid and took a healthy gulp as Dad shuffled in and shut the door behind him.

I watched over the rim of the bottle as he puttered around the counter and sat heavily on one of the barstools. His face looked flushed, and there was a fine layer of perspiration on his forehead from his trek inside. I couldn't tell if it was the strain on his body or the unbearable heat that had caused it.

I slid a look at him and gestured toward the fridge. "Want some water?"

He gave his head a little shake. "No, but I'll take some coffee if you've got some."

I blinked once, hard. He was fucking with me, right? What the hell was it with old people and coffee? He'd complained less than two minutes ago that it was too hot out, but thought it was totally normal to drink coffee now? I gave my head a little shake as a rueful laugh escaped my mouth. "I can make some for you."

He gazed around the room, and one eyebrow lifted at the sight of my single-serve brewer on the counter. "No, it's fine. I don't want to put you out any more than I already have."

"It's fine," I said. "I want you to feel at home here. Besides, it'll only take two minutes to brew a cup. Just tell me how you take it."

"No, don't worry about it," he replied.

"If you want coffee, I'll make the damn coffee," I snapped.

He huffed an irritated little sound and heaved himself off the barstool. "Just show me where the guest room is so I can rest up a bit."

I clenched my back teeth together, fighting back the urge to scream. I didn't know why he had to be so damn difficult all the time. He was my dad, and I loved him, but we'd never seen eye-to-eye; we never would. Not for the first time, I wished Whitney could be here to take him off my hands. She would know exactly what to do. I had a feeling the next week was going to be rough on both of us.

Shoving away from the counter, I strolled down the hallway toward the front of the house. I'd converted my office into a bedroom for him and had a bed and TV moved in so he wouldn't have to struggle up and down the stairs. There was a full bathroom one door down, so the setup was almost ideal. Or so I thought. Dad paused in the doorway and looked around, a frown tugging at his lips.

I felt my hackles rising as I watched his gaze sweep over the room. "Something wrong?"

He gave an abbreviated shake of his head. "Nope."

The tone of his voice told me he was lying, but I couldn't bring myself to care at that moment. No matter what I did, it wouldn't be right. I decided to take a step away before my anger got the best of me. "Make yourself at home," I said through clenched teeth. "And yell if you need anything."

Without giving him the chance to come up with anything else that aggrieved him, I jogged up the stairs to my room, pulling my cell from my pocket and dialing as I went. Whitney picked up just as I closed the bedroom door.

"Hey, big brother. How is Dad doing?"

"Ornery as shit," I replied. "Are you sure you don't want to take over for me?"

I could practically hear her eyes roll through the phone. "The only reason you guys don't get along is because you're so much alike."

"I take offense to that," I retorted. I'd admired my dad growing up. He was a hard worker and a good husband to my mother until she passed, and all I'd ever wanted to do, just like every other kid, was make my father proud.

From the time I was in middle school, I followed in his footsteps, playing peewee football, then becoming a high school quarterback and leading our team to state. After graduation, I spent two tours serving my country in the Marines, just like dad had. After I was discharged, I went to his alma mater and got a degree in law—just like him. And I hated every second of it.

It paid the bills and then some, and I enjoyed when people got what they deserved, but that wasn't nearly as often as it should be. I felt like something was missing from my life, maybe more than one thing.

I knew a lot of it had to do with Kate. Ever since I met her, I'd felt the urge to settle down, or at least turn my attention to a more serious relationship. Even though she'd been married at the time, I knew there was something different about her, that I wanted to explore it further. She had her reservations, but I hoped I would be able to convince her to give me another shot.

As for my job, I didn't know what to do. Larry had dangled the promotion in front of me like a carrot, but I wasn't sure I wanted it anymore, especially not if there were stipulations attached to it. I wouldn't whore myself out for a raise.

I hung up with Whitney, not feeling much more optimistic about the situation, then changed and headed back downstairs. I hit the basement for a quick run on the treadmill and was just opening the door into the kitchen when I ran into my dad. "Hey. I'm gonna change, then eat. What would you prefer—chicken or pork?"

The doctor had given strict orders for my father to follow a healthier diet to try to lower his cholesterol. Not for the first time, I wished Mom was still around. For the last year and a half since she passed away, I was certain he hadn't been taking care of himself. They'd spent so much time together, always going golfing or playing racquetball together, that it had never occurred to me to worry about his health.

Now, though, I was acutely aware of his age. He was looking older and more frail, almost depressed. Mom's battle with cancer had hit him hard, and I felt bad for not checking in with him more often.

He lifted one shoulder. "Whatever's easiest for you."

"Chicken it is." This time, I didn't even bother to argue. There was plenty of food in the pantry that he could make if he didn't like it.

Seated at the oak table, he threw a look my way. "Something going on with you and Dr. Winfield?"

I froze at the question. Why the hell was he asking? I knew Dad was astute enough not to have missed the exchange between Kate and me, but he'd never expressed any interest in my love life. I decided on an easy answer. "We know each other. She was a client."

My father grunted. "No wonder she ran away from you."

"Always assume the worst about me, don't you?"

Unfortunately, in this case, he was right. I'd hurt Kate, and I deserved her scorn. The way she'd looked at me in the hospital had nearly gutted me. I'd seen distrust and sadness, insecurity and accusation. But underneath all that, I'd also seen a glimmer of desire. This thing between us wasn't even close to being over yet.

I sidled up to the reception desk and peered at Mrs. Hodges. "I need to ask you a favor."

I hadn't been able to get Kate off my mind and, sometime during the past twenty-four hours since Dad had asked me about her, I'd finally come up with a plan. It wasn't my best work, but it was all I had at the moment.

"What's that?" The older woman turned an inquisitive gaze on me as I pulled up a chair and took a seat.

"I need you to call Dr. Winfield and have her come in."

Her graying eyebrows drew together. "Whatever for? I believe everything has already been settled and—"

I shook my head. "I need to speak with her."

Her eyes narrowed, then took on a speculative look as she tipped her head to one side. "Mr. Price—"

"Please," I said when I knew she was about to balk. "I need to see her in person. It's important. Whatever you want for Christmas this year, it's yours."

Her lips pressed into a thin line. "Dating clients is against our policy, let alone our ethics—"

"She isn't technically our client any longer," I argued. "And this isn't some whim. I promise," I added when she opened her mouth to admonish me again. "Tell her anything to get her in here. I just need to see her."

"I don't know why you can't just talk to the poor woman yourself," she groused.

"I don't want to scare her off," I admitted. "Her husband cheated on her, and she doesn't want to go through that again."

"Poor dear." Mrs. Hodges's eyes softened, and I knew I almost had her. "She's the sweetest thing."

I almost choked on my reply. Kate and sweet weren't exactly synonymous—in fact, her redheaded temper was one of the things I loved most about her. I managed to force down the laugh that had sprung to the tip of my tongue.

"She's... incredible," I amended. "Isn't your husband a fan of the Stars?"

I knew Mr. Hodges was an avid hockey fan, and I'd give them season tickets if I could just convince her to get Kate in here. It was underhanded, I knew, but there was no way she'd come if I asked. Not after last time. I knew she still hadn't forgiven me, hadn't thought I was sincere. I needed to apologize, but I had to get her in here first, somewhere private so I could speak with her one-on-one.

"Oh, all right." Mrs. Hodges threw up her hands, then shook a finger at me in warning. "But you'd better not hurt that poor girl."

I grasped her fingers and grinned widely. "Thank you, Mrs. Hodges. I owe you. Anything you want, let me know."

She pulled free and waved me off, a tiny smile curving her lips as she turned her focus back to the computer screen. "I have work to do."

Still grinning, I stood and strode from the room, already thinking about how I was going to convince Kate to give me a second chance.

CHAPTER
SEVENTEEN

KATE

I settled back against the imitation leather of our favorite corner booth and peered out the window. Victoria and I used to have lunch together every Friday, but with the craziness of the past few months, our routine get-togethers had fallen by the wayside. I'd spoken with her a few times, and we'd had dinner that disastrous night at Eros, but I was dying for some girl time.

She seemed to be truly happy with Blake, and I was excited for her—really, I was. But I couldn't help the little pang of envy that assaulted me when I thought of their relationship. I loved Victoria, and though I'd only spoken with Blake a few times, I felt that he was a genuinely good person. After all, he saved my life after the incident at the healthplex last month. That in itself told me just about everything I needed to know about him.

After everything she'd been through, Victoria deserved someone like him, someone who would love her and treasure her for who she really was. I thought I'd found that in Steve, but I was wrong. We had similar interests, and for a while, it was enough.

Unfortunately, our attraction and lust didn't have the power that I saw between Blake and Victoria. When Blake watched her, his face softened, and admiration and adoration filled his eyes. I wanted someone to look at me that way, like I was their single focus, the one person they would put before anything else.

My thoughts turned inexorably to Gavin and our chance meeting at the hospital nearly a week ago. It seemed that everywhere I went, Gavin just happened to show up. It felt like a kind of sign, but I wasn't sure what it meant. Either he was a sociopathic stalker or fate was trying to push us together. I had a gut feeling it was the latter.

I couldn't stop thinking about the night we spent together. The way he made me feel was terrifying. I had a sneaking suspicion that if I ever truly gave myself over to the sensation, I would never recover.

The front door of the café opened, and my eyes were drawn to Victoria's familiar form as she stepped inside and pushed her sunglasses to the top of her head. She held the door for the person behind her, a pretty young brunette with a baby in tow. To my surprise, both of them headed in my direction.

I slid from the booth and greeted Victoria with a hug. She pulled away and gestured to the woman standing just behind her. "I hope you don't mind, but I invited Lydia to have lunch with us."

I smiled and stuck out my hand. "Kate Winfield."

"I'm Lydia," she introduced herself, "and this is Alexia." She jiggled the little girl propped on her hip.

We took a seat in the booth, and Victoria turned to me. "Do you remember me talking about Blake's friend, Xander?" I nodded. "This is his wife and little girl."

"Oh," I said, finally making the connection. "It's nice to finally put a face to the name."

"You, too," Lydia said as her eyes darted toward my forehead. "I hope you're feeling better."

She had a savage-looking wound as well, and a small smile quirked my lips. "I am, thank you. But it looks like we could be twins."

She blushed and lifted one hand toward her head self-consciously. "Thankfully my hair is starting to grow back, so it's not as noticeable as it was."

I nodded. She swept her hair to the side, partially covering the wound, and she was right; unless you were specifically looking for it, it didn't stand out. She still seemed a little bit uncomfortable, so I moved the conversation along. "What do you do again?"

I couldn't remember ever hearing what she did for a living, but she seemed shy, and I wanted to draw her out of her shell.

"I own Something Blue, a bridal salon downtown."

I grinned and turned my attention to Victoria. "Well, that's convenient."

"I know, that's part of the reason I invited them," Victoria allowed. "Lydia will be designing my wedding gown. I hope you're going to be my maid of honor. I'd like her to design a gown for you too."

"I'd be thrilled," I said, and I meant it wholeheartedly. "So have you set a date yet?"

Victoria grimaced a little bit. "Not exactly. I want to keep it small, get married this fall, but Blake thinks it's better to take our time."

My brows drew together. "Is he having second thoughts?"

"No." Victoria rolled her eyes. "He says he wants to make sure it's what I want, and he's pushing for a long engagement."

"I can't blame him," I said softly. "He just wants what's best for you."

"I don't know why he's being so stubborn about it," Victoria griped.

I shot a look at Lydia, who looked a little lost. I tipped my head toward Victoria. "She balked last time, so Blake is dragging his feet now," I explained.

"I didn't balk," Victoria said with no small amount of disdain. "I just..."

I barely held back a snort. "You freaked out and ended your relationship when he told you he wanted the two of you to move in together. Of course he wants to make sure he doesn't screw up again." I turned to Lydia. "Right?"

She bit her lip. "I'm not sure I'm really the person you want to ask about relationship advice. I made a huge mess of things myself."

"Between you and Xander?" I asked.

"Yeah," Lydia breathed. "It's not exactly common knowledge, but..." She glanced between Victoria and me. "I'm sure I can trust both of you."

"Of course." We shared a look, then nodded, and Lydia continued. "Xander and I haven't exactly had a normal relationship," she stated slowly. "We met at my cousin's wedding in Vegas, then got to talking at the bar. Things got a little out of hand, and we... decided to get married."

I lifted my brows in surprise. She didn't exactly strike me as the type of person to do something rash and impulsive. "Well, that's one hell of a story to tell your grandkids."

"Yeah, well there's more." Her cheeks turned red, and she looked horribly contrite. "I woke up the next morning, then freaked out and told him I wanted a divorce. He was already heading back overseas when I realized that this little one was on the way."

She ran one hand lovingly over the baby's pale blonde hair,

then dropped a kiss on the top of her head. "We hadn't really taken the time to get to know each other, and I didn't exactly have a way to reach him."

All of a sudden, I knew exactly where the story was going. "How did he find out?"

She bit her lip. "His tour ended just a couple months ago, and he ended up moving back. I emailed him a couple times while he was out of the country, but he never responded. Then he tracked me down one day and saw Alexia at the salon with me, and he just... knew."

She gave a little shrug of her shoulders, and my heart went out to her. She looked genuinely distraught, as if she truly regretted what had happened. Determined to stay positive for her, I piped up.

"Well, it looks like everything worked out for you. That's all that matters. Besides, I have friends in the military who missed the birth of their babies. There's nothing to say he would've been able to make it back in time anyway."

"I guess," she said, though she didn't sound convinced.

Victoria turned her probing gaze on me. "Since we're speaking of men, how's Gavin?"

I speared her with a glare. "I told you—"

"Yeah, yeah. I know what you said. Now tell me the truth."

"There's nothing to tell."

She tipped her head and lifted one eyebrow as she studied me. "Liar."

"We..." I trailed off, trying to figure out exactly what to say. So much had happened, and I'd never filled her in on what exactly transpired that night at Eros. "We've been talking a little bit here and there."

Victoria glanced at Lydia. "She's crazy about this guy, but she won't admit it because he was the lawyer who represented her in her divorce."

"That's not—"

Lydia pursed her lips. "You're not talking about Gavin Price, are you?"

Immediately, every sense went on high alert, and I eyed her. "Why?"

I couldn't begin to explain the irrational jealousy that flared up when I heard Gavin's name fall from the other woman's lips. I tried to brush it off, but the prickly sensation remained.

"He was actually our lawyer, too—before we cancelled the paperwork."

"Small world," Victoria remarked as I let out a relieved breath. She turned back to me. "So, are you dating now?"

I cleared my throat. "Not officially." Not at all.

She just nodded, but her clear gray eyes held a mixture of concern and pity. Part of me wanted to ask for advice, but I couldn't begin to formulate my own feelings on the matter. One minute I'd decided I was better off without him; the next I was wishing that he was next to me again. I'd heard the expression "when you know, you know." Well, I didn't have a freaking clue. When the hell would it click for me? I felt like my emotions were all over the damn place.

"I'm still trying to work through everything," I admitted. "I'm not sure what I should feel or think. Part of me still feels guilty."

"Why?"

"You know." I leaned my elbows on the table. "I was still married. And even though Steve cheated on me, I always wanted to hold myself to a higher standard. Plus, a lot has happened between Gavin and me already. I don't know if it's fixable."

Victoria sucked her bottom lip into her mouth before speaking. "This is only my two cents, so take it with a grain of salt." I lifted a brow at her. "I can attest to the power of communication. I nearly ruined something good because Blake and I weren't on the same page. I don't know what's been said or what happened between you and Gavin, but I've seen the way he looks at you. I believe anything's fixable if you both want it."

I pondered her words for several long moments. I knew she was right. There was only one problem... I had no clue what I wanted.

"Just think about it," she said softly.

"I will." I let out a sigh as I glanced at my phone. "I've gotta go. I have an appointment in half an hour."

"Gavin?" Victoria turned her gray eyes on me, and I nodded.

"I just have to stop in to fix a billing issue."

"Good." Victoria's lips curled into a smile. "Then you can—"

I waved her off before she could tell me—again—how sweet Gavin seemed and how I should give him a chance. "I already know where you're going with that."

"Then you should know I'll just keep pestering you until you listen." She gave me a big phony grin when I glared at her. "Quid pro quo. You helped me with Blake. Now it's my turn to help you with Gavin."

I rolled my eyes as I scooted out of the booth. "See you later. Nice to meet you, Lydia. Thank you for not matchmaking like this traitor here." I jerked my head toward Victoria, and Lydia laughed.

"Good luck. If he's really as amazing as Victoria says he is, I think you'll need it."

Yeah. So did I.

CHAPTER
EIGHTEEN

GAVIN

I tapped my foot anxiously, every nerve ending buzzing with anticipation. The phone on my desk rang, and I snatched it up. "Price."

"She's in conference room A," Mrs. Hodges said on a sigh. "Don't make me regret this."

"I won't, I promise."

I hung up and straightened my suit jacket as I drew in a deep breath. Holy shit, I was nervous as hell. Mrs. Hodges had told Kate there was a discrepancy in the billing and that she needed to correct the paperwork. It was true, to a point. I'd foregone my usual fee, charging only what the firm required and nothing extra. I didn't want a dime of Kate's money. I wanted her fair and square, and I wanted us to start with a clean slate.

Grabbing up the envelope on the corner of my desk, I headed out of my office and down the hall toward conference room A. I'd chosen this room specifically because it was designed to accommodate only a few people. The last several times Kate had been here, we'd met in the larger room. I didn't want a single reminder of Steve or her divorce today; only us.

I paused a few feet from the doorway and drew a fortifying breath before stepping inside and closing the door. Kate's eyes went wide and round as I seated myself across from her.

"What are you doing here?"

I lifted a brow. "Last I checked, I work here."

She darted a glance toward the door. "Your assistant said she would be right back, so—"

I stopped her with a shake of my head. "She's not coming back."

Her mouth opened, then closed. She blinked once, then her eyes became narrowed slits. "You set this up."

"I did," I admitted. "I knew you wouldn't come otherwise."

She leaned back in her chair and crossed her arms over her chest. "You don't know that."

One brow arched toward my hairline. "Would you have?"

Her gaze skittered away, and I could see her tongue sweep over her teeth as she contemplated lying to me. Finally, her conscience won out. "Maybe."

"Maybe?"

"Fine." She exhaled, long and slow. "Probably not."

"I know," I said softly. "That's why I enlisted her help."

She looked at me like I was stupid. "Why?"

"Because I need to apologize."

She stared at me for a moment, then turned her attention to the table. "It's fine."

The two worst words in the English language, right behind the two I was about to say. "I'm sorry."

So totally inadequate, they didn't begin to conquer the hurt I'd caused her. She deserved so much better than the way

I'd treated her. Stung by jealousy, I'd immediately turned my attention to the woman in the bar, hoping that Kate would see me with her and make her realize what she was missing. But that look of hurt in her eyes had only made me feel guilty. I'd made it seem as if Kate were replaceable, which was the furthest thing from the truth.

"I... lost my head when I saw you with him. Thompson and I go way back, and..." I trailed off, not wanting to dredge up drama from twenty years ago. Those pretty blue eyes met mine, but she remained silent. "Anyway, I was jealous, and I wanted to hurt you. It was stupid—I was stupid—and you didn't deserve it."

She nodded a little. "Thank you. And I... I could have handled it better myself."

That wasn't technically an absolution, but she hadn't bolted for the door to escape me. We had a long way to go, but the fact that she remained seated across from me gave me hope. For a moment, we just stared at each other. Finally, I broke the silence. "I actually do want to give you something while you're here."

I slid the envelope across the table to her, and she stared at it. "Is this...?"

"It is." I dipped my chin. "It's over."

She lifted a hand and tentatively touched it. "Thank you."

"Of course."

I gave her a couple moments to absorb the information, then— "You shouldn't feel bad about what we did."

I knew she did though, and her cheeks blazed pink at my words.

I pushed my chair back and rounded the table. Kate grasped the arms of the chair like she was about to leap forward and run out the door. I was quicker, though, and I knelt next to her. "Tell me something."

"What?" She regarded me warily, and I gathered my words.

"I've thought about our night together a thousand times." I watched her swallow hard, her gaze dropping away from mine and fixing on my chest instead. "Something's been killing me, and I need to know—was I the only one who felt something?"

Her tongue darted out to wet her lips, and she took almost a full minute to respond. Her answer came on a breathy whisper, low and sexy as she shook her head jerkily. "It wasn't just you."

Thank God. "Kate..." I reached out and gently took her hands in mine. "I'll take this as slowly as you want. Just let me in. Just give me a chance to prove this is right."

"I... I don't know..."

It wasn't an outright refusal. "I know you're still hurting. But we're friends, right?"

Her brows drew together in confusion, and she finally met my eyes. "Yes?"

I bit back a smile. "Good."

She looked completely off-balance as I stood and pulled her to her feet. "Gavin...?"

"I know you're not ready for more—yet," I said as I walked her to the door. "But I'm going to be here when you are. We'll take it one step at a time, as slow as you need."

She turned to face me just before we reached the door. "Why are you doing this?"

I brushed a thumb over her cheek. "You don't know, red?" She shook her head, and I grinned. "Baby steps."

A tiny sigh of protest fell from her lips as I opened the door and guided her out of the conference room. I had her exactly where I wanted her; slightly off-balance, yet curious. I wasn't about to scare her off by telling her my plans. I'd spent the last six months dreaming about her. When she was ready, she'd come to me.

I opened the door and held it wide, then stepped into the hallway behind her—and almost right into Shannon.

"Oh! Sorry about that." Shannon put her hand on my arm. "I've been looking for you."

I watched Kate's eyes drop to where Shannon's fingers curled into the fabric of my jacket, and she subtly stepped away. I shifted toward Kate, effectively shrugging away from Shannon's touch. "As you can see, I was in a meeting with Dr. Winfield."

Her lips curled downward in a frown. "I thought everything for that case was taken care of."

Who the hell did she think she was? Partner's daughter or not, I wouldn't tolerate her insinuating herself in my business. I pinned her with a hard stare, and she cowered slightly under the scrutiny. I settled my hand on Kate's lower back. "You're correct. Dr. Winfield isn't a client anymore, but she is always welcome in my office."

Shannon's cheeks blazed bright pink at the implication, and her chin dropped a fraction.

At that very moment, Larry stepped out of his office, a curious look on his face when he saw us congregated in the hallway. Jesus. What the hell was this, a fucking party? I wanted to get Kate the hell out of here before one of these idiots gave her a reason to never want to see me again.

Larry looked from Shannon to me, my arm still around Kate, whose entire body had gone rigid. His gaze lifted to her face, and he extended his hand, pasting on the smarmy lawyer smile I'd seen more than once. "Good afternoon."

Kate tipped her head and returned his handshake. "Hello."

Larry passed the file in his hand to Shannon. "Would you mind taking care of this for me?"

With a quick nod, she grabbed it from his hand and bolted. Thank God. One down. I turned my attention back to Larry, my fingers curling slightly into the soft flesh of Kate's back. "Well, we were just—"

Larry's inquisitive gaze landed back on Kate. "Have we met before?"

"In passing, maybe?" she said with a polite smile. "I've been here a few times, so I'm sure we've crossed paths."

I didn't like the way he watched her, his eyes assessing, searching. Maybe it was a good thing he'd seen me with Kate. Maybe he could finally get it through to Shannon that there would never be anything between us. Stepping even closer to her, I spoke. "I know you need to get going."

My words seemed to jolt Larry from his reverie, and he flashed an insincere smile. "Enjoy your afternoon."

I nodded, then let out a pent-up breath as I guided Kate from the office and out to her car. I waited as she used the fob to unlock it, then opened the door. Her hand rested on the top of the door, and she paused as she climbed in, then turned to me. "It's not really my place to ask, but..."

She bit her lip, and I settled my hand over hers. "You can ask me anything, always."

Her eyes darted to the side before meeting mine again. "That girl. Are you...?"

"Never." I gave a quick shake of my head. "Not for lack of trying on her part. But there's only one woman I'm interested in, and it's not her. I think she finally figured that out today."

Kate blushed, and her gaze dropped to where our hands were linked. She nodded slightly. "Okay."

I wanted so badly to kiss her, but I forced myself to let her go. I had to remind myself that she'd agreed to being friends— nothing more. Yet. "Drive safe."

"I will." She slipped behind the wheel of the car, and I shut the door behind her. With a little wave, she drove off, and a smile curled my lips. As I watched her turn out of the parking lot, I was already calculating just how long to wait before I called her again and when I could next see her. There wasn't a chance in hell I was letting her slip away now, no matter what I had to do.

CHAPTER
NINETEEN

KATE

I shifted restlessly, trying to take the strain off my aching feet. I was already starting to seriously regret wearing the damn three-inch heels, but I wanted to look nice.

For Gavin? my brain whispered conspiratorially. I shook it away. I'd dressed up to look good for me and me alone. That's what I told myself—but I knew I was lying. I wanted him to desire me even if I wasn't quite sure what would happen between us, if anything.

Nerves battered my insides at the thought of seeing Gavin again. Though we'd texted and spoken on the phone several times over the past week, he'd never made any attempt at flirtation or tried to take things further.

I didn't know what to think about this meeting today. A coffee break at three o'clock was too late to be a friendly lunch, yet too early for an intimate dinner date. He'd thrown me for a loop, and I didn't like it at all.

I felt so much better knowing exactly where I stood with someone. I despised trying to read between the lines, as I had for so many years with my ex. Gavin had seemed so intent just a few weeks ago on dating seriously, yet he hadn't brought it up again. It was frustrating, and I hated myself for worrying over it. I was the one who'd told him it would never happen, and here I was, disappointed at the prospect that he wanted to just be friends.

I let out a disgusted little sound as I kicked at the sidewalk, scuffing the toe of the expensive stiletto. Scowling at the torn leather, I leaned against the rough brick building and let out a little growl. What the hell was wrong with me? I already knew the answer to that. I wanted Gavin, way more than I'd ever admit out loud.

I pulled my phone from my bag and checked the time again. He'd called half an hour ago to let me know he was running late, but it was already a quarter after three. My stomach twisted into a tight knot. I should be relieved. I should turn around, get in my car, and head home—alone.

But for some stupid reason, all I could think about was Gavin. He'd promised friendship because that was all I was willing to offer. Why was I so disappointed about that? I'd been divorced for barely more than a week. I couldn't even contemplate the idea of letting another man into my life yet, even one as sweet as Gavin.

As if my thoughts conjured him, I glanced up to see him round the corner of the building. I sank my teeth into my lower lip as my gaze swept over him from head to toe. Dressed in dark charcoal slacks and a blue shirt with the sleeves rolled up to his elbows, he looked sexier than any man deserved to. He'd removed his jacket and tie, and the collar of his shirt had been unbuttoned, giving me a peek at the deeply tanned skin at the base of his neck.

My heart thudded against my ribs as my gaze moved upward and caught the sexy curl of his lips. God, that smile literally made my knees weak, and I swayed slightly as he approached, thankful for the hard wall behind me, holding me up. His head turned, his attention moving toward the street, and the smile slipped from his face. "Down!"

Confused at his reaction, I followed his gaze to the car. The passenger side window had been rolled down, and the driver came into view as he pulled almost even with me. My eyes swept over the man behind the wheel. He was nothing more than a black blob, the hooded sweatshirt out of place in the sweltering heat of the summer afternoon.

His face was obscured by a ball cap and sunglasses, and I trailed my gaze lower, over his arm extended outward—toward me. Sunlight glinted off the black object in his hand, and my heart stopped.

He has a gun.

"Get down!"

I jumped at Gavin's harsh command, and I sucked in a breath as a loud pop splintered the quiet afternoon. Pain ripped through me as Gavin tackled me around the waist, taking me to the ground and stealing the breath from my lungs. It felt like a brick wall had slammed into my body, and a wave of fire shot down my arm.

"Fuck!"

Gavin's terse expletive cut through my delirium, and I blinked against the spots dancing before my eyes, unable to comprehend exactly what had happened. I flailed uncomprehendingly but was restrained by Gavin's heavy weight still on top of me. Suddenly, a second crack split the air and shattered glass rained down around us.

"Stay down!"

Gavin pushed my head back down, tucking me further into the protection of his large body, and I struggled to draw in a breath.

"C-can't—"

I bucked upward, and he lifted his chest from mine and

stared down at me, a question in his eyes. Relieved of the weight, I dragged in a deep breath and tried to sit up. My left arm refused to cooperate, and I struggled against him for a moment before falling to my back. Cries of fear and outrage rose around me, but I tuned them out as I stared up at Gavin, his face twisted into an expression of intense concentration.

"Just stay where you are," he commanded, flicking a glance around our surroundings once more. "The car's gone, but there's glass all over the damn place."

I nodded and licked my lips as blinding pain radiated down my arm. "Gavin..."

Not sparing me a glance, he pulled his cell from his back pocket and started to tap away at the screen. "Yeah?"

"My arm," I panted out. "It hurts."

Dark brown eyes laced with anger flitted over me as he sat back on his heels and rolled me slightly to the side. The phone fell from his fingers as he seized my left arm, his features twisting into a grimace. "Jesus!"

I closed my eyes against the fiery sensation, and a tiny whimper fell from my lips. Glass tinkled and crunched as Gavin shifted into a crouch beside me. I assumed a shard had sliced into my arm, causing the acute pain shooting through my triceps.

"Why didn't you tell me your arm was hurt?" Without bothering to unbutton his shirt, he ripped it open and stripped it off.

For a second, my attention was splintered. In my peripheral vision I could see him ripping off the sleeve to wrap around my arm to stop the bleeding, but I couldn't drag my gaze away from the sculpted muscles of his biceps and forearms exposed by the tight white tee shirt beneath. They rippled as he leaned forward and gently wove the fabric around my injured arm and tied it off.

I sucked in a breath at the sudden pressure, then forced a

little laugh as I forced myself to focus on his question. "My entire body hurts."

"Yeah, well, getting shot will do that." He gave a brief shake of his head, and I twisted my head toward my left arm.

Getting shot? "What?"

He was too busy inspecting my arm to reply, so I slapped my palm against his chest and shoved to get his attention.

His gaze snapped to mine. "It's just a graze."

"*Just a graze?*" My voice rose several octaves, fueled by indignation and bewilderment. He said it like it was no big deal, like it happened every day, and it served only to infuriate me more as the panic and fear leached away. "Are you kidding me?"

I struggled against him, intent on sitting up and assessing the damage for myself.

"Hold on, hold on." Gavin slid a hand beneath my back and levered me to a sitting position, taking extra care with my arm before placing it gently in my lap. The world spun for a moment, and I fought the nausea that roiled in my stomach. He wrapped an arm around my shoulders for support and cupped my face in one huge hand. "You good?"

I nodded shakily as everything righted itself and returned to normal—as normal as this situation could get. "I'm fine."

Gavin turned my chin toward him and searched my gaze for a long moment. Whatever he saw there must have assured him, because he gave a little nod, then picked up his phone. I rested my head on his shoulder and listened as he spoke with the 911 dispatcher, giving our location and details. When he hung up, he turned his head, and his chin brushed my hair. "Still hanging in there?"

I nodded against his chest, suddenly too exhausted to respond as the adrenaline wore off and my body began to crash.

CHAPTER
TWENTY

GAVIN

I cursed myself once more as I studied Kate where she sat on the bed of the small emergency room, feet crossed at the ankles, her face pale and drawn.

I couldn't fucking believe I left my piece in the car. The one damn time I should have had it, I'd forgotten to put it back on. I hadn't been able to take it with me to court this morning, and I was in so much of a hurry to see Kate that I had parked beside the coffee shop and practically jumped from the car.

I couldn't get the sight of her ragged, torn flesh out of my mind. It replayed on loop over and over, serving only to increase my fury. Thank God she'd taken a step to the side when she had. Just a few inches to the right, and the bullet would've pierced her heart instead of her arm.

Unbidden, my hands curled into fists at my side. The neighborhood the coffee shop was in was a decent one, but I wasn't a fool; I knew bad things happened everywhere. However, there was one detail that stuck out in my mind. As I'd lain there on the pavement, my body covering Kate's, I managed to glimpse the back of the car between the bumpers of two vehicles parked along the curb, and what I'd seen, or lack thereof, turned my blood to ice. The car's license plate had been removed.

Over the past couple of hours since the incident, I played several possibilities through my mind. It could've been a random drive-by shooting, but I didn't think gangbangers would be so cautious as to remove their license plate. The bullet could've been intended for someone else, except for the fact that, though there were several other people milling around on the sidewalk, no one else was even remotely close to her when the shot was fired.

I had to admit that it was possible the driver was shooting at the coffee shop itself, or someone inside, but the glare of sunlight on the glass more than likely would've obscured the driver's vision. It would have to be difficult to mark a target inside the building while in motion driving past. I didn't like the last remaining option, that Kate was, in fact, the intended victim. You didn't shoot that close to someone just to scare them.

Aside from her recent trouble at the healthplex, she hadn't mentioned anything unsettling. The attack nearly a month ago had resulted in several stitches, but the man who had attacked her was now dead, so that trail was cold.

Something else must've happened, and I wanted to know what it was. We'd relayed everything we knew to the detective who'd left just a few minutes prior. He seemed to be of the opinion that it was random, possibly gang-related, but promised to look into it.

My focus returned to Kate, bantering with the nurse who held out a sheet of instructions to care for the wound.

The nurse tipped her head at Kate. "I'm sure you know all

this, but no showers for twenty-four hours, and make sure to check for infection when you change the bandages."

"I appreciate it." Kate offered a smile that didn't quite reach her eyes.

I thanked the nurse and made sure the curtain was pulled shut before I turned back to her. Her gaze was focused on the industrial-style linoleum floor, and I watched her for a long moment before speaking. As a doctor, she was probably used to hospitals, used to procedures of this sort. But I had to imagine that this was the first time she'd been on the receiving end of something this serious, and she looked utterly calm. Too calm.

I stepped forward, right into her field of vision, and squatted in front of her, then waited for her to meet my gaze. "You okay?" I asked softly.

The corner of her mouth curled up, and her hands lifted in a shrugging motion. "I'm used to it. This is what I do."

I captured one hand and drew it between mine. "I know," I acknowledged. "But you're normally the one in control; you take care of everyone else, but who takes care of you, Kate?"

"I do," she whispered. "Only me."

For a moment, her eyes filled with pain so acute that I could feel it as it sliced through my heart. In those bright blue depths, I saw fear and worry and something else I couldn't quite name. I knew she wasn't used to having someone to count on, but I wanted to be that person for her. I wanted to be the man she turned to when she needed something. Whether she needed help or just wanted to talk, I wanted to prove to her that she could always count on me to be there.

Tears glazed the pretty orbs, and I stood, gently tugging her to her feet. I wrapped one arm around her waist and tucked her head against my chest as she leaned stiffly against me.

"Let it out," I whispered against her hair. "I'm right here. I won't let you go."

Her body shook, but her tears fell silently as she buried her head into me, clinging to my T-shirt for dear life. I'd always detested a woman's tears. I'd hated it when Whitney would come home from school sometimes, crying over the breakup of a boyfriend or the loss of a best friend. Though I comforted Whit as best I could and dropped a threat or two in the ear of whichever young, stupid jock had broken her heart, I'd always try to distance myself from her grief.

With Kate, though, I wanted to pull her into me, absorb her sorrow like it was my own and take all the pain away. As I knew she would, she pulled away much too soon and dabbed at her eyes with her fingers as she moved away, putting distance between us both physically and emotionally.

Despite every instinct inside me screaming not to, I allowed her to retreat. For now. There was a lot going on in her head and her heart at the moment, and she needed time to come to terms with all of it.

She looked down at the blue-and-white hospital gown in dismay, and I fought the smile that came to my lips. "I think you make the gown look good."

Her head tipped slightly to one side as she slid a glare my way. This time, I couldn't help the soft smile that curled my lips. After seeing her so vulnerable, it was a welcome relief to see the feistiness come back full force. "If you don't want to wear that hideous thing out of here, I think I can help you."

I scooped up the ruined shirt I'd been wearing earlier and held it up. "Missing a sleeve, but it'll do well enough. Should we make it match?"

A tiny smile touched her lips as she nodded, and I deftly tore the seam of the remaining sleeve.

"Turn around," I said softly as I twirled a finger in the air.

She followed my instructions, and I pulled the ties on the gown until it loosened up the back.

She threw a glance over her shoulder. "Promise you won't look?"

It was a ridiculous request, considering I'd explored every inch of her body at length during our night together a little over a month ago. Still, I couldn't help teasing her a bit. "Are you crazy? I've been dying to see you again."

Her cheeks flushed bright pink, and I decided to let her off the hook as I scooped up her bra from the pile of clothes discarded on the chair in the corner.

"I want you to know how completely unfair this is," I complained without heat. "I have to help you get dressed, but I can't look or touch? That's not very nice, Doctor."

Kate smiled a little at my teasing tone and met my eyes. She looked so damn gorgeous, I couldn't help myself. I took her chin between my thumb and forefinger, then leaned in and gently kissed her lips.

I met her eyes as I held her bra up between us, suspended from the tiny straps. She extended her arms and allowed me to slip it up and into place, then fasten it in the back. I helped her into my now sleeveless dress shirt, first her bad arm, then the good one. I buttoned it all the way up to her neck, then tied the tails at her waist.

She arched her neck and tugged at the stiff collar. "Did you have to button it all the way up?"

I lifted a brow at her. "Hell, yes. No one is going to see an inch of your body except me."

I grinned when she glared at me again, then gave a playful tug to the front of her shirt. "Come on, red, let's get you dressed and get out of here."

Holding up the pants she'd worn earlier, I helped her step into them, despite the fact that, just like mine, they were dirty and showed signs of holes. I scooped up her purse, flicked a look around the room to make sure we hadn't forgotten anything, then held out a hand for her to take. Reluctantly, she grabbed on, and we made our way to the elevator. I jabbed the down arrow, then guided her inside as the doors slid open.

I leaned against the railing as the car began its descent, and I watched Kate in the mirrored reflection across from me. Her eyes were closed, and her head tipped drowsily to one side. As if it were the most natural thing in the world, I slipped one arm around her waist and tucked her head against my chest. I loved seeing her in these rare unguarded moments, where her prickly demeanor slipped away, leaving only the open, desirable woman beneath.

"Tired?" My lips brushed her hair as I spoke, and her cheek rubbed gently against my chest when she nodded.

"I just wanna fall into bed and sleep for the next twelve hours."

The elevator dinged our arrival at the parking garage, and I curled my fingers into her waist. "Soon," I promised.

I gently propelled her forward, steering her toward my car. Though I'd been rather salty at the time, I was grateful I'd driven myself instead of riding in the ambulance. At least now we didn't have to call a cab or an Uber. Kate's SUV was still at the coffee shop, but I could arrange for that to be picked up tomorrow.

I used the key fob to unlock the door, then held it open and supported her as she lowered herself into the seat. Once she was settled, I closed the door and rounded the car, then slid behind the wheel. I knew where Kate lived from my previous visit, and a comfortable silence fell as we turned in that direction.

As I drove, I snuck peeks at her from the corner of my eye. Gradually, her lids lowered and her head rolled slightly to one side as she drifted off to sleep. Twenty minutes later, I pulled into her driveway, then turned to look at her. Faint scars were still evident on her forehead, and now she had new scratches and bruises to match.

A fierce protectiveness welled up inside me, urging me to reach across the console, pull her into my arms and never let go. She wouldn't appreciate the gesture, at least not yet. Despite the fact that she continued to deny it, I knew there was a connection between us, something special that I wanted to explore.

I reached out and gently brushed the backs of my fingers over her cheek. Her long lashes fluttered, and those pretty blue eyes slowly blinked open and met mine.

"We're here."

Her gaze left mine and darted toward the house, and she nodded slowly. By the time I climbed out and made it to her side, she had already unbuckled her seat belt and opened the door. I dug through her purse and fished out the keys to unlock the front door. I closed it up once she had entered, but I didn't bother to lock it. We wouldn't be here long enough to worry about it.

The soft scraping of nails against wood drew my attention as Peanut came tearing into the foyer. A bright smile lifted Kate's lips, and she scooped him up using her good arm, then cuddled him close. His little pink tongue darted out in frantic kisses, and Kate jerked her head away with a little laugh. "I know, I know. You need to go out."

Seizing the opportunity, I plucked him from her grasp. "I'll take care of it. Why don't you head to your room?"

After a moment, she relented. "Thanks."

When Kate turned down the hallway, I made my way to the backyard and let Peanut run around for a few minutes. After he relieved himself, I brought him back inside and began to gather his things. I carried his food and bowls out to the car, then left his leash by the door and headed toward her bedroom.

Kate exited the bathroom just as I rounded the bed, and I decided to bite the bullet. "Where do you keep your suitcase?"

Her brows pulled together, her expression turning first curious, then wary. "Why?"

Spinning on a heel, I turned toward her closet and threw the doors open. "Because you're coming home with me," I said as I scanned the shelves. I pulled down the first duffel bag I came across and tossed it on the bed.

Kate let out a disbelieving little laugh. "This is my home. I'm staying here."

"Not right now, you're not," I retorted as I strode to the dresser and yanked out several pairs of socks and underwear, then tossed them into the bag.

She immediately reached in to retrieve them. "I'm not going anywhere."

"In case you suddenly developed a case of amnesia to go along with your stubbornness, you were shot at today," I snapped. "You're out of your damn mind if you think I'm letting you stay here alone."

"Getting shot isn't something I'm likely to forget anytime soon," she said caustically as she rolled her eyes, "but I have neighbors right next door in case anything happens."

I jumped on her excuse. "So you'll put someone else's life in danger just to avoid coming with me?" Guilt clouded her features as her teeth sank into her lower lip, but I refused to give her an inch. "You're coming with me, and that's final."

I snatched the socks and underwear from her hand and tossed them back into the bag. "Now, tell me if there's anything specific you want, otherwise I'm just going to grab a bunch of random shit." Her frosty gaze narrowed on me, and she pressed her lips together defiantly.

She was spirited, I'd give her that. The woman was too damn independent by half and made winning her over all the more challenging. But I'd never given up before, and I wasn't about to now. I let my eyes slowly trail down her body and back up as I fought a smile. "Or you can be naked. Your choice."

That jolted her into action. She stomped to the closet and began to rip hangers from the rail, tossing them haphazardly over her shoulder. Nearly a minute later, she retraced her steps and flounced down on the edge of the bed, refusing to look at me in her fit of pique. She watched from the corner of her eye as I scooped each garment off the floor, removed it from the hanger, then folded it and placed it inside the bag.

"Toiletries?"

She popped up and stormed to the bathroom. I couldn't hold back my grin as bottles began to fly in my direction. I hastily fielded the projectiles and dumped them unceremoniously into the bag, thanking God that she only had one good throwing arm.

"Impressive aim."

It was apparently the wrong thing to say, because a dozen more bottles and tubes, half of which I was pretty sure she didn't even need, came flying in my direction. I snatched each out of the air and tossed it into the bag. I missed the hairbrush as it hit the ground at my feet and ricocheted against the bed. When nothing else came flying through the air, I met Kate's gaze where she leaned against the doorway.

"That all?"

Face set in a mutinous expression, she pushed off the doorjamb and started past me. I caught her around the waist and pulled her close, careful not to bump her injured arm. "Have I told you recently how much that temper of yours turns me on?"

"Have I told you how much I dislike you right now?" she shot back.

I couldn't help the laughter bubbling up. "Is it gonna be like this every time we fight?"

With an irritated little scowl, she pulled free and propped her right hand on her hip. "This is literally the stupidest thing ever. A hotel would be perfectly safe."

"You'll be safer with me."

Her lip curled up in disgust as her gaze swept over me from top to toe, letting me know exactly what she thought of my pronouncement. "I'd prefer a hotel."

She would have been safe enough in a hotel, that much was true. But the fact of the matter was, I wanted her in my house where I could see her and know she was safe, and I wasn't above playing dirty to get her there.

"Peanut!" I bellowed the dog's name and was rewarded a few seconds later when I heard the scrabble of little feet tearing down the hall. The dog skidded into the room, and I scooped him up. "Want to come have a sleepover at my place?" The dog licked my chin, and I turned a challenging gaze in Kate's direction.

She stared at me, unblinking. "Are you seriously threatening to kidnap my dog just to suit your own agenda?"

"I am. And what the hell kind of name is Peanut anyway? We need to come up with something new. You're a boy, right?" I asked the dog as I held him up to confirm. "You need a masculine name, like... Blade. Or maybe Thanos?"

The dog tipped his head to one side as he inspected me curiously, and Kate's scathing retort cut through the silence. "He's not a character in some stupid comic book."

Her cheeks were almost as red as her hair, and her eyes snapped with barely restrained fire. I loved that I could read every emotion flitting across her pretty face, and I loved to rile her, push her to the very brink of her patience until that aloof façade exploded. Intent on goading her further, I tried again. I turned back to the dog and scratched him under the chin.

"How about... Thor?" The dog let out an excited little bark, then lapped at my chin.

"Thor?" I tried again, with the same reaction. "Guess that settles it."

I turned a victorious smile on Kate, who looked like she would happily rip out my entrails and strangle me with them. "You're not changing my goddamn dog's name."

"Let's go, Thor. Time for a car ride."

The dog tore out of the room the moment his tiny feet touched the ground, then I turned my attention back to Kate. She blinked once, hard and slow.

If looks could kill...

Man down.

CHAPTER
TWENTY-ONE

KATE

I petted Peanut absentmindedly as I stared out the window, houses and buildings a blur as they passed.

Gavin reached over and squeezed my knee. "Still not talking to me?"

I shifted my legs to shake him off but didn't bother to respond. Hell yes, I was still mad. I was pissed that he had so expertly manipulated me into doing exactly what he wanted, and I wasn't nearly ready to forgive and forget just yet. Though the idea of spending the night alone in an empty house wasn't exactly appealing, I had several other options. I could've stayed in a hotel or, barring that, I had friends in the area or could've gone to my parents' house.

"We both know this is completely unnecessary," I snapped.

"I disagree." Gavin settled his elbow on the console between us, cautious to avoid jostling my arm. "We both know it's a big deal; you just don't like being told what to do."

"No kidding," I drawled and rolled my eyes.

I could see him flash an answering grin in the reflection of the dark windshield. "Tough shit," he replied.

I sulked in my seat and stared off into the darkness until Gavin turned into a driveway nearly twenty minutes later. I started to throw the door open but remembered Peanut on my lap at the last moment. I didn't want him to take off and get lost in some strange neighborhood. Gavin seemed to understand, because he grabbed my bag from the back, then scooped Peanut up and secured him under one arm.

Using his hip to prop open the door, he held out a hand. I stared at it for a long second, intent on refusing, before common sense kicked in. The low seats were a bitch to maneuver in, and I was grateful for the help. As soon as I was steady on my feet, he released me and closed the door, then headed to the house. I trailed behind, dragging my feet at the prospect of being stuck prisoner here. I followed him into the kitchen, where a familiar face came into view.

"Phil!"

The older man's gaze bounced between Gavin and me, then landed on my bandaged triceps. "What happened?"

"Just an accident," Gavin responded.

"I was shot." I said it as clinically as possible, like it was no big deal, even though the memory still had the power to send shivers down my spine.

Gavin glared at me, and I shrugged my good shoulder as Phil's eyes widened with disbelief. "You *what*?!"

"There was a drive-by at a coffee shop downtown," Gavin said before I had the chance to speak up. "Kate was grazed by a bullet, and she had to have stitches."

"You said you were running late," Phil accused with a withering glare. "You never said Dr. Winfield was injured."

"I didn't want to worry you," Gavin said as he strode toward the fridge and pulled out a bottle of water. He waved it in my direction, and I nodded. I wasn't so stubborn that I would refuse a drink, especially since I hadn't eaten or had anything to drink since lunch.

As if on cue, my stomach rumbled, and Phil's head whipped toward me. "You must be starving. There are leftovers in the fridge. Gavin, heat something up for Dr. Winfield."

"You can call me Kate," I offered with a smile. "And I can get my own food, it's fine—really."

"No, no." Phil waved me off, then gestured toward the table. "Come sit. Tell me everything while Gavin gets the food ready."

I shot a look at the man in question, who rolled his eyes as he took a pan from the drawer of the fridge. Heat raced through me as he briefly met my gaze, a tiny smile playing at the corners of his mouth. He was obviously used to his father's overbearing nature. I made a mental note to ask Phil later how he managed Gavin.

Over reheated lasagna, Gavin and I told Phil of the incident downtown, then gradually segued into other local news, including the remains they'd found a couple weeks ago.

Phil gave a little shake of his head. "What's this world coming to?"

I nodded in commiseration. People sucked.

"Well, I'm off to bed." Phil pushed back his chair and stood. "Glad you're okay, Doctor."

"Thanks. Sleep well."

I felt Gavin's eyes on me as his dad disappeared down the hall, and I finally worked up the courage to face him. "Well. I guess I should get to bed, too."

Those dark chocolate eyes stared intently into mine, studying me for several long seconds before he spoke. "How are you feeling?"

I notched up my chin. "I can handle it."

"I'm sure you can," he soothed softly.

My gaze narrowed on him. I hated being soothed, pacified like a toddler. "I don't want your pity, Price."

He blinked once, but his expression never changed. "Have I pitied you at all?"

"No," I snapped. "You just bulldozed your way into my house, then bullied me into doing exactly what you wanted."

One dark eyebrow lifted. "You mean, made sure you're safe? How awful of me."

His words were borderline condescending, and it made me see red. "Don't act like a fucking martyr."

"Don't be petulant."

"Petulant?" I stabbed a forefinger in his chest. "I am a grown fucking adult, and I can take care of myself."

"If you would stop being stubborn for two seconds—"

"God, you're so infuriating!" I started to whirl away from him, but he caught my waist and twisted me back to face him.

"Damn it, red. No—" He slapped a palm over my mouth when I started to speak. "Shut those pretty lips of yours and listen for once. I know your ex was a piece of shit. I know you have no reason to trust men, including me, but believe this—I will do everything in my power to keep you safe. And if that means pissing you off, then so be it. I don't give a damn. I'd rather you be angry than dead. Understand?"

I knew he would say anything to get me to acquiesce, but his words were so matter-of-fact that I couldn't help the little thump my heart gave in response. Not that I would ever say as much to Gavin, but I actually felt much better staying here, especially now that I knew Phil was here.

I would definitely be safer—in both senses. Gavin would protect me from any potential threats, and Phil would save me from Gavin. Or maybe he would be saving me from myself, because part of me still wanted to throw myself into Gavin's arms the way I had at the hospital and soak up every bit of strength and comfort those hard muscles had to offer.

The man was potent, and I had to constantly remind myself to stay on guard around him. He ripped away my defenses much too easily, stared into my eyes and read what I felt in my soul. Part of me wanted so badly to give in, but I wasn't sure I could trust him yet—or myself.

He lowered his hand, and I swallowed hard, then nodded as I pulled from his grasp. "I... I should go clean up."

"No showers, remember?"

"Thanks, Dr. Price," I shot back, but my words lacked heat. "Where's my room?"

"I'll show you." Gavin strode to the door where he'd dropped my bag on the way in, then hoisted it over his shoulder and headed toward the stairs. My shoulder throbbed dully as I followed him, each step jarring the aching muscle. I almost cried in relief when he flipped on a light in the second room we came to. "This one has its own bathroom, so you'll have plenty of privacy."

I peered around the doorway, my eyes sliding over the contents of the room. "It's not yours, is it?"

God, I couldn't handle sleeping in his room, surrounded by his tantalizing scent.

He shook his head and hitched a thumb over his shoulder. "Nope. I'm at the end of the hall."

That wasn't much better. There were barely twenty feet separating us. As if reading my thoughts, Gavin quirked a grin. "Want to see my room, red?"

"Ha." The derisive laugh came out much shakier than I'd intended. "No way."

"Your loss."

He pushed past me and set my bag on the bed, then turned to me. "Make yourself at home. Use whatever you need, and if you can't find something, don't hesitate to ask."

I nodded. "Thank you."

He dipped his chin. "Of course."

He started out of the room, but I lifted my good hand and stopped him as he drew even with me. "Seriously. Thank you. I really do appreciate it."

He stared at me for a long moment. "I just want you safe."

"I know," I whispered, unable to tear my gaze away.

One huge hand came up to cup my face, and his thumb swept over my cheek. His gaze flitted over my face before returning to my eyes. "You look exhausted. Why don't you take a bath, then get some rest?"

I nodded, and he dropped his hand away. "Night, Kate."

"Night."

I watched as he entered his room, closing the door behind him, and I let out a little sigh. I was just so... confused. He could be so high-handed sometimes, and other times he was so incredibly sweet. God knew I was attracted to him, and he wasn't shy about voicing his intentions for me.

Deep down, I still hurt. I wasn't sure I was ready to put myself back out there, even casually. My heart felt too fragile; Steve's betrayal had been bad enough, but I'd never felt about Steve the way I did about Gavin. There was just something between us—chemistry, hormones, something—that made my body come alive. If I opened myself up to Gavin and he broke my heart, I wasn't sure I would ever recover.

I filled the large tub with hot water, then stepped inside, careful to keep my bandage from getting wet. The warm water lapped over my skin as I tipped my head back, and I closed my eyes, barely holding in a little hum of pleasure. The slight pressure of a hand on my shoulder jerked me back to reality, and I realized I had dozed off.

Gavin's soft brown eyes met mine as he slid to his knees beside the tub. "You okay?"

"What are you doing in here?" I automatically moved to cover my exposed breasts with my good arm and sank a little deeper, trying not to get the bandage wet.

"Checking on you." His eyes held concern as they studied me. "I didn't hear any movement, and I wanted to make sure you were okay."

Since I'd fallen asleep, he was probably checking to make sure I hadn't drowned. His stare was hot and intense, and I had to clear my throat before speaking. "Yeah. I'm fine, thanks."

He tipped his head at me. "Do you want help washing your hair?"

I grimaced a little bit. I couldn't do it by myself, and I was sure that it was caked with dirt from having rolled around on the ground outside. "Would you mind?"

"Of course not. Hold on one sec." He braced his hands on the edge of the tub, then pushed to his feet. With a purposeful stride, he left the bathroom and returned less than a minute later, a plastic cup in hand.

"Here, sit up a little bit." He slipped one hand between my back and the wall of the tub and eased me forward. I tilted my face to the sky, and he dipped the cup into the water, then poured it over my head, soaking the long strands. He picked up my shampoo and squirted it onto my hair. With long, lean fingers, he massaged my scalp, rinsing out the debris and relieving some of the tension I'd been carrying all evening.

When he was done, he washed my back, then gently settled me so I was reclined against the wall of the tub. "Just relax."

His hands went to my shoulders, and he started off gentle, his touch becoming firmer and more sure as he attacked the knots that had built up in the muscle. I turned to jelly under his ministrations as he stroked along my upper back and shoulders, the base of my neck.

Cautious of my injury, he slid his hands over my good shoulder, kneading the flesh. The other hand moved forward, fingers teasing along my collarbone. He dipped lower, and I sucked in a breath as his thumb brushed my nipple. I shifted in the water, clenching my legs tight against the sensation that shot straight to my core.

I knew I should stop him, but it felt so good—too good. His hand curved around, curling under my breast to cup it as he continued to tease the tight peak. I bit my lip and allowed my head to fall to the side as he kissed my ear. The dark stubble of his five o'clock shadow was rough against my skin, and I shivered as he trailed his kisses lower, nuzzling against my neck.

His other hand left my shoulder and trailed downward, one long finger unerringly finding my center and dipping inside. The water sloshed precariously as my hips jerked in response. Oh, God. I had to stop this before we ended up in bed again. I slammed my legs together, trapping his hand as I tilted my head to look up at him. "Watch it, buddy."

Gavin offered me an unrepentant grin. "Just doing my duty."

I forced an unbelieving little sound from my throat. "I'd say that's taking it a little far."

One broad shoulder lifted in a shrug. "I take pride in a job well done."

Despite his hand being trapped between my thighs, he continued to torture the little bundle of nerves at my entrance. His thumb lightly circled my nipple, and the little bolt of pleasure that zinged through me stole my breath. It took me a moment to find my words. "Pride or pleasure?"

His grin grew. "Yes."

Reaching between my legs, I extracted his questing fingers and leveled him with a stare. "I did go to medical school," I reminded him, "so I know all the most vulnerable places on the human body."

Instead of pulling back at my threat, he let out a little

laugh and twined his fingers through mine. "Don't remind me. I've never enjoyed a woman's touch more than yours."

The compliment shouldn't have pleased me so much, but it did, damn it. I needed to turn this train around before it completely derailed. "Now you're just blowing smoke."

He lifted a brow. "You were there too, so I know you know that's not true."

I felt my cheeks heat as memories of that night rushed back. He was right; I'd thoroughly enjoyed touching him, and I reveled in his hands traveling all over my body, leaving no inch unexplored. I frantically beat the memories back and scrambled to my feet, keeping my good arm over my chest while my other hand covered my lady parts. "Could you hand me a towel please?"

He stared up at me for a long moment before slowly rising to his feet and pulling a clean towel from the linen cabinet. Instead of passing it to me, he carefully ran the fabric over my shoulders and back, then down each arm and across my stomach. He secured it around me, then lifted me from the tub and gently set me on my feet.

But he didn't let me go. Instead, he settled his hands low on my hips and dipped his head so his eyes were even with mine. "Fair warning, sweetheart: as soon as you're feeling better, I'm coming for you... and I will catch you."

CHAPTER
TWENTY-TWO

KATE

A groan left my mouth even before I cracked my eyes open. Holy shit. I felt like I'd been hit by a freight train. There wasn't a single inch of me that didn't ache. For several long minutes, I lay there, just staring at the ceiling and willing my muscles to relax. Finally, I rolled my head toward the nightstand, and I swiped out a hand, grasping the bottle of ibuprofen that Gavin had left there last night.

Awkwardly, I struggled to sit up, using my one good arm, grateful that he'd left the cap loosened for me. I popped two tablets into my mouth and swallowed them down with water. The hot bath last night had helped to ease some of my pain, but I had a feeling the next couple days were going to be brutal. I glanced at the nightstand, at the phone charging on the surface. I should probably call my parents and tell them what happened.

Even though it was only after eight o'clock, I dialed my parents' home phone number, the same one we'd had since I was a child. After only a couple rings, my mother answered, her voice chipper.

"Katie, honey, how are you?"

"Fine, Mom. How are you?"

"Oh, the usual," she said.

I fought the urge to roll my eyes. It'd been the same for the last thirty years. While my father went to work in his accounting firm, Mom stayed home and took care of the house. She came from the South, born of a generation who thought it was a woman's job to look after the house and family.

My sister was the same way. She'd been married to her high school sweetheart for nearly ten years, and they had the requisite house in the suburbs, two kids, and a dog. I was damn proud of what I'd accomplished, but I'd be lying if part of me said I wasn't at least a little envious of her.

My parents weren't happy about my divorce, but then they never really liked Steve to begin with. Mom didn't ask about it, and I didn't bother to offer any information. It was over, in the past, and that was all that mattered.

"I have something to tell you," I began slowly. "I wanted you to hear it from me before you found out from someone else."

"Oh? What's that?"

I heard the wary curiosity in her tone. "There was a shooting downtown near one of the coffee shops yesterday, and I was there."

"That's terrible!" She clucked a sympathetic sound. "What's this world coming to?"

"I don't know," I said. "It's pretty bad. Anyway, I was standing right outside, and I was kind of... hit."

"Hit?" my mother asked. "By what?"

"Um... the bullet."

On the other end of the line, my mother sucked in a

breath, and I could practically see her eyes widen in shock. "Oh my God! Are you okay?"

"Well..." I laughed. "I wouldn't exactly be calling if I wasn't."

"You know what I mean," my mother scolded. "Do you want us to come down?"

I picked at a thread on the blanket. "No, that's okay. I appreciate the offer though."

"Are you sure? Daddy can take some time off, and—"

"It's fine." I cut her off. "Really. I'm staying with a friend, so I'm perfectly safe."

"If you say so..." My mother trailed off.

"I am. I just wanted to let you know."

"All right," my mother acquiesced, sounding not at all happy about it.

"So tell me what else is going on." I changed the subject and listened as she prattled on about my nephew's football team for a few minutes.

"Anyway, they're already starting practices to get ready for the fall."

"Isn't it a little early?" Don't get me wrong. I was born and raised in Texas, and I loved football as much as the next girl, but seriously. The kid was only six.

"You know how it is," my mother said.

Unfortunately, I did.

A few minutes later, after getting all caught up on the drama, I hung up with my mom, then made my way downstairs to the kitchen. I smiled at Phil where he sat at the table, flipping through the morning paper. Gavin had told me to make myself at home, so I headed for the fridge and pulled out a jug of orange juice.

"Glasses are to the right of the stove. Need some help?"

"No, thanks. I think I've got it." I shot Phil a smile, and he turned his attention back to his paper. With one hand, I managed to unscrew the cap and awkwardly sloshed it into the glass.

"Something happen between you and Gavin?"

Oh, God. Had he noticed the tension between us last night? I cleared my throat. "No. Why do you ask?"

He speared me with a look. "I was born at night, but not last night."

I blushed fiercely and turned my attention to the jug of juice, taking an extra-long time to screw the cap on using only one hand. Not knowing what Gavin had said to his father, I couldn't exactly lie to him. "We dated once."

"Ah."

He went back to his paper, and my brows drew together. That was it? I felt the overwhelming urge to explain what had happened between his son and me. "He's a really great guy. I just... wasn't in a good place at the time."

The paper rustled, and Phil's voice floated over the top. "You're too good for him."

I opened my mouth, then snapped it shut. It was obvious that there was some kind of discord between father and son, but... "Why would you say that?"

Phil snorted. "He's too stubborn, too high-handed."

Well, I couldn't argue with that. "It's probably what makes him so good at his job," I pointed out.

"More to life than work," he remarked.

I didn't know how to respond to that, so I just nodded. I couldn't help but wonder what my family would think about Gavin. Knowing them, they'd probably think he was a total catch. And, truly... he was. He was handsome and successful, the epitome of the perfect man. He was just as incredible as he was infuriating, and part of me had to admit... It was kind of endearing. Okay, maybe a lot endearing.

I loved that he was straightforward and didn't beat around the bush. He knew what he wanted and went after it with single-minded focus. Despite my best efforts to push him away, he'd always made sure that I was taken care of. From my divorce with Steve to the shooting yesterday, he put me first and tried to do what he thought was best. He could be overbearing and controlling, but also so damn sweet sometimes that I wanted to melt into a puddle at his feet.

I finished my juice in silence, then excused myself from the kitchen. I took another long soak in the tub and spent a good portion of the day reading and relaxing, watching a couple of shows on TV. By midafternoon, the throbbing in my arm was back, along with an ache at the base of my skull. I popped a couple more ibuprofen, then curled up to take a nap, wishing not for the first time that Gavin was here beside me.

CHAPTER
TWENTY-THREE

GAVIN

Between court and getting caught up on my regular cases, I was late getting home. I entered through the garage, then made my way to the living room. Dad was in my favorite recliner, remote clutched in one hand, sawing logs louder than Sports Center blaring in the background. I hesitated for a moment, just watching him.

Something Kate had said a while back stuck with me. We were all getting older, and despite the fact that Dad and I didn't always get along, he wouldn't always be here. Even though he drove me crazy sometimes, he was still my dad, and I still cared about him. We may not be best friends, but I wanted whatever time we had left together, hopefully many years yet, to be better than the ones we'd put behind us.

As if my musing alerted him to my presence, he stirred in the chair. He glanced at me, then at the clock. "Long day."

"You know how it is," I responded. If there was one thing my dad understood, it was work. "Did you and Kate get into anything today?" I asked as I settled back on the couch and crossed one ankle over my knee.

He shook his head but remained silent. For several seconds, we both watched the TV, then he spoke up. "She's a good girl."

His words didn't surprise me, except for the fact that he'd never before taken an interest in my love life. "She is," I admitted.

"Maybe the forever type?" he asked.

"If she wants to be," I responded softly.

He gave another little nod. "I wouldn't mind having her in the family."

I smiled a little. "Yeah. Me, too. Where is she, anyway?"

He used the remote to gesture toward the stairs. "Said she had a headache and wanted to go lie down."

I braced my hands on my knees and pushed to my feet. "I'm gonna go check on her, then start dinner."

Dad turned his attention back to TV, and I strode through the house and up the stairs. I paused in the doorway of my room, a soft smile curling my lips at the sight that greeted me. Sure enough, Kate was asleep in the middle of my bed. She lay on her back, her knees tucked up to the side, a pillow clutched to her chest, her injured arm draped over top.

I crossed the room, then carefully crawled onto the bed and removed the pillow from her grasp. I lay down next to her and eased closer until she was almost in my embrace. I brushed a kiss over her forehead, and she stirred, then slowly came awake. Pretty blue eyes met mine before she closed them again.

I lifted one hand and brushed my thumb over her cheek. "Feeling better?" I asked softly.

"Mmm." She nodded slightly and stretched out her legs but didn't offer anything else.

I grinned. "We're not even married yet and you're already getting headaches?"

Her eyes slitted open to glare at me, but I could see the faint flicker of a smile at the corner of her lips. "In your dreams, Price," she quipped, then closed her eyes again.

"Are you always this cranky when you first wake up?" I teased gently.

Carefully avoiding her damaged shoulder, I trailed my fingers gently down her arm to the dip of her waist and swept my thumb over her stomach. "I wonder what you'll be like a couple months in."

Her brow furrowed in confusion, and she blinked at me. "A couple months in what?"

"When you're expecting our first kid."

Her eyes widened before she schooled her features into a remote expression, and one eyebrow ratcheted toward her hairline. "Our first?"

"Yep. I've got it all planned out."

She gave a little snort. "Do you now?"

She pressed her lips together to quell the smile threatening to break over them, and I grinned in return. "Sure. Been working on this for a while now. Date a little while longer—"

"We're not dating now," she pointed out.

It was my turn to lift an eyebrow. "You're living with me."

"Temporarily," she corrected, "and only out of necessity."

I waved her defense away. "For now. Anyway, date for a few more months, then convince you to marry me."

"Sounds like a long shot," Kate interjected, and I threw a mock glare her way.

"Don't interrupt. I figure we'll be married for a year or two before we start trying, so I'm not too old to play with the kids."

She blinked. "Wow. You've thought of everything, haven't you?"

"I've had a lot of time to think about it."

"Are you always this pushy?"

I grinned. "I think you knew the answer to that when you hired me."

She rolled her eyes playfully but couldn't contain the tiny smile that flitted over her lips. "This is true."

"What do you think?" I asked. "Did I miss anything?"

Her eyes held a glimmer of challenge as she looked up at me. "And, what? Am I supposed to put my career on hold to raise these imaginary children of yours and take care of the house like a good little wife?"

My face turned serious. "Not unless you want to. Do you really think I'll try to make you give that up?"

She studied me for several seconds, then finally shook her head. "No. I don't think you would do that."

Her answer filled me with relief, and I brushed a lock of hair away from her face. "Kate?" Her brows lifted slightly in question, and I met her gaze. "I want to kiss you."

It was both a declaration and a question. I wanted to push her, but never pressure her into something she didn't want. She hesitated for a long moment, then finally nodded. I slipped my fingers into her hair and cupped the back of her head, then dipped my head and kissed her softly. Just once, just enough to show her how much I cared.

I lightly slapped her hip. "I'm gonna head down and start dinner. Come on down whenever you're ready."

I started to roll to my feet, but one hand shot out and fisted in my shirt, halting my progress. She released me as if she'd been scalded, and I took her hand in mine. "You good?"

"Yeah." She nodded. "Just... thanks—for everything."

Not wanting to push her any more at the moment, I gave her fingers a gentle squeeze, then slipped off the bed and left the room. It'd always been my motto to leave them wanting more, and I smiled as I felt her eyes tracking me the entire way out the door and down the stairs.

CHAPTER
TWENTY-FOUR

KATE

Dinner was an uneventful affair, but both Gavin and Phil seemed more relaxed than I'd ever seen them. We kept up a healthy stream of conversation, everything from TV shows to politics to sports. I found myself glancing between Gavin and his dad, realizing just how similar they were despite their insistence to the contrary.

When we were all finished, I stood and began to gather dishes to take them into the kitchen. I was juggling mine one-handedly when men both waved me back into my seat.

"Sit down, sit down," Phil blustered. "You're a guest here. I'll take care of it."

"You're a guest, too," Gavin pointed out as he stood.

"Yeah, but you cooked dinner," Phil retorted cantankerously.

I bit my tongue, bemused, and watched the two men face off—one was a younger version of the other, but his glare was no less powerful.

"I'll just—"

I grabbed my plate, but both men turned to me in unison. "No!"

They turned back to each other, and the glare continued for another few seconds before Gavin finally threw his hands in the air. "Fine. Have at it."

Phil looked pleased to have won, and I couldn't help the tiny smile that curled the corners of my lips. Gavin shot me a look across the table, and I rolled my lips together to contain the laugh welling up. It really was amazing how stubborn these two were.

When all the dishes had been collected, Phil retired to his room, and Gavin stood, holding out a hand in my direction. "Come sit with me?"

I allowed him to help me up, then followed him into the living room, where he sank down into his recliner. I started to move past toward the couch, but he caught me around the waist and pulled me backward.

"Gavin..." I warned.

Hands framing my hips, he smiled up at me. "You promised to sit with me."

I rolled my eyes. "That was before I knew what you intended."

"Too bad," he said as he pulled me down sideways across his lap. "No reneging on your promises."

He flipped on the TV, then settled on some show about natural disasters and sat back to watch. After a few minutes, I gradually began to relax and laid my head along his shoulder. I felt his lips brush a kiss over the top of my head, and I smiled at the sensation.

The show went to a commercial a couple minutes later, and Gavin hit the mute button. "How are you feeling?"

I tipped my chin up to look at him. "Still a little sore, but it's not terrible."

He studied me. "Do you need your medicine?"

"No, I'm good," I responded.

He cocked an eyebrow. "Is that Dr. Kate refusing treatment, or is this real Kate?"

I rolled my eyes even as a smile curved my mouth. "I'm pretty sure you knew I was a terrible patient before you dragged me over here."

"I do. That's why I'm asking."

I delivered a little slap to his chest, and he laughed before his eyes turned serious. "I'm not just talking about your arm, you know. How are you really?"

I fiddled with one of the buttons on his shirt. "I'm... okay."

"Hopefully we'll have an answer soon." His breath stirred the hair next to my ear when he spoke. "The police will do whatever they can."

All the thoughts over the past couple weeks came spilling forth. "What if it wasn't random?" I asked.

His expression darkened. "If by some chance someone actually meant to do you harm," he replied, "I'm going to do everything in my power to put them behind bars for a long damn time."

"Can I ask you something?"

"Anything." His fingers trailed up and down my arm, sending ripples of pleasure through my body.

"You introduced me to a man the day I left your office. Who is he?"

"Larry?" I nodded. "He's my boss, one of the partners. Why?"

I lifted my shoulders in a little shrug. "No reason. I just... He looked familiar."

Gavin took my chin between his thumb and forefinger and directed my gaze to his. "Did something happen? Did he say something to you?"

"No." I shook my head, and his hand fell away, settling on

my thigh. "Nothing like that. But I think I saw him at the VA one day."

"Like, as a patient?" Gavin's brows drew together, and I shook my head.

"No, I... The day your dad was admitted to the hospital, I overheard Dr. Coleman arguing with someone. I think it was him."

"What were they arguing about?"

"I'm not entirely sure, but I think they were discussing a patient," I admitted. "The guy—Larry—sounded like he was accusing Dr. Coleman of not doing his job. Said he couldn't just apologize and make it all go away."

Gavin's expression turned pensive, and I studied him. "Does that make any sense to you?"

"I don't really know," he responded slowly. "Maybe it was nothing—just a coincidence, or maybe it wasn't even him."

I didn't like the way it felt, but there was also no evidence of any wrongdoing. Larry hadn't said a single word to me, hadn't even really acknowledged me beyond our introduction that day in Gavin's office. Maybe I was overthinking things. Or maybe I really did have something to worry about. Either way, it was worth looking into. Better safe than sorry.

I smiled at Gavin. "I'm sure you're right. Like you said—just a coincidence."

CHAPTER
TWENTY-FIVE

GAVIN

Coincidence, my ass. The fact that she'd run into Larry at her place of work, along with his strange behavior recently, threw up all kinds of red flags.

I'd managed to gently coax out of Kate the details of the argument she'd overheard. They'd supposedly mentioned a patient—who the hell could it be? No one in his immediate family had passed away that I was aware of, but I knew better than to dismiss anything. The details were vague, but I trusted Kate, I trusted her instincts, and if she felt that something was wrong, it was.

I filled out the paperwork, then carried it back to the reception desk, where Abby flashed me a grin. "I'll let him know you're here. Make yourself comfortable. It should only be a couple minutes."

I inclined my head at her. "Thanks."

I took a seat on the sofa along the wall, then crossed one foot over my knee and settled in to wait. The lobby was purely functional, not a single decoration on the walls except for the handful of knickknacks Abby had scattered over her desk. Everything looked completely new though. From what Xander had said, they'd been in the building for a very short period of time and were just getting the business off the ground.

I heard the soft approach of footsteps along the carpeted hallway, then a dark-haired, dark-eyed man stepped into the lobby. He tipped his head at me. "Mr. Price?"

As soon as I saw his face, it clicked. I'd first met Connor Quentin on an extraction we'd worked in Kabul. I rose and crossed the room to take his extended hand. "Gavin Price."

I was sure he'd already run background on me before conceding to this meeting, so I didn't bother with more of an introduction. He released my hand and gestured down the hall. "Let's head into the conference room, and you can tell me what you know." I preceded him into the room, then took a seat at the small round table and waited until he sank into a chair across from me.

"How have you been?" he asked, acknowledging our prior acquaintance, brief though it was.

"Good." I gave a tight nod. "I put in my time, then came home to go to school."

"Lawyer, right?" The faint twist of his lips hinted at a smile, and I took the friendly jab good-naturedly.

"Dad's footsteps." I shrugged. "What can you do?"

Con tipped his head like he understood perfectly. "McLean said he was a client of yours."

"That's actually how I found out about you. How long have you been in business?"

"Last tour ended about a year ago, so it was kind of a process getting everything all together, finding a place for a home base, all that good stuff."

He piqued my curiosity. "What do you do? Besides the obvious," I added.

"Long-term, I'd like to land a government contract. To be honest, though, right now we'll take anything pretty much just to get our name out there. We'll be offering some self-defense classes soon, as well as firearms instruction, and we've assisted the locals on a couple cases."

I knew he was referring to both Victoria and Lydia. "Well, those are both commendable endeavors, so I'm sure you have clients lining up."

He lifted one shoulder humbly. "We're doing okay so far."

I took the hint and didn't pry, but something he said sparked a memory. "Actually, Kate said at one point she'd like to take some self-defense classes."

Con nodded knowingly. "Any training is better than nothing, especially these days. What happened recently?"

"Someone shot at her a couple days ago outside a coffee shop."

His brows lifted toward his hairline. "You're sure it was meant for her?"

"I was only a few feet from her, but it looked pretty damn deliberate to me. The PD seems to think it may have been gang related. There was no license plate, and even though we have the model, there's a good chance that car's sitting in a chop shop somewhere right now. It's like searching for a needle in a haystack." He raised a brow, and I shrugged. "The coffee shop released the camera footage, but without evidence..."

"Says the lawyer," Con shot back.

"You know how it is," I grumbled. "They don't have the time or resources to look too deeply into it." It was a fact of life, and one I fucking hated. Kate could've been killed, yet I seriously doubted they'd ever find the person responsible.

"So we'll just have to find some evidence," Con supplied, as if it were just that easy. "Anyone suspicious, anyone who might want to hurt Kate? I remember there being an ex-husband."

"They just divorced," I confirmed, "but they ruled him out since he was out in public with his new wife."

The normally unflappable Marine's eyes widened. "He's already remarried?"

I couldn't help the scowl that took up residence on my face. "He's a piece of shit. But that's neither here nor there. He's out of her life, and that's all that matters."

"Okay," Con said slowly. "Anyone else who stands out?"

This was the tricky part. "This is kind of convoluted," I warned, then told him about the conversation she'd overheard at the VA between Dr. Coleman and Larry Raines. I wasn't sure what the hell to think, but coupled with his strange behavior recently, I couldn't discount anything.

"Raines. Any idea who this guy is?"

I blew out a breath. "Yeah. My boss."

Con absorbed that for a long moment, then— "Fuck."

"Yeah." It always sucked when lawyers were implicated, because most of them, myself excluded, were slimy as shit. They would have to be careful to cross every *t* and dot every *i* if Larry were responsible in any way.

"Motive?"

I lifted a shoulder. "No fucking clue."

Elbows braced on the arms of the chair, he steepled his fingers and peered at me. "What about the other guy—Coleman?"

"I don't know anything about him. But he works with her every day," I pointed out. "If he thought Kate had overheard something, it makes sense that he'd want to silence her. But if that was the case, wouldn't he have tried something before now?"

"Hard to tell. Did either of you get a look at the shooter?"

I nodded. "Hoodie, ball cap, glasses—but it definitely

wasn't Coleman." I'd looked him up on the website, and the doctor was older and more heavyset, while the gunman had been leaner, younger-looking.

Con looked up at the ceiling in thought. "Interesting.

"Something's up with Raines, I just can't figure out exactly what it is. His daughter works at our firm now, too. He said he wanted to "keep it in the family," and it's been... *implied* that my partnership is dependent on being with her."

One nearly black eyebrow ratcheted toward his hairline. "He wants you to marry the girl to get a promotion?" I pressed my lips together into a firm line, and he snorted. "What the hell is this, 1950?"

"Things have felt... different over the past few weeks. He's had a hair-trigger temper, been more of an asshole than usual."

Shannon had actually avoided me like the plague since our run-in the day Kate had stopped by the office. I was relieved, and I prayed that she'd given up any dream of us being together. I couldn't tell if Larry's actions were driven out of a desire to do what he thought best for his little girl, or if he was trying to deflect attention from something else.

Whatever was going on, it wasn't good. Larry was an asshole on the best of days, but he'd never been as preoccupied and eccentric as he had been recently. He obviously had something on his mind, or he was caught up in something he shouldn't be. I didn't believe it was a coincidence at all that his change in attitude had happened about the same time Kate overheard him arguing with Dr. Coleman.

His expression turned contemplative. "Could be embroiled in something."

"Anything's possible. That's why I need you guys to check him out, see if you notice anything suspicious."

"Didn't you do some recon in your day too?" he asked with some mirth.

"I've been out of the game so long…" It did sound damn good though.

Con studied me from across the table. "I'm always looking for a good addition if you're looking for a real job. Get you out of that courtroom."

"Yeah, I hear ya," I answered with a little shrug. "It pays the bills."

"If you change your mind, I'll make you a damn good offer."

"I appreciate that." I stood, and he followed suit, stretching one hand across the table to shake.

"Let me introduce you to the guys before you head out. Most of the guys are here today, with the exception of Vince Incarnato. He's working security detail for Gemma Malone."

I lifted a brow. "The singer?"

"That's her."

That was pretty impressive. I followed Con down the hall where he punched a code into a steel door, which opened with a beep. I gazed around the large room as we stepped inside, and my attention snagged on a couple familiar faces. Xander. Blake. Cole Thompson, and his brother, Clay.

Fuck.

My entire body went rigid, but I lifted my hand in greeting. Clay smirked at me from his spot, relaxed back in a chair, feet propped up on the desk.

Xander greeted me with a handshake, as did Blake and Cole. Con introduced me to two more guys, Jason Doyle and Dane Sullivan. Clay smiled lazily as he climbed to his feet. "How's it goin', pretty boy?"

I couldn't help the contempt I felt for the man, but I schooled my expression. I didn't know if he and Kate had ever actually been together, but it didn't really matter at this point. I was rewarded by the fact that she was with me now and not him. "Fine."

His gaze swept over me from head to toe, taking in my suit with no small amount of disdain, judging from the sneer on his face. He met my eyes, and his mouth twisted into a smirk. "How's Kate?"

I fucking hated the sound of her name passing his lips, but I'd be damned if I ever let him see how much it got to me. I dredged up every ounce of control I possessed. "Got clipped by a bullet a couple days ago, if you want to know the truth."

The snide look immediately fell away, replaced by a mixture of anger and concern. "What the fuck happened?"

I tipped my chin up. "Guess you're not close enough for her to tell you herself."

"Don't fuck with me." He took a step toward me, and I lifted a brow as my shoulders tensed and my hands clenched into fists at my side. "Who the hell shot at her?"

Blake and Xander both straightened in the background, now standing at attention and watching with wary expressions.

"Don't know." I didn't relax my stance as I tipped my head toward Con. "That's what I hired him for."

From my right, Con cleared his throat and shifted his focus to Clay. "I was going to assign this one to you, but not if you're going to kill each other."

Fucking awesome. Just what I needed, to deal with this asshole on top of everything else. Clay held my gaze for a long moment before I finally shook my head. "He's fine."

Clay's eyes narrowed, filled with undisguised scorn and mistrust. I didn't give a damn if he hated me. All that mattered was keeping Kate safe. "Do your job, and we won't have a problem."

Those hard amber-colored eyes held mine. "Take care of her."

"Always." My reply was curt, and we stared at each other

for a long moment. Whatever he saw in my eyes must have reassured him, because he finally nodded.

I turned to Con. "Do you need anything else from me?"

"Nope." He shook his head. "We'll run some of the info you gave us, then we'll be in touch."

Even though I knew she was safe, I was eager to get home to Kate. God only knew how long she'd be staying with me, and I didn't want to waste a second of the time we had together. One way or the other, I was going to win her over again, no matter how long it took.

CHAPTER
TWENTY-SIX

KATE

Phil sent a warm smile my way as I stepped into the kitchen. "Good morning."

I smiled in return. "Morning."

From his place at the table, he nodded toward the coffee pot on the counter. "It's fresh. I just made it about half an hour ago."

"Great, thank you," I said gratefully as I pulled a mug down from the cupboard. I stood at the counter as I sipped at the brew, waiting for the caffeine to send its familiar jolt of awareness through my veins. Feeling a little more awake, I sauntered to the table and took a seat across from Phil. The surface was scattered with various sections of newspaper, and he shoved them in my direction.

"I'm done with those if you want them."

"Thanks," I said. I wasn't much of a newspaper reader, so instead I turned my gaze out the sliding door to the verdant view of the backyard.

With the rain that had fallen yesterday, I hadn't gotten a

chance to go outside. The backyard was well manicured, filled with flowering shrubs and bushes, and a picturesque little gazebo sat in the middle, practically calling to me. Maybe I'd try to dig up a book and go outside and read for a while. It'd been a long time since I had more than just a few moments to myself.

I set my cup on the table, and my gaze slid over the rim to the headline on one of the sections of newspaper. The word "remains" caught my attention, and I turned the paper around to read the article. According to the report, the second victim had now been identified as a 56-year-old male resident of a neighboring suburb.

"Did you see this?" I tapped the newspaper and Phil glanced up.

"I did. Damn shame."

I pressed my lips together, thinking of the day I'd found Mr. Tripp in the cornfield just a few weeks ago. I wondered if the police had any leads yet and if this case was related. The article didn't say as much, but I wasn't surprised by that. No need to spark unnecessary panic if they didn't absolutely have to. I glanced at the man's name again, committing it to memory. Merrill Keane.

I shook my head and pushed the newspaper away. "I hate reading the news. It's so depressing all the time."

He nodded in commiseration. "There is so much evil in the world."

Eager to change the topic, I focused on Phil. "How have you been feeling?"

He tipped his head from side to side. "Getting old, Doc. You know how it is."

I couldn't tell if he was brushing me off or not. I studied him. "Have you been taking it easy?"

Phil huffed a little laugh and set down the newspaper as he regarded me. "Are you kidding? My son won't let me do more than lift a plate around here, like he thinks it's going to break me."

I offered a soft smile as I sat back in my seat. "That's only because he cares about you. We both do."

His dark, intelligent eyes met mine. "I appreciate that. It's been nice having you around. I think you're good for my boy. He's used to being in charge all the time. It's nice to see someone give him a run for his money. He's always been a stubborn one."

I barely managed to hold back a laugh. From what I'd witnessed over the past few days with the Price men, the apple didn't fall far from the tree. "We'll see what happens," I said smoothly.

I wasn't ready to admit the possibility of a relationship with Gavin to myself, let alone anyone else. The last thing I wanted to do was get Phil's hopes up. I genuinely liked the man, and I didn't want him to be disappointed if things didn't work out.

"What's your plan for the day?"

He lifted an eyebrow at my change of subject but went along with it anyway. "Same as yesterday and the day before. I'll probably watch some TV and relax."

"I think that sounds like a good idea, actually," I said. "I was thinking about doing some reading myself."

We went our separate ways, and I found myself in the cute little gazebo half an hour later. I'd pilfered a thriller novel from Gavin's office, but fifteen pages in, it still hadn't grabbed my attention. It wasn't the author's fault; my attention kept drifting back to the newspaper article I'd read this morning.

Merrill Keane. I don't know what it was that drove me, but I found I needed to know about the man. Maybe it was a sense of remorse at his loss, or guilt that we hadn't been able to stop his murder. I closed the book then went inside.

Gavin's downstairs office has been converted into the spare

bedroom for Phil, so Gavin had moved his computer and important files upstairs to his bedroom. He'd given me carte blanche to use whatever I wanted, and I picked up the laptop from his nightstand, confident that he wouldn't care.

I googled the man's name and sifted through several newspaper article accounts of what they supposed had happened. The exact cause of death was not disclosed, though the police suspected homicide.

Apparently badly decomposed, his body had been found near Oak Creek—less than two miles from Hartwell Road where I'd found Mr. Tripp, and a little over a mile from where the third body had been recovered. On a map, they made a neat little triangle right around the small creek that coasted through the landscape.

Clicking out of the *Dallas Repository's* webpage, I went back to the main search bar. Keane had several social media accounts, and curiosity prompted me to open them. In life, it seemed like Keane had enjoyed a good laugh. His page was filled with jokes and memes, and I couldn't help but chuckle aloud as I scrolled down.

A photo at the bottom caught my attention, and I clicked on it to get a better look. Four men in fatigues smiled at the camera, and despite the grainy, blurry photo, I immediately recognized Keane's face. Taken probably decades ago, he looked incredibly young and happy, his arm slung around another soldier's shoulders.

I sat back in the chair, my eyes riveted to the photo. What reason would anyone have to kill Keane, or Tripp for that matter? Both had been military, but different branches. From what I gathered, they lived in different parts of the city, nearly thirty miles from each other.

I felt like I was missing something, but I wasn't quite sure what. Keane and Tripp didn't look the same, but that didn't really mean anything. I didn't know anything about modus operandi or victimology except what I'd learned in a criminal justice class I'd taken years ago. I knew it wasn't my job to figure out who killed them—that was for the police—but I couldn't help the curiosity driving me. I wanted it to make sense, and right now, there were so many unanswered questions. Could they have been saved, somehow?

With a sigh, I closed out of the browser and closed the lid of the laptop. A dull ache radiated from my shoulder, but the wound felt significantly better than it had the past couple days. Pushing out of my chair, I went in search of some ibuprofen to take the edge off. Within a few days, I figured I'd be almost back to normal, and I couldn't wait to get back to work. I hated feeling useless and cooped up. I wasn't even supposed to run, so I decided to take a walk around the subdivision.

It was sunny but scorching hot, and I returned to Gavin's house, exhausted. Just as I was jumping into the shower, a text lit up my phone.

Gavin: I have another appointment after work, so I'll be home late

Me: That's fine

Gavin: I hate leaving you there all alone

Me: No worries. I'll be fine with your dad

Gavin: You feeling better?

Me: Just took some ibuprofen, but it's much better

Gavin: Good. I've gotta run, but I'll see you when I get home

I tossed my phone on the bed. Looked like it was going to be another long night alone. I should be grateful that he was giving me space, but I kind of missed his presence. Yeah, he was overbearing, but he was also sexy and funny and... sweet.

Damn it. I didn't want to be falling for this man, but I was terrified that the way my heart plummeted in my chest meant exactly that.

CHAPTER
TWENTY-SEVEN

GAVIN

I hadn't mentioned it to Kate when I texted her earlier, but Con was already digging into Larry and had asked me to stop by at some point. I found myself once more in the lobby of Quentin Security after work. The same pretty little brunette behind the desk greeted me by name, then called Clay to let him know I was there.

A few moments later, the steel door swung open, and Thompson appeared. "Price." He gave me a quick nod. "Come on in."

I pushed off the counter and followed him through the doorway into the bullpen area I'd been in the last time I was here. Xander and Blake tipped their chin at me in greeting, and I offered one to the other men in the room.

Con stopped beside Clay's desk and pulled up another chair. "I'd like to go over this with both of you."

"Sure."

Clay lifted an eyebrow as I slid into the seat, almost as if he were challenging me to request someone else. I honestly didn't give a damn who was working it as long as we got some answers. Clay was just as good as anyone; the fucker was one of the smartest men I knew—he was just a complete asshole.

Ignoring Clay, I turned my attention to Con. "What did we find out?"

He lounged back in his chair and regarded me. "Doyle did a little digging on Larry Raines. He and Coleman go way back, apparently. Went to school together, were even roommates in college. Unfortunately, nothing suspicious. Finances, from what we can tell, appear to be in order."

"That doesn't eliminate the possibility of blackmail," I pointed out. "Greed is a pretty damn good motivator."

"It is," Clay agreed. "So is hate."

I tipped my head in question. "The argument?"

Con nodded almost imperceptibly. "What did Kate say she overheard again?"

I drew back on the conversation. "Something about blaming Coleman for the death of a patient."

"We may have the answer to that," Clay said, taking over the conversation. "Raines's primary residence is over on Waterton."

I'd been there a couple times, several years ago when I'd first joined the firm. Larry liked to entertain and show off his wealth. "Yeah, I know it."

"According to the records, he also has a small home on the opposite side of town."

I contemplated all the possibilities. The most likely was that it was a rental, or he could have a little side piece he kept there. Wouldn't be the first time it'd happened, and I couldn't completely discount the theory. I shrugged. "Okay. That doesn't tell us much."

"Maybe not," Clay agreed, "but I took it upon myself to scope the place out yesterday."

I dropped my head back. "Jesus, Clay. Better hope to hell

you don't get caught. He'll sue your ass for breach of privacy and anything else he can throw at you."

He made a face like it didn't matter one way or the other, and I rolled my eyes as he continued. "Do what you gotta do. Anyway, apparently Raines's wife was living there up until two days ago."

My brows drew together. So, no mistress then. "I'd heard rumors that they had a huge blowup sometime last year and that she wanted to leave him. I guess she did."

"Not exactly." Clay picked up a pencil and tapped the eraser on the desk. "There was a company there moving medical equipment out of the place. Hospital bed, machines, all kinds of stuff."

"Okay..." I drew out the word, unsure exactly where the hell he was going with this. "So you think his wife is sick?"

Piercing golden eyes met mine. "Not sick—dead."

I reeled back in surprise. "You're shitting me, right?"

He never mentioned anything about Meredith being hospitalized or terminally ill. Jesus. Had he hurt her? The thought made me sick. But if he was capable of hurting Meredith, he was more than capable of hurting Kate, too, if he thought she was in the way.

"Do we have any idea what actually caused her death?"

Clay gave a brief shake of his head. "Not yet. We'll probably have to wait another couple of days until the death certificate is officially in the system."

I mulled that over, something not making sense. "Why would he blame Coleman? He's been at the VA, right? She certainly wouldn't have any reason to be there."

"We're checking into both of them, but it may take a while to get hospital records and such," Con said. "We did run a cursory check on Coleman, and it looks like he was a vascular surgeon prior to transferring to the VA roughly five years ago."

I'd remembered seeing Meredith roughly a year ago, right

around the Fourth of July, and she'd seemed to be perfectly healthy. What the hell had happened in such a short amount of time?

I sighed and glanced at my watch. "I've got a client dinner in half an hour, so I gotta bolt. Keep me posted?"

"Give us a few hours."

"Thanks."

I left QSG with more questions than answers, still stunned about the news of Meredith's death. Were these incidents separate, or was her death some sort of catalyst? Either way, we needed to figure it out sooner rather than later—before Kate got caught in the crosshairs again.

CHAPTER
TWENTY-EIGHT

KATE

After a quiet dinner with Phil, I headed to my room. I climbed into bed, wondering where Gavin was and who he was with.

He had texted me intermittently throughout the evening, taking a little sting out of the jealousy that had reared up. I knew he took clients out to dinner from time to time—I'd run into him at Eros while he'd been doing the same thing. But the idea of him sitting across from a pretty female client in a romantic restaurant folded my stomach into knots.

He'd said he would see me when he got home, but he hadn't specified when that might be. Tonight? Tomorrow morning? I wasn't going to show my cards and give him the satisfaction of looking for him. I'd been bored out of my mind sitting here all day, even with Phil's company.

Worse, I couldn't get Gavin off my mind. Surrounded by his things, it was even harder than usual. I thought of the past couple days and how attentive he'd been, and I realized I was in deep trouble. I wouldn't be able to hold him off much longer.

If I was entirely honest with myself, I wasn't sure I wanted to. He was sweet and funny and sexy as hell, even if he did try to change my dog's name. Peanut, or Thor as Gavin liked to call him, had made good friends with Phil, and he'd spent the last couple of nights sleeping in the spare bedroom downstairs.

I picked up the book on the nightstand and began to read but couldn't focus, my thoughts continually drawn back to Gavin. My life was rapidly spiraling out of control, and there was nothing I could do to stop it. I knew the police were doing everything they could to find the person responsible, but I also knew it was a long shot. For better or worse, I was stuck in Gavin's house for the foreseeable future.

I felt on edge, and though a huge part of that was due to the shooting at the coffee shop, I knew this sexual tension building between Gavin and me was a contributing factor. It was thick enough to cut with a knife, and my skin ached with the need to be touched. I'd stopped him a couple nights ago; now I wished I hadn't. I was on fire for him, but I didn't want to give in. I was afraid it would make me look easy in his eyes, and I hated the idea.

With a harsh exhale, I tossed the book on the nightstand and turned off the light. The darkness only made it worse. The room felt empty, and I craved his touch. The soft sheets caressed my body, and the scent of laundry detergent wafted up to me from the pillow, reminding me of the way Gavin smelled—manly and fresh. Damn the man.

I closed my eyes and indulged in the fantasy of Gavin sliding into bed next to me. I could practically feel his lips on mine, his hands skimming over my flesh. My body warmed, and I sneaked my hand below the waistband of my panties. Spreading my legs, I bit my lip as I dipped a finger between my folds. As good as it felt, it was nothing like the way Gavin had touched me. When I finally came on a brief cry, I felt strangely unfulfilled and slightly disappointed.

I curled onto my side and lay there for several minutes, staring into the dark. I felt more alone than I did even when Steve and I had first separated. I couldn't explain it, and it sounded stupid to my own ears. I'd chosen this; I'd kept Gavin at arm's length, and he wouldn't make a move until I gave the green light.

At some point over the past few weeks, my heart had begun to heal. If I hadn't known all along that Steve and I weren't meant to be, being with Gavin solidified it. We'd only been intimate once, but there was an inexplicable connection, an indefinable emotion between us. And even after everything, he'd never wavered from his course.

Most men would have thrown in the towel and walked away. But not Gavin. He said he wanted me, would wait forever—and he'd been true to his word. We'd had our hiccups, but I knew he was loyal. If I gave him my heart, he would treasure it, do his best never to hurt me.

A knock on the door startled me, and I practically jumped from the bed. Worried that Phil might need something, I quickly yanked on my robe and crossed to the door. I opened it a few inches and peered through the dimly lit space, my heart jumping as Gavin's face came into view.

"Hey," he said quietly. "Just wanted to check on you before bed."

This side of him made my knees weak, and I wrapped my hand around the edge of the door, using it to steady myself. "I'm fine," I whispered.

"Good." He reached out and tucked a strand of hair behind my ear. "Were you bored today?"

"A little bit." I shrugged and leaned my head against the back of my hand where it curled around the door. "But your dad was here to keep me company at least, so it wasn't too bad."

"I'm glad." He stared at me for several long seconds. "I like having you here."

His admission made my heart swell. "Me too."

He leaned forward a little bit, then froze, nostrils flaring slightly as his gaze dropped to my fingers—fingers that had just been inside me only moments before. Completely mortified, I immediately straightened and dropped my hand to my side.

"I—I should get to bed," I stammered.

I tried to shut the door, but Gavin stopped it with his foot, a slow smile spreading across his face. "What's wrong, Kate?"

I shook my head emphatically. "Nothing. Just tired."

"Is that all?"

I started to nod, and he snatched up my hand. I tried to pull it back, but his hold was too firm, and he tugged me closer. "What did you do today?"

"Oh, you know." My gaze darted around the room as I stalled for time. My eyes moved back to his, and I found myself frozen in place as he lifted my hand to his lips. Eyes locked on mine, he took my index finger in his mouth. His tongue curled around it, and I felt the light sting of teeth as he scraped along my flesh.

I let out a little whimper, and he chuckled. "Did you miss me?" Somehow, I managed a tiny nod, and his eyes seemed to darken further. "You're all I think about."

He nipped my finger again, and I fought to hold in a whimper as heat raced through me. "Did you take the edge off?"

My gaze skittered away as I licked my lips and reluctantly nodded.

"Were you thinking of me?"

I swallowed hard and managed another tiny nod.

"Did it help?"

I met those unfathomably dark eyes again, and our gazes held for a long moment before I shook my head.

"I can make it go away."

Yes, please. My body literally ached for him; all I had to do was say one little word, and he would make the pain go away. We stood barely a foot apart, yet I felt as if we were on the precipice of a great divide. The time had come to either risk everything and jump or turn away. For the first time in a long time, I shut off my brain and listened to my heart.

"Yes."

One dark eyebrow lifted toward his hairline. "Yes what?"

"I want you."

Gavin slipped between the narrow space, then closed and locked the door behind him. "God, Kate, I've missed you so much."

"Wait—what about your dad?" I whispered as he attacked my neck.

He broke the kiss long enough to speak. "Don't worry. He's on the other side of the house. He won't hear a thing. Now..." He gripped the hem of my shirt and gave it a little tug. "Let's get you naked."

CHAPTER
TWENTY-NINE

GAVIN

My blood felt like it was on fire, and I couldn't wait another second to be inside her. Thank God for the loose shirt she chose to sleep in. I tore it from her body, and she stood in front of me perfectly, gloriously naked. I wanted to touch every inch of her, use my lips and tongue to trace each curve—later. Right now, I just needed to be inside her before I exploded from wanting her.

"Bed—now," I managed.

She let out a tense little laugh. "You sound a little worked up."

"You think?" I chuckled as I took her hand and guided it to my groin. Beneath the fabric I was swollen with arousal, painfully hard. "God, I've been waiting for this for weeks. I've been jerking off at least once a day thinking of you."

She cocked a brow. "What about your other women?"

"There was never another woman—I told you that." I took her in my arms. "There hasn't been since I met you, and there won't be another."

Her teeth sank into her lower lip as she stared up at me. "Really?"

"Promise." I cupped the back of her head possessively. "You're it for me."

She sat heavily on the edge of the mattress, then pushed herself backward, bracing herself on her elbows as she watched me from beneath hooded, sultry eyes.

Fishing out the condom I'd been carrying around for the past couple of days—just in case—I shucked my pants and socks in one fluid movement. Stroking my hard-on with one hand, I ripped the foil packet open with my teeth and rolled the condom over the swollen head, then levered myself over her. "Your shoulder's okay?"

"Yeah, it's—" Her words splintered into a low moan as I lightly bit the spot where her neck met her shoulder.

"Good." I soothed the sting with my tongue. "First time's gonna be fast and hard. Can't go slow—it's been too damn long."

"For me, too," she said as her head dropped back and she reached for me, her fingers wrapping around my biceps. "I want you so bad."

Hearing her say those words—admitting that she felt the same way I did—made my heart swell with satisfaction. I kneed her legs apart, then settled between her silky thighs. Her hands coasted upward and curled around my shoulders as I rolled my hips, nudging her soft opening. The head slipped an inch inside, and she let out a little sigh. She was wet, soaked and ready for me. I pressed forward and I hissed in a breath as she took me all the way in with one hard stroke.

Sliding one hand beneath her hips, I lifted her to meet each thrust, sinking deep inside, unable to get close enough, deep enough. I wanted to feel every inch of her wrapped around me, wanted her to feel me for days. I hammered into her hard and fast, claiming her mouth and drinking in her cries of pleasure.

Her nails dug into my back, and her thighs tightened around my hips. I could feel the tension in her muscles as she raced closer and closer to the edge. Her heels dug into the back of my legs, and she finally went over, sinking her teeth into my shoulder to stifle the sharp cry of release.

Her muscles tightened around me, spurring me on, and I let myself go. Four deep strokes, and I came with a groan and steeled my muscles to keep from smashing her into the mattress. My body felt drained, and it took every ounce of energy I had to climb from the bed to dispose of the condom. On shaky legs, I made my way back to the bed and slid in next to her, pulling her close.

She came to me like she couldn't stand to be away for one more second, her body molding to mine as I pulled her in close. I turned my face into her hair and breathed deeply, inhaling the scent of her. For the rest of my life, I knew each time I smelled that jasmine-scented shampoo, I would think of Kate. I traced little circles on her shoulder as I spoke. "I missed you."

She tilted her face to mine, a small smile playing over her lips. "I've been living with you for the past three days."

"Not like that." I turned slightly to face her and gestured between us. "This. When you're open and unguarded."

The smile slipped away, and she rolled to her back. "I'm just..."

She trailed off, and I grasped her chin, guiding her back to me. "Just what, sweetheart?"

"I don't know." She licked her lips. "Everything with you feels like it's too good to be true."

"Why?"

"I've never felt this way before, and it's scary."

"I can understand that. You've been hurt before, and you

want to protect yourself. But it's just me, babe. You'll learn to trust me."

"I do trust you. It's just... I don't know how to act, how to... *be*."

"Just be with me." I drew one finger over her nose and across her cheek. "We'll take it slow, no pressure."

Yet, I silently amended. There wasn't a single moment when I couldn't envision her by my side, and I wanted it all with her—marriage, kids, everything. Over the past few months, I'd come to know more about her than she realized. I might not know her favorite movie or which foods she hated, but I knew *her*.

I knew she was fiercely independent but loyal to those she cared about. She was stubborn, strong, and spirited, and she would fight for whatever she felt was right. I wanted a lifetime of fighting and making up, falling more in love with her each day.

"You're perfect just the way you are, and I love you for it."

She sucked in a breath and dropped her gaze away. I gave her a second, gauging how far to push her before I slipped my finger beneath her chin and lifted her gaze to mine. "For the record, that was me telling you how much I care about you. You don't have to say anything"—I swept my thumb over her lips when they parted—"I just wanted you to know. I'll wait as long as you want; I'm not going anywhere."

She burrowed her face against my chest, her arms coming up to embrace me. I held her tightly to me, stroking her hair, silently offering comfort and support. Finally, she pulled away.

"I'm sorry I pushed you away."

"It's fine. I—"

She shook her head, those big blue eyes boring into mine in the pale moonlight. "It's not fine. I was wrong. I..." She blew out a breath. "I just kept thinking there's no way you could want me when you could have any girl out there. All I could think about was getting close to you, then being cheated on, like last time. And when that girl from the bar came along—"

Guilt slammed into me at her words. "Kate—"

"I was terrified."

"Because you thought I'd proved you right," I stated softly.

"Not just that, but..." She bit her lip. "When I saw you with her, it hit me hard just how much I was already falling for you, even then."

It was an admission I wasn't expecting. "Sweetheart..."

She placed her palm over my heart. "I was so worried about being hurt again that I completely shut you out, and it wasn't fair. I'm sorry for making stupid assumptions and comparing you to my ex. I thought if I kept you at a distance, it wouldn't hurt so badly when you left."

"I'm not leaving." I brushed my nose over hers. "You got a raw deal, and I'm sorry for that. I'm not like him, and I hope you realize that."

"I do."

"I know this isn't ideal," I murmured softly as I played with a lock of hair that had fallen across her cheek. "I just want you to be safe."

Her eyes drifted away, and her expression turned pensive. "I haven't heard anything from the police yet."

Levering to my elbow, I propped my head on my hand. "I'm sure they're working on it."

She nodded a little and opened her mouth to speak, then slammed it closed again. I lifted a brow at her. "Something on your mind?"

She shook her head, and I framed her face in one hand. "You know you can talk to me about anything, right?"

She rolled her lips in, then took a deep breath. "I just... What happens when it's over?"

I didn't pretend not to know what she was talking about. "What do you want to happen?"

She lifted one shoulder a little, her gaze fixed on my chest. Her question about the future gave me hope, but at the same time, I didn't want to push too hard. I'd already told her I loved her tonight; would she freak out if I told her I wanted her right here by my side every single night? Probably. I settled on the best response I could come up with on the fly. "All I want is you. Wherever you are, that's where I want to be."

Blue eyes lifted to mine, liquid in the pale light of the moon. "Okay."

It was a step in the right direction, and a smile curved my mouth. "Okay."

She lifted her chin, offering her mouth to me, and I met her halfway, pouring all the words I couldn't say into that kiss.

CHAPTER
THIRTY

I kissed Gavin goodbye, then closed the garage door behind him as he reversed out of the driveway. I immediately headed upstairs to my room and peeked out the window to make sure he was gone before I grabbed my phone from my nightstand.

I'd thought about it off and on for the past twenty-four hours, and something about the situation just didn't sit well. I brought up the home screen on my phone, then selected the number for the VA. After making my way through the automated system, I tapped my nails impatiently against the nightstand as I waited for the call to connect. Three rings later, Stella's honeyed voice floated over the phone.

Relieved that it was she who answered, I let out a little sigh. "Hey, lady. It's Kate."

"Oh," she breathed. "How are you feeling?"

"I'm good, thanks. Still a little sore, but it shouldn't be anything to worry about."

"That's good. When are you due back?"

"If everything goes well, probably another week or so."

Sooner if I could swing it. I hated sitting around with nothing to do. "I actually have a favor for you in the meantime, if you don't mind."

"No problem," Stella replied readily.

"If possible," I said slowly, "I'd like to keep this just between us. I don't want anyone to think I'm working off the clock." I use the excuse that would hopefully make sense and not rouse any suspicions.

"You got it," Stella replied. "What do you need?"

What I was about to do was a horrible idea, not to mention completely illegal, and I mentally crossed my fingers, hoping that she wouldn't ask too many questions. "Well, since I've got some time off, I offered to take a look at something for a friend's father. I was wondering if you could check the system for a patient.."

I already knew Tripp's file was in the system, but what about Keane's? Though I knew he had been in the military at one point, he may not have utilized the VA. All I knew was, I needed to get my hands on his chart to see if there was some kind of link.

Was there anything outstanding in their medical history? Were they a rare blood type? All I really needed was to determine if Keane was in the system. If he was, I would have Stella print off a copy for me so I could pick it up. While I was there, I could make a copy of Tripp's file in the data room. I didn't want to involve Stella anymore then absolutely possible, and this was the safest way.

"Okay..." I heard the hesitation in her voice, and I bit my lip, hating to drag her into this without any evidence of what exactly I was looking for. "Patient name?"

"Merrill Keane."

"Let me check." I heard the keyboard clicking in the background as Stella worked her magic. After a long moment, she came back on the phone. "You're right. He was actually a patient of Dr. Rodriguez at the branch over on Pennsylvania Avenue."

I closed my eyes, unsure of whether that was a good thing or bad. "I really appreciate your help, Stella. Would you mind printing off a copy of his file and just leave it in my mailbox? I can swing by later and pick it up."

"Do you need anything else?"

"No," I replied. "You've done enough. Thank you so much."

Well, shit. What the hell did this mean? It could still be a complete coincidence. But something felt... off about this whole thing. Three sets of remains found close together, two of whom were ex-military and patients of the VA. I knew it was a stretch, but I had to know for sure if there was a connection here, no matter how small. It could be nothing— or it could be everything.

I tapped my nails on the screen of my phone before drawing a deep breath and heading downstairs. Phil had removed himself to the living room in front of the huge TV, and I took a seat on the edge of the couch. "I need to drive over to the VA and pick up some files. Would you like to get out of the house for a bit and come with me?"

"Sure, if you wouldn't mind some company."

I smiled as he lowered the recliner and pushed to his feet. "Of course not."

Together we made our way to my car, which Gavin had retrieved from the coffee shop a couple days ago. I slipped behind the wheel, feeling more than a little guilty for not telling Gavin what I planned to do. He would literally kill me if he found out I'd left the house.

So, he just wouldn't have to find out—at least, not yet. It was part of the reason I'd invited Phil. I knew the older man was feeling cooped up, being stuck here in a house that wasn't his. I knew that feeling well. Besides, having Phil with me made me feel better knowing that I wouldn't be alone, even if I was only going in for a few minutes.

Forty minutes later, I parked in the lot behind the VA and turned to Phil. "Would you like to come in or stay here?"

He waved me off. "I'll just stay here if you don't mind."

"Not at all." I left the car running and the air conditioning on as I opened the door and slipped out. "I'll be back in just a few minutes."

I felt exposed being out here in the open all alone, and I hurried around the building, breathing a sigh of relief once I was inside. It was irrational, I knew, but I couldn't help it. The last time I was out in public I was shot at—I really didn't want a replay.

Stella lifted her gaze when she heard the door open, and she greeted me with a smile and a little wave as I approached the desk. "You look great."

"Thanks." I returned her smile. "Have I missed anything?"

"Same old thing here," she said. Then, almost as an afterthought— "Oh, I almost forgot." She searched her desk for a moment then handed a card to me. "Chris's mother passed away, if you'd like to sign this."

"Of course." I opened the card and wrote a little sympathy message, then signed it and handed it back. "How's he holding up?"

Stella lifted one shoulder. "I don't know. I'm really not even sure what happened."

"Sucks." I made a little face, then tipped my head to the side. "Anyway, I'll let you get back to it. Thanks again for your help earlier."

"Anytime."

She winked, and I slipped behind the little fold-down counter and into the small room where we kept patient records. Quickly, I skimmed the shelves for the "T" section, then pulled the file folder containing Robert Tripp's information from the bookcase.

Shooting a quick glance around, I copied each page of his chart, then replaced the folder. Scooping up the small stack of papers, I slung my purse over my shoulder and slipped out of the room. I grabbed the rolled-up files from my mailbox as I passed, then made my way around the counter.

As I left, I waved to Stella, who was engaged on the phone. She shot me a smile and a wave, and I turned to head out. As I did so, I almost bumped into Dr. Coleman.

"Whoa." He put a hand on my shoulder to steady me.

"Sorry about that." I took a quick step backward and forced a smile to my face, though my heart was racing in my chest.

Coleman studied me for a long moment. "How are you feeling?"

"Good, thanks."

"You sure? You look a little pale."

I let out a strained little laugh and made a fanning motion near my face. "Must be the heat. It's miserable out there today."

He nodded a little, and his gaze dropped to the papers in my hand, then went to the records room. His eyes met mine again, sending my pulse into a flurry. Oh, God. If he discovered I was taking patient files, I could not only lose my job but face a lawsuit for breach of privacy. I needed to get out of here—now.

"Well, anyway, I just had to stop in for a few things." I made a show of fishing for my keys. "See you later."

I clutched the papers tightly in my hand and turned, fighting the urge to run as I headed out the door, all the while feeling his eyes painting a bull's-eye on my back.

CHAPTER
THIRTY-ONE

GAVIN

The sound of the TV in the living room greeted me when I stepped inside the house. A delicious, spicy smell lingered in the air, and I tossed my briefcase and keys on the table before striding toward the stove. Someone had made stir-fry, and the remnants sat on the burner, the lid on the pan to keep them warm.

I pulled a fork from the drawer and scooped up a couple mouthfuls, leaning one hip on the counter. Aside from the TV playing in the living room, the house was quiet. I wondered if Kate was taking another nap. I stabbed another piece of chicken and shoveled it into my mouth, then headed toward the stairs to check on her.

I left her in bed this morning, warm and soft from a night of lovemaking, and I'd be lying if I said I didn't hope to get her back there again. I slept in her room last night, and I looked forward to doing it again. Now that she was starting to come around, I refused to backtrack. The only change I was willing to make was moving her into my room. I wanted her in my bed and in my house—permanently.

Though I had alluded to a serious relationship before, I knew she was still skittish from her divorce. I felt like every time I took one step forward, she took two steps back. After last night, something between us had changed. The wall around her heart had cracked and begun to crumble, and for the first time in more than a month, ever since our first night together, I got a glimpse at the real Kate. She was funny and smart and so damn sexy. I wasn't going to rush things with her. As long as she was here with me, that was all that mattered.

I jogged quietly upstairs and peeked into the guest bedroom, my eyes sweeping the empty room. Cocking an ear, I listened for any movement in the attached bath, but it remained quiet. I headed to the end of the hall where my room was located and paused in the doorway, a smile curving my mouth.

She sat cross-legged on the bed, my laptop, her phone, and a few papers spread out in front of her, and for a moment I just watched her. My eyes skimmed over her from head to toe, taking in those long auburn locks that fell in unruly waves down her back and over her shoulder. She wore a tank top and sweats, but her feet were bare, and I smiled at the sight of the soft pink polish tipping her toes.

Her head lifted when she noticed my presence, and her mouth curled into a small smile. "Oh, hey. I didn't hear you come in."

"Hey, beautiful." She slipped off the bed as I approached, and I pulled her into my arms, tipping her head up for a kiss.

The kiss turned deeper, more passionate, and I slid one hand under her shirt, my thumb caressing the soft skin of her lower back. She tasted so good and felt even better. I wanted to strip her bare and tumble her back onto the bed she'd just vacated. Somewhere in the back of my mind, common sense reared up, telling me to slow down, and I reluctantly broke the kiss.

"How are you feeling?"

"Good." Her hands came up to my chest, her fingers stroking over the silk of my blue tie.

"Stay out of trouble today?"

Automatically, she stiffened, and I regretted whatever it was I'd said. I mentally played my words back as she pulled out of my arms and sat on the edge of the mattress.

I pushed the papers aside and took a seat beside her, my gaze riveted on her face. "Kate?" She finally lifted her gaze to mine. "Is everything okay?"

She nodded, concern clouding her eyes. "Have you heard anything about the man who shot at me?"

So, that's what this was all about. I'd told her last night when we were lying in bed that I'd reached out to Blake and his friends to do some digging. I'd left out the fact that they were currently running background on Coleman as well. Turning to face her more fully, I pulled a knee up between us and cupped her face with one hand. "Not yet, sweetheart. But they're working on it, I promise."

She bit her lip. "What if they don't find him? Or what if they're chasing the wrong person?"

I stroked my thumb over her cheek. "They're good at what they do, red. Between Con's guys and the police, they'll figure it out."

"I just..." She trailed off, seemingly having some sort of internal debate with herself. Finally, she continued. "I don't know if this is just a fluke, or if I've totally lost my mind, but I don't know who else to talk to about this, and I don't want to sound neurotic or anything, but I feel like there's something here."

She took a deep breath, finally out of steam, and I lifted

my brows in question as I gazed at her, still trying to process her words. "What are you talking about, babe?"

She stared at me for a long second. "Can I show you something?"

"Of course."

"So, you've heard about the bodies they've found recently. Remember the first victim—the one I found in the cornfield?"

I nodded. "The police suspected homicide, right?"

"Yes. His name was Robert Tripp." She picked up a couple of papers from the bed, then handed them to me. "This is his medical chart. His name came up in conversation right after he was identified, and one of the nurses mentioned that he was a patient at the VA."

I quickly scanned them as she spoke. "Crazy."

"I know, right? Well, if you remember, a second body turned up a couple weeks ago, just a few miles away from the first victim." She handed me a second chart. "Merrill Keane. They don't know for sure, but they suspect he may have actually been killed before Mr. Tripp but wasn't found until later. Same with the most recent victim."

"Okay?" I wasn't quite sure where she was going with this. It sucked, but people died all the time, in all manners.

She laid a hand on my arm, insisting on my attention, and I met her serious gaze. "You can't repeat any of this, okay?"

I nodded, confused. "Of course."

She drew in a deep breath. "When I found the first victim—Tripp—the medical examiner on the case noticed something strange. All of his vital organs were gone."

I quirked a brow, surprised that she was telling me all this. "Gruesome. Animals?"

"Removed—surgically," she added as my stomach twisted. "Organs can fetch a pretty hefty price on the black market, so it's a good possibility he was killed and his organs harvested for profit."

I scrubbed a hand over my face. "That's... revolting."

"Right." She sighed. "Well, this may have been the same scenario. I was curious about Merrill Keane, and when I googled him, I happened to find out he was a veteran of the Gulf War. According to news reports, his body was badly decomposed by the time he was found, so there's no conclusive evidence that they were removed. But..."

She stared at me. "That makes three bodies found within a three-mile radius over the past month. Both of the men identified had type O blood—which would make them universal donors."

"You think they're connected," I said, understanding dawning.

She nodded. "The third victim still hasn't been identified, but Merrill and Keane were both patients at the VA. Keane was from a different branch, but his information was accessible. Both men's charts say they're single with no next of kin listed. What if someone targeted these men on purpose— say, a doctor who could perform the surgery?"

"It's possible," I admitted. "What are you thinking?"

Her teeth sank into her lower lip. "Remember that argument a while back? Coleman made it sound like they were talking about a patient, but now..."

Oh, Christ. I saw exactly where she was going with that. "You think Coleman's responsible."

"Maybe." She lifted one hand. "But I have no proof. I just... have this gut feeling. He has access to patient records, and God knows he's capable of surgical procedures."

Son of a bitch. This whole thing became more and more tangled each day. We'd already determined that the gunman wasn't Coleman himself, and I knew from the man's build that it wasn't Larry. So who was it? It was possible that the shooting at the coffee shop was totally random, but I seriously doubted it. If Coleman or Larry were involved in something of this magnitude, they certainly weren't doing it alone.

"So... Do you suppose they're in on this together? Or Larry could be blackmailing Coleman for whatever reason," I mused.

"Anything's possible." A tiny shudder ran through her. "But I'm glad you don't think I'm crazy."

"No, you're definitely not crazy. I don't believe in coincidences, especially ones as glaring as this. Besides..." My next words died on my lips as something suddenly occurred to me, and I held up Keane's chart. "Wait—didn't they just ID this guy?"

"I believe so, yes."

My gaze narrowed on her. "Then when the hell did you get these, and how?"

She stared at me for several long seconds and rolled her lips together before answering. "Today. At the VA."

"Goddamn it, Kate—"

She pressed her palms to my chest as if she could physically hold down the anger rising within. "Just hear me out."

I dipped my chin and glared at her, sarcasm dripping from my tongue. "Great, I can't wait to hear what excuse you have for putting yourself in the same building as a man who *probably tried to kill you.*"

She crossed her arms over her chest, frosty eyes narrowed. "Don't be dramatic. I was perfectly safe. Your dad went with me, and—"

"Oh, my God, I should have known." I dragged one hand through my hair.

I grabbed up my phone and called Clay, who answered on the first ring. No greeting, he launched right in. "Hey, I was just getting ready to call you. We found out that Meredith Raines was in a car accident a little over a year ago."

"I had no idea." Why hadn't Larry said anything? That

was right about the same time they'd separated. What kind of husband would leave his wife after that?

"Apparently she'd been drinking and slid off the road and sustained some pretty severe trauma when the driver side hit a tree."

I winced. "That sucks." Car versus tree was never a good outcome.

"Doesn't stop there. Guess who was with Meredith at the time?"

My gut tightened, and I had a feeling I already knew the answer before I asked. "Who?"

"Dr. Elijah Coleman."

Motherfucker.

"He was treated for mild injuries and released, but hers were much more significant. According to the report, she was driving and lost control. The car hit a tree, did a lot of internal damage."

I closed my eyes. "Well, that answers some questions." I explained what Kate had just shown me. "I'm going to the police station with Kate, then I'll be over."

"Don't bother," he said. "Tomorrow's the funeral. I'm gonna hit it up."

So he could see who showed up. Meredith was being laid to rest tomorrow, and news of her death had finally begun to whisper its way through the office. I wanted to be there, too. "I'll meet you there."

I'd bet my last dollar that Coleman and Meredith had been having an affair. What I didn't know was how she was tied into everything, if at all. It seemed significant somehow, but it was just one more piece of the puzzle that didn't fit. One thing I did know was, something strange as shit was going on, and I wanted to get to the bottom of it before Kate ended up hurt again.

CHAPTER
THIRTY-TWO

KATE

I extended my hand to the detective in charge of Mr. Tripp's case, and he offered me a kind smile. "How are you feeling?"

"Still a little sore," I admitted. He released my hand, and I sank into the seat across from him, Gavin in the chair next to me.

Mayfield's gaze bounced between the two of us before he spoke. "I don't have any news yet, if that's why you stopped in."

I bit my lip. "It actually is, kind of."

His head tipped slightly to one side in question, and I slanted a look at Gavin before speaking. "I feel really stupid coming to you like this, but I don't know what else to do."

"I'll do my best to help," he said as he reclined back in his chair and folded his hands over his stomach.

I took a moment to gather my thoughts, then dived in. "Do you remember me telling you that I was the one who found the body out on Hartwell about a month ago?"

He dipped his chin. "I remember you saying as much."

"So..." I dragged out the word, sure that he would laugh at me when I told him my suspicions. "You've found two other sets of remains so far, right?"

His dark eyes pierced mine. "We're still investigating to see if they're connected in any way."

"I'm not fishing for details," I assured him. "It's been on my mind a lot lately, especially after the shooting at the coffee shop, and..."

I trailed off, and Gavin draped an arm over my shoulders, lending comfort but allowing me to take the lead. I shot him a grateful smile for his unwavering support, then drew in a deep breath and turned back to the detective. "I honestly don't know what this means, but I thought I would bring it to your attention."

"What's that?" Cool and controlled to the core, Detective Mayfield's expression remained completely impassive.

"I work at the VA on the south side of town, and a couple of nurses were discussing everything that had happened. The news was on during our lunch break, and I saw that they had identified that first victim, the one I found in the field."

"Mr. Tripp," Mayfield confirmed with a tight nod.

"Right. Well, we got to talking, and I discovered that he was a patient there prior to his death." He nodded slightly, his expression bland as if he was waiting for me to eventually make my point. "Anyway, the incisions made on Mr. Tripp were precise, surgical."

His brows drew together. "Do you know that for a fact? None of the details have been made known to the public."

"I happened to be there when Dr. Pratt discovered the organs were missing, remember?" I reminded him. "Plus, there is a distinct difference between a surgical incision and a tear in the tissue from, say, animals feasting on it."

"Fair enough," he said mildly. "Continue."

"Anyway, I know Dr. Pratt suspected it was made by someone who's had medical training, like a doctor. When the subject of Mr. Tripp came up, I got to thinking about everything that's happened. As soon as they identified the second victim, Mr. Keane, I noticed that he was a patient, too. I didn't say anything at the time, because I didn't think it was relevant, but I overheard an argument at the VA between Dr. Coleman and another man just a couple weeks prior to me being shot at."

"What was the argument about?"

"It seemed innocuous enough," I said. "A man came in and blamed Dr. Coleman for what I believed at the time was the death of a patient. Larry said that Coleman would "pay for it," whatever he'd done. As it turns out, the man—Larry Raines—is my boyfriend's boss."

I tipped my head in Gavin's direction. "I found out that his wife was in an accident a while ago, and she'd been receiving medical care at home. I don't know the extent of her injuries, but it seemed to be pretty bad."

Mayfield stared at me for a long moment, looking almost bored. "Could be a complete coincidence."

"Could be," Gavin spoke up from beside me. "But I have it on good authority that Coleman was with Meredith Raines at the time of the accident."

"Here's the thing," I said slowly. "She wasn't dead at the time, and Meredith was never a patient of his. I don't know how she fits into this, but I've been thinking back on that altercation between the two men. That argument could have been about her or... something else."

"Such as?"

"Whatever happened, Larry was furious. Maybe mad enough to lash out at Coleman or try to blackmail him. Coleman has medical training and access to patient records.

What if one or both of them are involved in smuggling organs?"

Mayfield his eyes flared wide for a moment. "That's quite an accusation."

"It could all just be a coincidence, but..." I pulled out Tripp's and Keane's patient files and spread them on the desk.

"Not only was Tripp a patient at the branch where I work, but Keane, who was just identified a couple days ago, was a patient at another branch." I pointed to the part of the file with the emergency information. "Blood type for both men is O-negative, and their files list them as single with no next of kin."

Mayfield's gaze dropped to the papers on the desk, and I could practically see the wheels turning. "So, Raines blames Coleman for his wife's accident and subsequent death, but how do we jump from a disgruntled husband to a smuggling scheme?"

"Maybe it's not related at all." I lifted a shoulder. "I know how crazy this all sounds, believe me. I tried to talk myself out of coming here, but I feel like it's too... bizarre to just be a coincidence."

"Other than the shooting, have you noticed anything out of the ordinary?"

"Raines has been acting strangely for the past several weeks," Gavin stated. "Could be the complications with his wife, or it could be... something else. If he's been blackmailing Coleman, it would explain the argument they had. Maybe he's worried about being found out."

Mayfield stroked his jaw, then pointed to Keane's file. "Do you mind if I make a copy of these?"

I shook my head. "Just keep them. All I ask is that you keep an open mind."

"I'll do what I can," he promised.

I had to take the man at his word. He wouldn't tell me

about an ongoing investigation, but I truly hoped he followed through with it.

"Thank you." I stood and shook his hand one more time. "I really do appreciate your help."

"Anytime," he acknowledged.

CHAPTER
THIRTY-THREE

GAVIN

The day was clear and bright, completely incongruous with the somber atmosphere of the crowd gathered around Meredith's gravesite. Behind a pair of dark shades, I scanned the solemn faces around seated in the white plastic chairs as the pastor gave his eulogy. Clay was seated toward the front, and I knew he was doing the same.

So far I'd spotted Larry and his children, Shannon and Christopher. He'd remained dry-eyed and stoic throughout, while Shannon dabbed primly at the occasional tear. Christopher seemed the most broken up, his face red as he tried to control himself. I felt bad for the kids. No matter what had happened between Larry and Meredith, Shannon and Christopher had just lost their mother.

Afterward, we formed a line and, after a final prayer, began to toss roses on top of the casket. I added mine to the pile, then headed toward my truck. Clay was already ahead of me, and my phone vibrated an alert in my pocket. I pulled it out to discreetly read the text.

Thompson: Silver truck, far left

I glanced around, then finally spotted it parked at the very end of a long line of cars along the side of the road winding through the cemetery. I climbed inside, obscured by the heavily tinted windows. "You see anything?"

Clay Thompson sat in the driver seat, one hand on the wheel, the other in his lap, looking as condescending as ever. "Nothing. You?"

"Nope." I turned my attention back to the gravesite. "Keep an eye on them."

"Trying to tell me how to do my job?"

I threw him a bewildered look. "Why do you always have to be such a dick?"

His mouth kicked up in a smirk. "I ask myself the same question all the time, pretty boy."

"Pretty sure I murdered somebody in a past life," I grumbled. What the hell did I do to deserve being saddled with this giant asshole?

Clay let out a mirthless laugh, and we lapsed into silence for several long moments as we watched people slowly make their way away from the gravesite toward their cars. I wasn't sure exactly what I was looking for, but I had a feeling I'd know it when I saw it. Larry and his children stood next to the casket, accepting sentiments of sympathy from the guests, and Coleman remained off to the side, still seated in one of the plastic chairs.

"How's Kate?" Clay broke the silence, sounding genuinely concerned, and I shot a look in his direction before responding.

"Still sore, but she says she's okay. Hasn't been sleeping well."

"I imagine." Clay let out a little snort. "You always did get the pretty ones."

My hackles rose as jealousy engulfed me. "What the hell is that supposed to mean?"

"Not a damn thing."

I couldn't miss the bitter resentment in his tone, and I turned fully in my seat to face him. "What the hell is your problem? You've had a stick up your ass since we were kids. Don't you think it's about time to get over whatever adolescent drama you've got going on?"

"You think I'm the dramatic one?" His lip curled up in a sneer. "You always had your head so far up your daddy's rich ass that you never could see anyone but yourself."

I stared at him for a second. "Is that what the hell this pissing contest is about? You spent the last twenty years hating me because my family had money and yours didn't? I never did a goddamn thing except try to help you."

"Don't need your kind of help, pretty boy," he shot back.

"Jesus Christ," I replied. "I've never known anyone so smart who acts so stupid."

He turned a lethal glare on me. "Call me stupid one more time and see how it works out for you."

I rolled my eyes at his egotistical display. "I said you acted stupid, asshole. You were one of the smartest people I knew, could've done anything you wanted. Jesus, you were probably smarter than our valedictorian. You just never gave a shit about anything."

A cocky little smirk lifted his lips, infuriating me further. I don't know why it bothered me so much, except I hated to see someone with so much talent waste every opportunity presented.

"I never could figure that out about you," I said as I studied him. "Aside from being brilliant, you were the best damn athlete I'd ever seen—football, baseball, didn't matter what it was; if there was a ball involved, you had it nailed. You could've had a scholarship to any school you wanted, but you threw that away because you're lazy."

The smile slipped from his face, and his eyes took on a flinty expression. "Go fuck yourself, Price. I didn't want anything to do with you and your little asshat buddies, not even when your coach came crawling to me, begging me to join."

"Who the fuck do you think told him about you?" I exploded. "Think he just figured it out on his own?" I let out a little half laugh as I leaned back against the door panel and shook my head. "Should've known not to expect anything more from you."

For the next couple minutes, we were both silent, watching the stragglers by Meredith's grave. Finally, I snuck a look at him. For the first time ever, his cockiness had leached away, leaving his expression thoughtful and borderline insecure.

I scrubbed one hand over my face, feeling like a complete asshole. I didn't know why I hadn't seen it before. Yeah, he'd been a dick, and though I didn't know much about his past, I knew his home life hadn't been the greatest. The kids in school had been assholes to him, and he'd retaliated the only way he knew how—by being defensive and aloof.

"Sorry, man." After a long moment, he gave a small nod, and that was the end of it. I blew out a soft breath as the last of the guests strode away. All that remained were the caretakers, Larry, and his family. Coleman stood off to the side, next to a tree, and I wondered if he'd wait until they lowered her into the ground before leaving. Had he been in love with Meredith? It was all kind of tragic in a way. "Do you think—"

My train of thought was abruptly cut off as I watched Larry stalk toward Coleman. Even from here, I could tell he was pissed. His arms moved in erratic, furious arcs. "Whoa. Check that out."

"He looks pissed," Clay acknowledged.

I watched as Raines's son stepped between the two men and practically dragged Larry off. Shannon covered her face, shoulders hunched. Larry threw one more angry look at Coleman, then looped an arm around Shannon and guided her away.

"Interesting," I said as Clay put the truck in drive and pulled out. There was definitely some bad blood there. I wondered exactly when the police would bring him in for questioning. We'd spoken with Mayfield early this morning, but I'd turned down Kate's offer to join me here today. I wanted her at home where I knew she was safe, and right now, all I wanted was to get back to her.

CHAPTER
THIRTY-FOUR

KATE

Gavin's fingers slid through my hair, and his skin was warm against my cheek, his heart thudding softly next to my ear. For the past couple of days, things between us had been... perfect.

He was more than I dreamed he would be, better than anything I could've ever hoped for. We'd settled into a rhythm as naturally as if we'd been together forever. I entertained myself while he was gone, then we had dinner together and spent most of the evening talking and laughing before we fell into bed together.

Though I was content, I couldn't help the feeling of worry that consumed me when I thought about what might happen when I returned to work. As soon as all of this was over, I would be able to move back to my condo. The idea didn't hold the same appeal it had a mere week ago. Not wanting to disrupt the tenuous balance between us, neither Gavin nor I had broached the subject again. He'd made his intentions clear; now I just had to make up my mind.

His deep voice broke the silence. "I talked to Clay today."

From my spot draped over his torso, I angled my head up to look at him. "What did he have to say?" I was curious to know if they had learned anything since Meredith's funeral.

"I don't have good news for you." Gavin let out a sigh. "According to him, the police picked Coleman up for questioning yesterday after the funeral."

As far as I could tell, that was a good thing. It meant the detective was seriously considering what we'd told him, and I was both grateful and worried. What if Coleman was actually accused of doing something so heinous? And how many times had he done this? I already pitied his poor family. The investigation was only the beginning of what could be a very long and emotional process for everyone involved.

"They questioned him but couldn't find enough evidence to get a warrant or book him."

Everything in me stilled as I processed his words. "What does that mean?"

Dark eyes met mine. "There was nothing conclusive tying him to any of the crimes, and his wife alibied him for the time of the shooting. They had no choice but to release him last night."

Rolling away from him, I sat up and dragged a hand through my hair. I felt Gavin's heat at my back as he moved closer. "I'm sorry, babe. I know you wanted this to be the end—we both did."

He was wrong. I couldn't stand the thought of Coleman being responsible for the murders of those poor men. I only wanted justice, but the primary suspect had just been released.

Gavin dropped a kiss on my shoulder. "They're checking several other leads. Clay told them about the altercation between Larry and Coleman after the funeral."

I threw a look at him over my shoulder. "That doesn't

mean anything. He could just be pissed they were having an affair."

After I'd learned about the connection between Eli and Meredith, Larry's words made more sense. Meredith had been lost to him months before she'd passed away—and he'd blamed Eli for all of it.

"What do we do now?" I heard the helplessness in my tone, and Gavin wrapped an arm around my waist.

"C'mere, babe." He tugged me back down and pulled me close to his side, tucking my head against his shoulder. It felt like something a parent would do for their child, and my first instinct was to rebel. His hand swept down my spine, and I relaxed against him, allowing myself to wallow in the comfort and security of his embrace.

"We'll figure it out." He spoke quietly against my hair. "I promise."

It was on the tip of my tongue to demand how he knew, but a sudden realization stopped me. I trusted him, and if he believed they would find the person responsible, so then did I.

I turned my head and kissed the base of his neck. "Thank you."

His arms tightened around me, and I felt myself begin to drift off. Sometime later, my phone vibrated on the nightstand, jerking me from sleep. The sun had just begun to peek over the horizon, and I didn't recognize the number on the screen. Gavin's arm tightened around my waist, and I snuggled against him as I hit the button. I was almost asleep again when the phone beeped an alert that I had a voicemail.

Who the hell would be calling me this early in the morning? Heaving myself up on my elbow, I listened to the short message from Becky, the HR director at the VA.

"Kate, this is Becky Statler. I know you're scheduled to be out for the next week or so, but we've kind of had an emergency situation, and I'm looking for someone to take over some patients. Could you please give me a call back when you get this?"

Curiosity piqued, I slid from the bed and called her back. Her tone was weary when she answered.

"This is Becky."

"Hi, Becky, it's Kate calling you back."

"I'm sorry to call so early," she apologized, "but you're kind of my last resort. I know this isn't ideal, but I'm looking for someone to take over Dr. Coleman's position."

"Oh," I said, concerned. "Is he sick?"

Something that sounded like a soft sob filtered through the speaker. "I... I'm sorry. I thought maybe you'd seen the news."

Goosebumps rose over my flesh. "No. What happened?"

"Dr. Coleman isn't coming back. He's..." Becky drew in a deep breath. "He passed away last night."

I sucked in a breath, and I heard the rest of the sheets behind me. "Oh, my God." My mind spun uncontrollably, and I tried to make sense of the words. "I'm so sorry. I had no idea."

"It was a shock to all of us," she said sadly. "I don't want to rush you, but if we don't have enough coverage, I'll have to let his patients know."

"Yes, of course I'll do it," I blurted without thinking.

"Are you sure?" she asked. "I don't want to rush you."

"Yes," I said decisively. I couldn't turn her down; it was the right thing to do. "It's no problem at all. I'll see you soon."

I hung up, then turned to meet Gavin's curious stare. "Looks like we can cross Coleman off the suspect list."

"Why?"

"Because he's dead."

His eyes flared wide. "You're shitting me."

I let out a mirthless laugh, still half in shock, and shook my head. "No. She said he passed away last night."

His brows dipped, and concern clouded his expression. "I wonder what the hell that means."

I shrugged. "I have no idea. But I've got to take his patients today."

At that, he bolted upright. "Not a chance in hell."

"I have to do this," I argued. "There are people counting on him, on me, and—"

"Jesus, Kate." His tone was exasperated as swung his legs over the edge of the bed and grabbed my forearms. "You were just shot at a week ago. I don't want you going out until they figure out who the hell it is. Especially after this whole ordeal with Coleman. He was the only viable suspect, and now—"

I understood where he was coming from. "Listen. The office is never empty, between the staff and the cleaning crew. I'll be safe enough with them there." Gavin shot a hard look at me, and I stared right back. "Really, though. It'd be stupid for someone to try something while I'm at work, surrounded by a whole bunch of ex-military men all day long."

His chin dipped, and one eyebrow lifted toward his hairline. "Not making me feel any better."

"You know what they say about a man in uniform…" I couldn't help but tease him a little, and I pressed my lips together to contain a small smile when he let out a little growl and lightly smacked my ass.

"I'm the only man allowed to touch you." His expression turned serious again almost immediately, and he stared up at me. "I really don't like the idea of you going back there yet."

I felt strange, caught halfway between wanting to laugh or cry. Coleman was dead, which meant that our only suspect was now gone. Had Coleman killed himself out of guilt, or was it some natural cause? The timing seemed too coincidental, and that worried me immensely. I tried not to let it show as I leaned into Gavin.

"Honestly. It'll be perfectly fine." I hoped it would, anyway.

He frowned at me, then as if realizing it was a losing battle, he let out a low sigh. "Fine. But I'm taking you to work and I'll be there when you get off."

"Deal." I leaned down to kiss him. "Don't worry. Everything will be fine."

GAVIN

So, we were back to square one. Coleman had been found in his vehicle yesterday evening after leaving the precinct, dead from a single gunshot wound to the temple.

"Foul play?"

"Looks that way. There was only a small amount of gunshot residue on his hands—not enough to indicate that he pulled the trigger."

Son of a bitch. So, someone had killed him at point-blank range—probably someone he'd trusted, if he'd allowed the person to get in the car with him. "Have they questioned Raines yet?"

"They brought him in this morning. Apparently he owns a Smith & Wesson 9mm—the same caliber bullet they found in Coleman. It was also," Clay continued, "the same slug they dug out of the brick after Kate was shot at."

Fucking finally. "So they brought him in?"

"Yep. Apparently, he has no alibi for the time of the murder." Clay leaned back in his chair and propped his feet on the desk. "According to my guy at the PD, he's denying everything except his arguments with Coleman. Police got a warrant to search the house but haven't found the gun yet."

I scowled. "Has to be there somewhere. And, seriously? Nobody heard a fucking gunshot in the middle of the evening?"

What the fuck? In a world where everyone had a goddamn cell phone, no one had seen a damn thing, hadn't captured anything on camera or on video?

Clay spread his hands wide. "What do you expect?"

Not a damn thing, honestly. As much as I wanted to make it easy and blame him for Kate's incident, I had to look at it objectively. He didn't have an alibi, but they also hadn't found the gun to positively match ballistics. "We can't go off half-cocked and accuse Raines of anything. It won't fly in court. If Larry's responsible for shooting at Kate, I'm gonna make damn sure he doesn't get off on a technicality."

Con smirked at me from where he rested one hip against the desk. "Sure you don't want to come work for me?"

"I'm seriously considering it," I murmured. If Larry was found guilty of murder—attempted or otherwise—or God knew what else, the firm would likely collapse. We'd lose all credibility. "Is that offer open-ended?"

"Always."

I nodded. "I appreciate it. So, where do we stand with Raines?"

Clay shrugged one shoulder. "They can hold him for twenty-four hours. After that..."

Yeah, I knew the drill. And, if what he said was true, that there was no evidence of his involvement, they'd release him just like they had with Coleman.

"This guy might not be involved at all," Clay offered, echoing my thoughts.

"I know," I responded. "It just seems like too much of a

coincidence to ignore." Something just didn't shake out with that.

"When was the first time?" Con asked.

"First time that I know of was at the VA," I said. "Supposedly he was arguing with Coleman. Second was at my law office a week later."

Clay's phone vibrated an alert, and he made a face as he read the message. "Fuck."

"That your guy at the PD?"

"Yep. They found a couple sets of prints inside Coleman's car, but none of them belonged to Raines."

"He could've worn gloves or something." Hell, some people even used superglue to minimize their fingerprints and eliminate the oils from the skin.

"Possible, but they also found a hair that doesn't seem to match Raines, either. Raines is mostly gray. This is short, likely a man's, but dark blond or brown."

Jesus Christ. Couldn't we catch a break? I pressed the heels of my hands against my eyes. I knew the police were doing everything they could, but in the meantime, whoever had killed Coleman was still running loose. I wouldn't let him get to Kate next. "Okay. So Raines didn't kill Coleman. What do we know about an organ-smuggling ring?"

"Bad news on that." Con grimaced. "PD thinks whoever is harvesting the organs is working with Escobar Valdez."

I dropped my head back on a groan. This shit just kept getting better and better. "The goddamn cartel? Please tell me you're kidding."

"Nope." Jason Doyle rolled his chair over. "Got a tip from an acquaintance that the feds are on his trail."

I lifted a brow. "Nice of them to join the party."

The former FBI agent's lips quirked up in a wry smile. "Don't expect too much. It could take years to build a case."

"Tell me something I don't know." I crossed my arms over my chest. "This is a fucking shit show."

"Anyone else with motive?" Con asked me.

"Not that I can think of, but Kate was pretty adamant it's someone with medical experience."

"So, we're operating under the assumption that she overheard something she shouldn't have? Maybe Raines and Coleman were working together."

"That's my best guess."

"But Coleman was cleared," Clay reminded us, "so either they didn't find any evidence, or he really was clean."

"I'm guessing clean," I replied. "Why else kill him, unless he was on to whoever was responsible?"

Doyle glanced between the three of us. "Do we think Raines is involved in the smuggling ring, or maybe someone else Coleman worked with? Another doctor from the VA, maybe?"

"Possibly," Con spoke up. "But she works there every day. If it was someone from there, she most likely would've recognized them. Plus, why wait so long?"

"But for what purpose?" I said as I raked one hand through my hair. "She hasn't done anything."

"Doesn't mean someone doesn't think she saw or heard something she shouldn't have," Con spoke up. "It's just a matter of figuring out what."

Doyle nodded. "I'm running background on employees at the VA right now. They were done at the time of hire, but God only knows how long ago that was for some of them."

With the number of people Kate interacted with on a daily basis, I had a feeling it was going to be like looking for a needle in a haystack.

CHAPTER
THIRTY-SIX

KATE

I peeked out of my office and glanced up and down the hall, but everything was clear. Everyone else had already left, and I'd seen Magda come in just a little bit ago to begin cleaning. I left the records room and started down the hallway toward the offices.

Gavin had texted a little while ago and told me he was running late, so I decided to do a little digging of my own. I tried to justify it by telling myself it wasn't that bad. All I wanted to do was find out if Coleman had kept any records anywhere, any indication of who may have been responsible for his death. By now, we all assumed that it was tied in together. Like the police said, it was probably someone we both knew.

I rounded the nurses' station where Magda stood disinfecting the counters. "Hello, Dr. Winfield."

I shoved my hands in the pockets of my jacket and smiled back. "Hi, Magda. How are you?"

"Fine, thank you. Such a shame about Dr. Coleman," the woman clucked. "Such a nice man."

Sympathy seized me, along with shame for what I was about to do. "I know. I feel terrible. I'll be taking over a few of his patients, and I need to get a few things from his office." I prayed the woman wouldn't read into it and wouldn't question me for being in his office instead of my own.

"Well, don't let me bother you," she said. "We weren't sure what to do with it, so we just left it alone."

I nodded, grateful that HR had decided not to clear it out just yet. I wondered if the police had searched it, or if they would need to now that he'd been killed. That made me feel even worse, but I was tired of waiting around for something to happen. "That's perfect. Thank you."

Leaving Magda to her work, I meandered down the hall to Coleman's office and veered straight to the window. After the blinds were in place and I was sure that no one could see inside, I crossed the room again and flipped on the lights. Leaving the door open so as to not raise any questions, I glanced around the space.

It felt oddly empty without Coleman here, and the realization that he would never sit behind that desk again sliced through me. Though I hadn't known him all that long, he'd been a nice enough man. I still wasn't sure if he was involved in whatever was happening; we might never be sure. It only made my reason for being here more resolute. I was determined to find anything I could to help the investigation along.

I pushed down the guilt I felt at snooping around the dead man's office, and with a deep breath, I dived right in, starting with the desk first. I sifted through the contents of the drawers, inspecting everything, unwilling to disregard anything. The drawers were cluttered with paraphernalia, from notepads and pens to nail clippers and stock supplies like fabric tape and bandages. There seemed to be no rhyme or reason to his storage methods, and the next three drawers were almost identical.

In the fourth though, I found a worn paperback copy of *Jane Eyre*. It seemed incongruous with its surroundings, and I flipped through the pages. As I did so, a small rectangle slipped out and fluttered to the ground. The watermark on the back identified it as a photograph, and I turned it over.

The pretty blonde's face took my breath away. She was beautiful—captivating, really. There was something light and airy, inherently good about her. From her manner of dress, I speculated the picture had been taken a decade or more ago, and as I studied her features, I realized something else—this was not Coleman's wife.

I lifted my gaze to the framed photographs on the bookshelf behind me. Eli's wife was pretty enough, with curly brown hair, but she looked nothing like the woman in the photograph. My eyes dropped to the blonde again. Who was she? Whoever it was must've been important to him. She obviously meant enough for him to secret away a picture of her in his desk. The book made sense as well. It looked well loved, a timeless romance read and reread by someone in love.

I sucked in a breath as realization hit hard. What if this was Meredith—Larry's wife. They'd been together at the time of her accident, obviously very much in love. Part of me felt sad for them; both were married to other people, but they'd never been able to let go of one another. If they hadn't been in the accident, would they be together today?

I was so caught up in my musings that the soft pop from the vicinity of the lobby barely penetrated my consciousness. I glanced toward the doorway, expecting to hear someone or something, but silence reigned. I opened my mouth, then snapped it shut to keep from calling out. Uneasy and on edge, I crept toward the hallway.

Peeking around the doorframe, I searched for Magda. The building remained quiet—too quiet. Moving slowly and keeping my back to the wall, I walked silently toward the lobby. I had just reached the nurses' station when something on the floor caught my attention. I froze in place and leaned forward as far as I could, straining my neck to see around the corner. Blood pooled on the floor around Magda's body, and I slapped a hand over my mouth to keep from crying out.

Quickly, I ducked down out of sight and fought to get my emotions under control. My breathing seemed to echo in my ears, and I forced myself to calm, listening intently for any movement.

"Kate." A soft voice lilted on the air. "I know you're in here."

Without thinking, I scrambled on my hands and knees into the closest exam room and ducked behind the patient table. Seconds later, the soft rustle of material met my ears, and I knew the person was right outside the door. My heart threatened to beat out of my chest, and I drew a deep, even breath in through my nose, then expelled it slowly out my mouth, fighting to keep my body from shaking.

"Kate." The voice was closer this time. I pressed myself back against the table, and the traitorous paper stretched over top crinkled slightly. Every muscle in my body coiled with tension, and I prayed he hadn't heard the slight movement. The soft scrape of footsteps against the rough industrial carpet resumed, and I let out a measured breath. I remained still, tracking his movements, trying to gauge where he was going.

As silently as possible, I duck-walked toward the doorway and, keeping low to the ground, peaked around the doorjamb. The man's back was to me as he moved around the nurses' station, checking beneath the desks. As he turned slightly, his profile came into view.

Chris.

I felt absolutely blindsided, my mind spinning as I tried to understand. Why would he do something so terrible? He glanced upward, almost as if feeling my presence, and I jerked backward out of sight.

Shit. I couldn't stay here and risk being found, but he was blocking the main exit to the lobby. There was an emergency exit on the other side of the facility, and I plotted how to best get there. I peeked around the doorjamb and watched as Chris turned his back to me again. I had to make a decision, and now. Repositioning myself in a low couch, I got ready to run.

As quickly and quietly as possible, I bolted from the room and sprinted down the hallway away from Chris, staying bent at the waist. I heard a harsh expletive behind me, but I didn't slow down. The hallway that led to the emergency exit came up on my right, and I got ready to turn. Just as I started to slow, a shot rang out, and sheetrock exploded near my right shoulder, sending a flurry of powder into the air.

Instinctively throwing my body away from the path of the bullet, I kept running. The door to the supply closet was just ahead on my left, and I seized the handle as a second shot rang out. My fingers shook as I tapped in the three-digit code, then shoved the door open and threw myself inside. In my peripheral vision, I watched as Chris bounded down the hallway toward me, his feet slapping against the floor, the sound warring with the rapid heartbeat thudding in my ears.

I managed to slam the door just as Chris heaved himself against it. My gaze dropped to the floor, and I noticed a small rubber door stopper. I hastily shoved it underneath the door, and the low beeping tones, along with the click of the lock disengaging, reached my ears just as I kicked the door stopper into place. Chris threw his weight against the door, but it only budged an inch, thanks to the door stopper.

Shoving away from the door, I frantically pulled at the bins on the shelves, searching for something to defend myself.

Items clattered to the floor, and I seized a disposable scalpel sleeved in red plastic. I jumped as a heavy thud came from the door again, and Chris's laughter trickled in.

"I've got you now," he taunted. My gaze flew around the room, and I stared at the large shelving unit in front of me. Approximately seven feet tall, it stood in the middle of the room all by itself. If I tipped it over, it might prevent the door from opening.

I shoved the scalpel in my back pocket, then darted around the huge steel frame. Bracing my hands against the middle shelf, I shoved as hard as I could. It didn't budge. Tears sprang to my eyes as pain shot down my arm, and I let out a little growl of frustration.

"Come on, damn it!" Another thud sounded against the door, and it squeaked open another inch.

Shit, shit, shit! Another shelving unit lined the wall behind me, and I stepped up on the second shelf, using the extra height for leverage. Suspended between the two shelving units, I rocked my body back and forth, trying to sway the shelves in front of me. It rocked precariously, and hope flared as it slammed heavily back to the ground. I pushed again as hard as I could and felt myself start to fall as the feet left the ground and the unit began to topple forward.

At the same moment, the door to the supply closet flew open, and Chris launched himself inside. I braced myself for the fall, and I watched in horror as Chris's eyes met mine through the gaping hole of the shelf as I tumbled toward him.

He threw his hands up, but it was too late. The shelf hit him hard, knocking him to the ground, and I landed with a jolt, sprawled over top of the shelving unit. The wall stopped its progress, and my chin glanced off the steel shelf, sending stars dancing in front of my eyes.

Quickly regaining my wits, I scrambled up the incline of the shelving unit and slid through the doorway. As soon as my feet touched down, something wrapped around my ankle, stopping my progress. Fingers curled tightly into my skin, and I lost my balance as Chris jerked me toward him. His shoulders appeared in the triangle between the wall and the shelving unit, and a cruel smile transformed his mouth.

"I like when they put up a fight."

He was too big, too fast; I knew he would catch me before I even made it down the hallway. I kicked at him, and he let out a little grumble but didn't let go. Something poked my lower back, and I hastily reached into my back pocket to withdraw the scalpel just as Chris emerged from the rubble. Pushing the blade up, I stumbled to my feet and swung upward, aiming for his neck.

Understanding flashed across his features, and he threw himself to the side just in time. The scalpel sank into his skin, stopping when it collided with his collarbone. His eyes widened in disbelief, and he let out a harsh grunt of pain.

I stumbled backwards, trying to get my feet underneath me so I could run. In front of me, eyes locked on mine, Chris climbed to his feet and wrapped his fist around the scalpel. He yanked it out and tossed it to the ground with a little shake of his head. "You're only making it harder on yourself."

Heart jumping into my throat, I threw myself into action and propelled myself away from the wall. I tried to scream as a heavy weight slammed into my back and knocked me off my feet. Pinned to the hard floor, I writhed and twisted, trying to throw him off, but he was too strong.

I let out a muffled shriek as one hand fisted in my hair and slammed my face into the floor. A sharp, stinging pain stabbed into my neck, then radiated outward. I went limp as the sensation burned through my veins, and my body gave over to the pain.

CHAPTER
THIRTY-SEVEN

GAVIN

I pressed down on the accelerator, heart racing as the brick building came into view. I'd been about six blocks from the VA when Doyle called with the information we'd been waiting on all afternoon.

"Police are looking at Christopher Raines," he said. "Works at the VA. Dropped out of medical school a couple years ago and got his RN instead."

"You're sure?"

"No DNA match—that'll take weeks. But hair seems to match, and he had access to his father's residence where the gun was stored."

I couldn't believe the quiet young man was responsible for something so horrific. I'd only met him once that I remembered, but he'd always been reserved and polite. He'd even broken up the fight between Coleman and his father after Meredith's funeral. "What's the motivator?"

"Possibly money," came Doyle's response. "He was the medical power of attorney for Meredith after the accident.

Apparently, Christopher convinced his father that he was more qualified to make decisions on her behalf. According to his finances, there's a shit ton of money here unaccounted for."

Jesus. I swung into the parking lot and slammed the car into gear, then hopped out, already jogging toward the building before the car door shut. "Headed into the VA now. I'll call you as soon as I get Kate and get back on the road."

I ended the call and shoved my phone into my back pocket, hoping to hell the churning in my gut wasn't age-old instinct screaming that something was wrong—very wrong.

As I approached, I could see the lights were on inside, and I tentatively pushed against the door. With little pressure, it swung inward. I choked back the urge to vomit as the smell assaulted me the moment I stepped into the lobby. It was too distinct not to recognize, and I covered my mouth with one hand. My gut roiled with nausea, worry twisting it into knots as I crept forward.

The body was partially concealed by the hallway that ran perpendicular to the lobby, and fear clutched at my throat as my gaze landed on the pair of legs twisted at an awkward angle.

I paused midstride and shoved my hands into my hair. Oh, God. What if it was Kate? What would I do? The despair that crashed over me was almost crippling in its intensity, and my heart hammered against my ribs. I stood frozen for several long seconds before forcing my feet to move. I had to look—I had to know.

Throat thick with fear, I crept forward, already palming my phone in one hand. As I neared, two things became apparent. The first was that the woman, whoever she was, wasn't Kate. I damn near cried at the relief that rushed through me. The second thing I noticed was the blood staining the carpet and the gunshot wound that had ripped a hole in her torso. She was beyond saving. Which raised my next question—how long ago had she been shot, and by whom?

Taking a deep breath to try to slow the rapid pace of my heart, I tuned my ears to my surroundings. All was still. Pulling my phone from my back pocket, I quickly brought up my messaging screen and tapped in both Clay and Con's names, keeping it brief and succinct.

Me: At VA. One dead. No sign of Kate yet

Oh, God. What if Christopher had gotten to her? I threw a look at the woman at my feet, praying that she was the only victim here. I prayed that I wasn't too late, that Kate wasn't lying in one of the offices off the long hallway, gasping her last breath. I needed to find her—now.

Tucking my phone away, I pulled my Glock from the holster at my lower back, then slipped my finger forward to the trigger guard and held it low as I quietly made my way forward. I knew that Con would call in the woman's murder, so I didn't bother to contact the police. I also didn't want to draw any attention to my presence if the killer was still here.

I peeked in each doorway I came to, but each room remained dark and empty. About halfway down the hall, I spotted something lying on the floor. As I drew closer, I realized it was a scalpel. Blood stained the blade, and I sucked in a breath when I glanced in the open doorway of the supply closet. The shelving unit inside was skewed, as if someone had knocked it over, and materials had been spilled all over the floor.

I peeked around the doorjamb, but the room—like the others—was devoid of life. I quickly cleared the rest of the floor, but whoever had been here was long gone. Part of me was relieved; the other part was ready to jump out of my skin at what that might mean. Goddamn it. Where was Kate?

I dialed Con, who answered on the first ring, no preamble. "What did you find?"

"Not a soul here, other than the dead woman." Frustration seeped into my tone. "Any word of Christopher yet?"

"Not yet."

I didn't like the way he said it, and I immediately went on attack. "We need to find him—both of them. What if he has her?" I couldn't help the hysteria rising up, threatening to choke me.

"We'll find her." Con's voice was firm, confident. "Doyle's cross-checking everything, and the police are checking Christopher's known residences. We'll find her one way or another."

The sound of approaching sirens drew closer, and I tucked the Glock in my waistband as I made my way toward the door. "Police are here. I'm headed back your way as soon as I'm done here. Find her."

I didn't bother to wait for an answer before I hung up and stowed my phone in my back pocket. I was already waiting, hands in front of me when the police entered the building. I recognized one of the cops from a few days ago, and he gave me an appraising nod. "You found the body?"

"Yes, sir." I explained how I'd come to pick Kate up and found the woman dead. "I've got my concealed carry on me, so you can check ballistics."

He nodded, jotting down the information as I relayed it to him. "I'm worried he has her."

The cop eyed me shrewdly. "We're examining each lead, and we'll do our best—"

I was already shaking my head. Sometimes the best just wasn't good enough. The police were bound by policy and red tape—but I wasn't. "I'm telling you—he has her. He's—"

My phone vibrated in my pocket, and I met the detective's steely gaze. "Can I get that?"

He dipped his chin, and I slowly reached back to retrieve

it. Con's name flashed on the screen, and hope flared in my chest as I swiped my thumb over the screen. "News?"

"Police are checking his house now, as well as the home where Meredith had been staying. Doyle also found an old trailer registered to Peter Raines—Christopher's paternal grandfather."

They would search the obvious places first, the places Christopher frequented. They couldn't waste time running off to check every little thing with no evidence.

"Where?" He rattled off the location, and my gut twisted even as I prayed I was wrong. It was an isolated area, private and secluded—perfect to carry out a murder. "I'll meet you there."

I hung up with Con the same time the detective's phone rang. "Am I free to go?"

He held the phone away from his ear as he spoke to me. "We'll be in contact if we need anything."

I left the building at a dead run before he'd finished speaking. We were going to find her one way or the other. I just prayed it wouldn't be too late.

CHAPTER
THIRTY-EIGHT

KATE

Tears burned my eyes, and I watched with an odd sense of detachment as Christopher slowly rounded the metal table. I saw every movement, but I couldn't move, couldn't fight back. My eyes remained frozen open, the paralytic rendering my muscles completely useless.

We'd barely made it inside before he'd injected the neuromuscular blocking agent into my system, and I'd gone limp within seconds. I prayed that, like the drug he'd used to knock me out at the clinic, it would wear off quickly. I was still slightly disoriented, but fully aware of the pain coursing through my body.

I could still feel the tiny bits of gravel scraping over my back and sides from when he'd dragged me from the car, across the overgrown drive and up the stairs of the small porch. I'd felt each jolt as my back and head collided with the steps, unable to scream through the tape covering my mouth. He'd used the same medical tape to bind my wrists and ankles, hampering my ability to fight back. Every inch of me ached, and I couldn't even shift my weight to alleviate the worst of it.

As soon as the paralytic had kicked in, Christopher had ripped the tape from my mouth and cut my hands and feet free. He wasn't a big man, and he'd damn near knocked me out trying to get me up onto the table. I almost wish he would have, knowing what was coming next.

My head lolled to the side like a broken doll's, my limbs just as limp and useless. From my vantage point, I had a view of what must have been the kitchen. The trailer was small and appeared to have been gutted of everything, save the stainless steel table and a variety of instruments scattered across the cracked yellow Formica countertop.

I felt the restraints snap into place around my wrists, then my feet as he moved to the end of the table. Out of my range of sight, I heard Christopher rustling around behind me. My heart damn near stopped when he turned back, scalpel in hand. I couldn't tear my eyes away as he lowered it to my chest, and I braced for the pain.

Was he going to kill me now? I hoped he would make it quick instead of dragging it out, but I knew better. If he'd wanted to kill me right away, he would've done so back at the VA. Instead, he'd drugged me, restrained me so I couldn't fight back but would still be aware of everything around me.

The sound of ripping fabric filled my ears, and my vision blurred with tears as cool air washed over me. I wanted to be brave, but fear stole into my heart, taking over. I hated him for that.

He leaned forward and swiped up a tear trailing down my cheek. "What's this?"

He rubbed it between his thumb and forefinger, a cruel smile twisting his mouth. "You called me a coward. Remember that, Kate?" He chuckled softly. "Who's the coward now?"

He paused, then stared down at me. "Have you ever loved someone so much that you'd do anything for them?" He let out a wistful little sigh. "I'd give anything to have my mother back."

So that's what this was all about. I wished I could speak, but my tongue remained thick and unwieldy. I wanted to keep him talking, ask about his mother and her injuries, what he'd meant by doing anything to save her.

"She deserved the best, but I never would've been able to afford it. And my father didn't care," he replied bitterly. "Eli loved her, but in the end, he gave up on her, too. All she had was me. I had to take care of her."

I took his words apart in my mind, reassembled them, put them back together. Finally, it clicked. Eli—Dr. Coleman. Had he been involved, too, or was he just collateral damage? Had Christopher killed him out of resentment because he'd given up on Meredith ever healing?

"Do you have any idea how expensive those machines are?" He gave his head a little shake. "How do they expect people to pay for that? It's like they don't actually want patients to get better."

He'd been smuggling organs to... pay his mother's medical bills? The irony was not lost on me, and it made me ill all over again.

"Everything was perfect—until you came along." He rested one hand on the table and leaned further over me. "No one suspected a thing, exactly the way it was supposed to be. Of all people, *you* had to be the one to find that body." He gave a rueful shake of his head. "And what were the odds of you coming to work at the VA?"

"Thank God you suspected Eli first." He laughed. "Such a smart girl. But I'm always one step ahead, Kate. You want to know a secret?"

God, no. I wanted to shake my head, terrified of the

answer. He leaned so close that his nose almost brushed mine, his voice dropping several octaves. "I like it."

Those icy eyes met mine. "Do you know how hard it is to do all that work by yourself? Harvesting the organs and transporting them in a timely manner? Then having to get rid of the body without anyone finding it or seeing you in the process?"

"Eli was on to me. Did you know that? I had no choice but to take care of him when he confronted me. Can you believe the idiot came to me first, instead of going to the police?" He tapped the end of my nose with the flat edge of the scalpel. "You almost ruined it for me, Dr. Winfield. I think you should make it up to me."

My stomach tightened in fear at the implication. He must have seen something in my eyes, because he grinned. "It'll be so much more special with you. Now that there's no rush..." He shrugged. "I can take my time."

I watched, unblinking, as he lifted the blade, flashing in the glow of the industrial lighting overhead, and lowered it toward my torso. Silent screams filled my head as the blade burned a path down my sternum.

"Feel that, doctor?" Another tear leaked from the corner of my eye and he smiled. "Where should we start, do you think? Liver?"

I felt the blade slice into my lower stomach and fought the nausea rolling in my belly.

"Hmm..." He hummed a little sound, then shook his head. "No, I don't think so. Don't want you passing out on me just yet."

Reaching off to the side somewhere, I heard the soft clank of metal before he turned back to me. He held up some sort of device that resembled an ice cream scoop.

Oh, God.

Inwardly, I thrashed as it moved closer to my face. Outwardly, my body didn't even twitch.

"Such pretty eyes, Kate." The cool metal pressed against the skin near my temple. "Someone would pay a pretty penny for those."

He lifted the instrument closer to my face, allowing it to hover over my eye socket. A feral smile curled his lips as he lifted it away. "Maybe not. I want you to have a good view."

Motherfucker. I fought against the drug coursing through my system, trying to spur my muscles into moving, but they remained infuriatingly still. Christopher turned away again, and a tiny spasm rolled through the muscle of my forearm. I anxiously held my breath, praying for it to happen again.

There.

Just the slightest twitch, but my heart leaped as the index finger on my right hand moved. I tested it again, and I felt the cool brush of metal against my fingertip as I stroked the surface of the table. I focused as hard as I could, channeling all of my energy on trying to move my other fingers, my toes—anything.

To my left, Christopher was still rustling around, digging for something. Finally, I was rewarded by a tiny twitch of my foot. I was restrained, so I wouldn't be able to just hop off the table and run away, even if I did have control of my muscles, so I focused on the next best thing.

I pushed my tongue forward, trying to get it to cooperate. I hadn't seen much as he'd carried me into the trailer, but maybe if I could scream for help...

My hope was short lived as Christopher towered over me once more. "Open wide, doctor."

It took barely more than a second for his words to sink in as he pried my jaw open and lifted the channel locks he held. I tried to scream as the cool metal pushed past my lips, but nothing came out.

The scrape of metal against bone filled my ears, and I mentally cringed as the grooves of the instrument grasped for purchase on my saliva-slickened tooth.

His face contorted in concentration as he adjusted his angle and pulled. The pressure was so intense it lifted my head off the table.

Christopher chuckled. "Sucker's really in there, isn't it?"

Tears burned my eyes and slipped down my cheeks as he pressed one hand to my forehead, holding me in place. "Don't worry, Dr. Winfield. It'll be over in… just… one… second."

Blinding pain swept over me like a tidal wave, paralyzing in its intensity. I couldn't breathe, couldn't think, couldn't do anything except taste the metallic tang of blood filling my mouth and tremble from the pain radiating through my body.

The pliers were suspended in midair, the tooth clenched tightly between them, and I watched as a trickle of blood slipped down the side and fell out of sight. Every muscle in my body tensed, and my lungs contacted as a scream started low, then worked its way up my throat. It bellowed up and out of my mouth, startling us both when it coincided with the sound of screeching metal and splintering wood.

CHAPTER
THIRTY-NINE

GAVIN

I threw my weight against the door, and it finally gave way with a loud screech as the metal bent and the wood of the doorjamb cracked. My heart hitched, and the scene in front of me stole my ability to breathe.

The inside of the small trailer was almost completely empty. The floors were covered in cheap vinyl, stained dark in places with God knew what. The only thing of substance in the room was the stainless steel table in the middle of what should have been a kitchen, dated cabinets lining the wall. But that wasn't what grabbed my attention.

Kate lay on the table, wrists and ankles bound, stripped down to nothing but her underwear. The red trails of blood were stark against pale skin that had been sliced open. She was still—so still. She didn't move, didn't scream, didn't even look my way. Those azure eyes I knew so well stared vacantly at the ceiling, and a trail of blood trickled from the corner of her mouth, down her cheek and onto the table beneath her.

I felt my lungs constrict and my heart tighten as fury

billowed up, radiating through every inch of my body. Ripping my gaze away from her, I slowly lifted it to the man standing over her. His eyes were crazed, his cheeks flushed pink, and in his hand he held a pair of channel locks. And was that...?

Oh, Christ. It was a tooth. Kate's tooth.

I still couldn't believe I'd beaten the police here, but I'd left the VA and driven like a bat out of hell, bent on reaching here before... I swallowed hard. Before this. This was the worst possible scenario, finding her too late. Even when I'd first broken down the door, I'd planned to hold the man until the police arrived. I told myself over and over what I needed to do—what I should do—but seeing Kate's broken body lying there so lifelessly, all my plans flew out the window.

"You motherfucker!"

Christopher hurled the channel locks at me, probably hoping to slow me down, but I dodged them as I lunged forward. I slammed into him just as he snatched something from the counter behind him. We went down in a tangle of limbs, landing hard on the floor. He twisted beneath me, and I jerked backward as he swung at me.

The glint of metal flashed in the light and I jerked to the side as the scalpel sliced through the air a second time, heading right toward my face. Grasping the man's forearm, I dug one knee into the cavity of his stomach and fought the upward arc of the blade as he swung at me.

His free hand wrapped around my throat, and I used the opportunity to drive my fist into his face. He let out a grunt of pain but didn't let go. Using all my weight, I threw as much power behind my punch as possible, this time connecting with his jaw.

The scalpel waved perilously close to my face, and I lurched away from it, shifting my weight over his body. I let out a hiss of pain as the blade arced through the air and connected with my forearm, slicing through the fabric of my shirt and across my flesh.

Motherfucker. I gritted my teeth and landed another punch to his jaw. His head snapped to the side, and I grasped one of the fingers wrapped around my throat, yanking it backward as hard as I could. He let out a sharp cry and pulled his hand away from my throat before his finger snapped under the force of my hold.

He fought against me, shoving the scalpel at me, and I shifted my weight, trying to keep him pinned to the ground. His hips bucked upward, causing me to lose my balance, and I grabbed his arm for support as I fell forward. Under the force of my weight, the hand holding the scalpel sliced through the air, and there was a whisper of sound as it sank between his ribs and into his heart.

"Fuck!" I scrambled off of him, staring at the scalpel and the blood slowly saturating his shirt. Christopher's eyes went even wider, and a gurgling noise welled up and out of his throat. His stunned gaze met mine, and his fingers tightened around the handle protruding from his chest.

"No, don't—"

Before I could get the words out, he yanked the blade free, and blood spurted from the wound. It was my first instinct to put pressure on it to stop the bleeding, but my hand froze halfway to his chest. If the asshole wanted to take the easy way out and hemorrhage all over the floor in front of me, that was his choice. He didn't warrant another second of my time.

Scrambling to my feet, I fought the fear and apprehension clutching at my throat as I turned my attention to Kate. Still frozen in that same position, she hadn't moved an inch, hadn't uttered a sound. I'd begun to think the scream I'd heard was just a figment of my imagination. I couldn't bear to think of never seeing her smile again, never feeling her in my arms.

"Please..."

I blinked away the burning sensation in my eyes as I gently reached out a hand and settled it on her chest. For a moment, there was nothing. Then, as if God had answered my prayers, I felt a slight lift of her chest as her lungs filled with air.

Holy shit. She was alive.

I placed my hands on her cheeks and stared into those huge blue eyes. "Kate, can you hear me?"

She blinked once, long and slow, as if it took all the effort in the world, and relief flooded me.

I fumbled with the restraints as I released her hands and feet, all the while assessing her injuries. The sight of the deep cuts on her torso made my throat tighten with emotion. I wanted to scream, to lash out and strangle Chris with my bare hands. He'd kept her awake, fully aware of everything going on while he'd planned to torture and kill her.

The sound of sirens met my ears as I struggled out of my dress shirt and draped it over her. Seeing her like this, so helpless, I resorted to the only tactic I knew. "Always gettin' me out of my clothes, babe."

I tried for a teasing tone, but my levity fell flat as a tear escaped the corner of her eye and trickled down her temple, landing on the table with a tiny splash.

That tiny drop broke me, and everything in me shattered. "God, sweetheart. I'm sorry. I'm so sorry."

I bent over her, fighting the burning in the backs of my eyes as I gripped her hand and rested my forehead against hers. Her fingers twitched against mine, and I lifted my head to look into her eyes. There were no words of comfort that I could offer her. I refused to let her see my weakness—I had to be strong for her, make her believe that everything would be okay. Somehow.

"Never again," I promised. "I'll never let anyone hurt you again." I squeezed her fingers and lifted her hand to my lips. "We'll get through this—together."

KATE

I stared at the mirror, studying my face as I finished applying my makeup. The swelling in my jaw had gone down, but the implant the oral surgeon had inserted still felt strange inside my mouth, and I ran my tongue over the rough surface.

Feeling a presence behind me, I met Gavin's familiar brown gaze in the reflection.

His eyes were filled with concern. "Are you sure you'll be okay?"

I set the mascara down and turned to him with a small smile. "I'm sure."

It'd been nearly two weeks since the incident, and Gavin hadn't let me out of his sight more than absolutely necessary. He'd even taken several days off work before I finally threatened to move back into my condo if he didn't go back.

Since he very much liked having me in his home and his bed, he was less than pleased with my ultimatum. I wasn't altogether sure that I would follow through with my threat, because I liked being here with him more than I probably should have. We hadn't spent a single night apart for more than three weeks, and the idea of sleeping without him next to me was strangely disconcerting.

I lifted one hand and smoothed the twin lines of worry that had appeared between his brows. "I promise. Everything will be fine."

Though this was my first foray out of the house since the incident with Christopher, I wouldn't be alone. Victoria had invited me to go dress shopping with her, and I wasn't about to turn down the opportunity to watch my best friend pick out her wedding dress.

My phone vibrated on the counter behind me, and I turned around to read the message on the screen. I tapped out a reply, then stowed my phone in my back pocket and faced Gavin again. "Victoria is here. I'll be back by the time you get home from work."

I stretched up on my toes and planted a quick kiss on his lips, then started toward the doorway. Gavin's arm shot out and wrapped around my waist, pulling me back to him. His free hand lifted to my face, his thumb slipping beneath my chin and raising my face to his. Dark brown eyes stared into mine for several long seconds. "I just want you safe," he said softly.

I leaned into him and slid my arms up his chest until they were laced behind his neck. "I know. Both Victoria and I will be together at Lydia's shop. Xander's got plenty of security there, so we'll all be safe."

The threat of danger had passed, but Gavin was still intensely worried for my well-being. As much as it drove me crazy, I appreciated it at the same time. I knew he cared deeply for me, and over the past couple weeks my feelings for him had become crystal clear. I hadn't found the right time or words to tell him, but now wasn't the time either.

"Text me when you get there and when you leave." I

cocked an eyebrow at the demand. A small smile crooked his mouth. "Please."

I grinned, then planted another swift kiss on his lips. "I don't want to keep Victoria waiting. Have a good day at work."

He still held my face cradled in one large hand, and he pulled me back to him, brushing his lips over mine in a sweet, lingering kiss. He broke away, then studied me for a long moment before finally releasing me. "Have fun."

With that, I skipped downstairs and out the door, pausing briefly to pet Peanut on my way out. Victoria's car was parked in the driveway, and I waved to her as I hopped down the front porch steps and cut across the lawn to meet her. I slid into the passenger seat, and she reached over the console, wrapping me in a welcoming hug. "I'm so glad you could come."

"Are you kidding?" I said as I pulled my seat belt across my chest and snapped it into place. "I wouldn't miss this for the world."

Our small talk turned to discussion of the wedding as we drove to Lydia's bridal salon, discussing her venue, colors, and a million other tiny little details. Half an hour later, we parked along the street outside the salon, and Victoria looked over at me. "So, how are you? For real?"

The words stuck in my throat. What could I tell her? That I woke sometimes in the middle of the night on silent screams, tied to that table while Chris sliced through my flesh and ripped my tooth out? That wasn't going to happen.

I shook my head, unable to stop the tears from welling in my eyes. "I can't."

She leaned over and pulled me into a tight hug. For several minutes, we remained that way. Finally, I dragged in a ragged breath and swiped the tears from my cheeks. "I'm sorry. I just..."

Victoria peered at me. "Whenever you're ready, I'll be here."

If there was ever anyone who understood what I'd gone through, it was Victoria. I tried to smile but knew I failed miserably. "Thank you."

Lydia herself greeted us with a smile as soon as we stepped in the door. She opened her arms for a hug and held me close. "You look amazing."

I knew she'd been through trauma herself, so it meant the world to me that she offered a compliment instead of sympathy. "Thank you." To deflect the attention away from myself, I gestured toward Victoria. "I can't wait to see her in some gowns."

Lydia's grin lit up her whole face. "I have a few picked out, but feel free to take a look around. If you find something you like, you can bring it to the dressing room right over here." She pointed to a room with the raised dais in front of it.

I meandered the racks for a few moments while Victoria went inside the room to get changed, and I fingered one of the model gowns with reverence. I remembered being young, with stars in my eyes, more excited about dressing up for my wedding than the man I was marrying. The lace was soft and delicate beneath my fingers, and I couldn't help but wonder what Gavin would think of it.

My attention was splintered when Victoria swept out of the dressing room wearing a stunning ballgown. "Oh," I breathed. "It's beautiful."

"Not too much?" she asked. Knowing how self-conscious of her voluptuous figure she was, I shook my head.

"I think it's absolutely perfect. But try on a few more just to make sure."

She inspected the gown from several different angles before retreating into the room. My gaze went straight back to the lace gown on the mannequin, and I heard soft footsteps approach as Lydia reached my side. "Would you like to try it on?"

I smiled ruefully. "I really shouldn't."

"It looks even better on," she said. "And the ivory would really complement your skin."

"You're not helping my willpower," I said with a roll of my eyes.

Her smile only grew, and I finally relented. "Oh, all right."

She carefully lifted the gown from the mannequin, then carried it to the dressing room next to Victoria's. Victoria stepped out, this time in a pretty sheath dress, and we admired the gown before she went into change again. Lydia tipped her head toward my dressing room, and I took the silent cue to enter.

I'd be lying if I hadn't thought a lot about my relationship with Gavin over the past couple weeks. Things had happened between us so quickly, but I couldn't imagine not having him in my life at all. He'd implied before that he wanted marriage, but he hadn't said anything since the incident. I had a feeling he was waiting for me to come around to his way of thinking. The more I stared at the dress, the more I began to think it sounded exceptionally good.

I quickly shucked my clothes, then stepped into the dress, zipping it up as far as I could before stepping out. Victoria was already on the small round dais, and her eyes widened, her hands flying up to cover her mouth when she saw me. "Oh, Kate."

Tears welled in her eyes, and I let out an uncomfortable little laugh. "That bad?" I joked.

There were no mirrors inside the dressing room, so I hadn't had a chance to see what the dress looked like yet. My heart raced with anticipation, and I braced myself, then slowly turned around to meet my reflection. My breath caught in my lungs, and I froze. Lydia had been right. It did look even better on. It fit perfectly, and it felt like a dream.

"I love that look," Lydia said quietly, a soft smile on her face.

I couldn't tear my eyes away from the mirror. "The dress?"

"Your expression," she clarified.

I met my gaze in the mirror, wondering exactly what it was she saw. My eyes were bright, my cheeks flushed. I looked happy. I looked like...

"A woman in love," Lydia said, finishing my sentence for me.

She was right; I was in love. I wasn't about to let a man like Gavin slip through my fingers.

CHAPTER
FORTY-ONE

GAVIN

I'd invited Dad to stay with us, but he'd declined—thank God—saying that Kate and I deserved our privacy. I didn't mind having him around as much as I thought I would, and things between us were definitely better.

When I walked in that afternoon after leaving the office, the house seemed too quiet. I wasn't sure if Kate was home yet, since she'd ridden with Victoria to the salon today. *Home.* I liked the sound of that, maybe a little too much. We'd been sharing a bed for the past twelve nights, but I hadn't officially asked her to move in with me. Not wanting to push her, I hadn't broached the subject since the incident.

I couldn't even think of it without getting pissed. More often than not, most nights I dreamed of walking in on that scene, Kate strapped to the table and unable to move. More than once I'd dreamed that I was too late, and I'd woken in a panic, sweating and reaching for Kate to make sure she was still there. She had nightmares, too, but she seemed to be handling it like a trooper. I felt like a goddamn mess, and I wanted to lock her away in our room where I knew she'd be safe forever.

Realistically, I knew she'd never put up with it. She needed to go back to work soon, and there was no reason for her not to, except for my own insecurity. I hated the thought of what she'd been through, and the shit luck she'd experienced lately. She'd been attacked in her old office at the healthplex, then again at the VA.

I'd gone back with her once, a couple days ago, when she'd had to turn in some paperwork. She'd tensed walking through the lobby where Magda had been murdered, but a few minutes later she'd been right back to normal. I wasn't sure I'd be the same in her shoes. She was stronger than anyone I knew, and I loved her all the more for it.

Loosening my tie, I meandered upstairs to change before dinner, pausing as I crossed the threshold to our bedroom. Kate stood next to the closet, and I watched as she tucked something inside, then straightened. She turned and startled when she saw me, her hand flying to her throat.

"Oh, my God, Gavin!"

"Sorry, babe." I pushed off the doorframe and strode toward her, pulling her against me as she melted into my embrace. "Didn't mean to scare you."

"You're too quiet," she complained without heat, turning her face into my throat.

I ran my hands over her back, enjoying the way she felt against me. "How was your day?"

She leaned back a bit and tipped her chin up to me, an indecipherable look in her eyes. "Good."

"I'm glad." I dropped a kiss on her lips. "Thank you for texting me and letting me know where you were."

"Only because you asked so nicely." Her lips curled into a smirk. "And I hadn't even had a chance to tell you I was home yet. I only beat you by a few minutes."

I'd been wondering, but I didn't say anything. I opened my mouth to ask about dinner, but I didn't have a chance.

"It's occurred to me that you've been very—" She cleared her throat. "—*vocal* about your feelings, but I haven't. And I should. I mean, I need to. I've been thinking about us a lot recently, and I... I really like you. Even though it's only been a few weeks, I feel like I can see something between us—a future, maybe."

She paused and licked her lips, but I didn't dare interrupt. I knew how monumentally important this moment was, that she come to terms with her feelings all on her own. This was a huge step for her—putting herself out there and offering herself to me, heart and soul. I stared at her, and she shifted uncomfortably, her gaze darting over my shoulder as she bared herself to me.

"I just... I really like you. I know I already said that, but I mean it. I know you care about me, and I... care about you. I feel closer to you than I've ever felt with anyone else, like you just... get me."

"I like to think so," I murmured, my hands tightening on her waist.

"So, um... I hope you don't mind me using your closet," she said, indicating it with a jerk of her head.

My eyes narrowed at the abrupt change of topic. "It's yours as long as you want it."

She peered up at me. "I bought something today."

For some reason, it seemed important to her that I know this. "Glad your shopping trip was beneficial."

"I bought a dress."

Not quite following, I started to nod, then froze as the implication sunk in. She'd spent her day at a bridal salon.

"A white dress," she clarified, still watching me closely.

"Oh?"

Not the most intelligent response, but I couldn't come up

with anything else at the moment. I wanted to ask her exactly what that meant, what she wanted, but I let her lead the conversation, gradually taking me wherever she wanted to go.

"I just... I wanted to tell you that I..." Her voice cracked, and she licked her lips before she continued. "You told me you loved me."

Her gaze darted back to mine, and I nodded slightly but stayed silent. "I didn't say it back to you then, but I should have."

I opened my mouth to speak, but she stopped me with a brief shake of her head. "I was scared—afraid of putting myself out there again and getting my heart broken. I think I've known for a while, but I wasn't ready to admit it. But I don't want to spend another day without telling you how I feel," she whispered shakily. "I don't want to spend another day without you."

I admired her so much for being brave enough to trust me with her heart. "You'll never have to," I promised as I cupped her beautiful face in my hands. "I will never hurt you, and I'll never leave you."

She stared up at me, her teeth cutting into her lower lip, looking vulnerable as hell. "I love you."

My heart swelled at the softly whispered words, and I pressed my forehead to hers. "I love you, Kate."

Her lips were soft and sweet beneath mine as I dipped my head and our mouths came together. Her lips parted on a sigh, and I curled my tongue over hers, stroking and tasting. Before I was ready, I forced myself to pull back.

"You said you bought a dress?"

Her cheeks flushed pink with embarrassment. "I know it sounds crazy and impulsive, but... yeah. I did."

"Good." I gave a single nod, then grabbed her hand and hauled her across the room toward my dresser. I dug inside for a moment as I spoke. "Then it'll go perfectly with... this."

I held up a small blue box, and her eyes widened, her free hand coming up to her mouth. "Are you... Is that...?"

I released her hand just long enough to open it, revealing the diamond inside. "I told you I was serious. I knew you were the only one I wanted." I dropped to one knee and gestured between us. "I just want you to know, this is not at all how I pictured this happening in my head."

A huge smile exploded over her face. "It's perfect."

I pulled the ring from the box and grabbed her left hand. "Kate Winfield, would you do me the honor of being my wife and spending the rest of your life with me?"

"Yes!"

Her hand trembled in mine as I slipped the ring on her third finger, then rose to my feet and pulled her in close. "I love you so much."

"I love you, too." She stretched up to kiss me before pulling back and admiring the diamond that sparkled in the light. "I can't believe this. It's so... wow."

"I had a really awesome proposal planned," I complained good-naturedly. "Now you'll have to tell everyone I proposed in the middle of the afternoon in our bedroom."

Her eyes turned dark with desire, and her teeth raked over her lower lip as she planted her hands on my chest and pushed me toward the bed. "Let me make it up to you—in our bed."

And if that wasn't the best thing I'd ever heard, I didn't know what was.

EPILOGUE

GAVIN

I stood at the window, adjusting my cufflinks as my gaze skimmed over the guests assembled in the white chairs that had been placed in curved rows around the gazebo in the backyard. The slight breeze lifted the ribbons, making the flowers dance as the late afternoon sun spilled its golden glow over the yard.

In another hour or so, it would be dark and all the tiny white lights strung overhead would illuminate the small dance floor and the dozen tables that had been set up for dinner. Though I'd have gone along with whatever she wanted, Kate had chosen to keep things simple. She loved the gazebo in our backyard and thought it was the perfect place to get married.

I had to agree. It was now strewn with ribbons and flowers, and a long white aisle runner led from the back door of the house up to the steps of the gazebo. In less than half an hour, I'd be standing at the end of that runner, getting married to the love of my life. I couldn't fucking wait.

"Last chance."

I swiveled my head toward Rob, who lounged in the doorway, a teasing smile on his face as he flipped his keys around his fingers.

"Get the fuck outta here."

He laughed and pocketed the keys before coming closer. "You know I'm kidding. I wouldn't let you run out on her."

I knew he wouldn't. Besides, I'd have to be cold and dead in the ground to ever give Kate up. She was it for me, and I couldn't wait to have her by my side for the rest of our lives. The past three months had been a whirlwind of activity as we planned the wedding, but I got to come home to her every night, so I was calling it a win.

Kate was still at the VA, but I'd resigned from Walker and Raines. Larry hadn't been charged with anything, but I hadn't been able to lie to myself any longer. A little over a month ago, I'd taken Con's offer and now worked for QSG, primarily covering the firearms classes as well as offering legal counsel when needed. I planned to keep my license so I could continue to practice—on my terms this time.

Rob adjusted my tie. "Jesus. Did you get dressed in the dark?"

"Whatever." Part of me was nervous as fuck, and my hands were still shaking. It wasn't the marriage part that worried me, exactly. I couldn't explain it. I was a ball of nerves, nervousness and anticipation and a little fear all mingled together rolling around in my stomach.

"I'm just messing with you." Rob stepped back to inspect me, then clapped a hand on my shoulder. "You all good?"

No. "Yes." Or I would be as soon as I saw Kate.

"Good. I'll see you down there."

My best man headed out the door, and the sound of his footsteps trailed off as he headed downstairs. I drew in a deep breath and glanced out the window again. I recognized Xander, Lydia, and their little girl, Alexia, in the front row,

Blake seated next to them. I imagined Victoria was with Kate, helping her get ready. My sister and her family were there, as well as Kate's family. We'd cut the guest list at fifty people, and it looked like they were all here.

"Can I come in for a second?"

I turned to my father. "Of course."

He stepped close and gazed out the window. "Looks like everything's ready."

"Yep."

He stared outside for another long moment before meeting my eyes. "You all ready?"

"I am."

"Good." He gave a little nod. "I'm glad you chose her."

"Me, too." Kate meant more to me than anything, and I would spend the rest of my life showing her how much I loved her.

"Your mother would be happy."

Emotion clogged my throat at the mention of my mother. She'd only been gone for a little over a year, but her absence today was profound. I wished with all my heart that she could have had the chance to meet Kate, because I was sure they would have loved each other. I swallowed hard. "I think so, too."

He pulled me into an awkward hug. "I'm proud of you."

Emotion burned at the backs of my eyes, and I tightened my hold on my dad. Hearing him say that meant everything.

A long moment later, he pulled away and tipped his head toward the window. "I'd better get down there. Good luck, son."

I nodded, still trying to get my emotions under control. Glancing in the mirror one last time, I took a deep breath and checked my reflection. I smoothed my suit jacket, then straightened my tie one last time before I got ready to head downstairs. A soft click drew my attention to the door—closed now, Kate leaning against it.

My gaze flitted over every inch of her, clad in a lacy white dress. I struggled for words. "Don't you know it's bad luck to let me see you before the wedding?"

"I don't care." She pushed off the door and I met her halfway, pulling her into my arms. "We'll make our own luck."

I stared down at her. "Is everything okay?"

"I just needed to see you."

Not wanting to smear her makeup, I dropped a soft kiss on her forehead. "I'm right here, babe. I'm not going anywhere."

"Ever?" She tipped her head up, a little smile teasing the corners of her mouth. There was no mistaking the worry in her eyes, though, and I lifted my hands to frame her face.

"Ever. You." Disregarding the pink lipstick coating her pretty lips, I dipped my head and kissed her between words. "Are. Mine."

I pulled back to look at her, those big blue eyes cutting straight to my heart as a smile lit her face. "You ready to do this?"

I dropped my hand and laced my fingers with hers. "Let's go."

Hand in hand, we headed down the stairs and toward our future—together.

Get ready to dive into the next steamy book in the Quentin Security Series! With a stalker closing in, pop star Jana Malone cooks up a marriage of convenience with her grumpy, tatted up bodyguard. Turn the page for a sneak peek of <u>Heart of a Devil</u>!

HEART OF A DEVIL

VINCE

I was seriously not cut out for this shit. The bar crowd had never been my scene, and it was even less so now that I was surrounded by a bunch of immature twenty-somethings who thought they were God's gift to the world.

I fought to keep my expression neutral as I watched the scantily clad bodies dry humping each other on the dance floor. Ripping my eyes away from Gemma, I glanced around the crappy little hole in the wall bar. Louie's was a favorite post-show hangout, but for the life of me, I couldn't figure out why. The place reeked of booze, sweat, and perfume, and a sticky substance that I prayed was alcohol coated the floor in spots.

My boots made a disgusting sound as I shifted, returning my gaze to Gemma. My principle—the woman currently under my protection—was on the dance floor shaking her skinny ass to some country pop song one of her friends had released a few months ago, and the dude behind her was doing his best to get his hand up her short as fuck Daisy Dukes.

Gemma Malone's band members were scattered around the small club, each scouting a new piece of tail to take home for the evening—or the morning, in this case, considering it was past midnight. I'd spent the last ten hours at the venue playing babysitter for her during the final show of her tour. As if that wasn't bad enough, I'd been obligated to accompany her to Louie's when she decided she wanted to come out and unwind with the rest of the band.

It was fairly local, thank God, so I was only about an hour from home. All I wanted to do was herd Gemma out the door, drop her off at her house, then pour myself into bed for a couple of hours before I had to be back at her place. It was already creeping close to one o'clock, and I was supposed to be back over there by eight to take her to the studio.

The guy plastered to Gemma's back was getting bolder, his hand moving between her thighs, and I wondered if she was stupid enough to let him feel her up on the dance floor. Gemma was the chosen poster child for Magnolia Way records and a supposed role model for little girls. I snorted. She wouldn't be much of a role model for long if one of the people standing around the floor waving their cell phones got a picture at just the right angle.

Unfortunately, it was my job to keep her safe, both from the person sending her threatening letters and from herself, so I stomped across the dance floor and wedged myself between them. "Time to go."

Big blue eyes glared up at me. "What the hell, Vince?"

I tipped my head toward the door. "Let's go before you get in trouble."

Her face fell into a petulant expression. "I wasn't doing anything wrong."

"Yeah, come on, man," the drunk kid wheedled. "We was just havin' fun. Right, babe?"

We both ignored the drunken idiot, and I focused on

Gemma. "You were practically fucking him on the dance floor. Unless you want to end up a headline on tomorrow's tabloids, I suggest you get your shit and go."

She rolled her eyes and stomped away, but not in the direction of the front door as I'd hoped. I followed her to the bar where one of her fellow bandmates sat with a beautiful brunette draped over his lap, her tongue currently trailing up the side of his neck. A tumbler of what appeared to be whiskey sat on the bar in front of Brandt, and he lifted a hand, signaling for the bartender to deliver another as he watched Gemma approach.

He slid the glass her way, and she slammed it back, then wiped the back of her wrist across her mouth, all the while glaring at me. Brandt Meacham smirked, his gaze bouncing from me then back to Gemma. "Bodyguard cracking down again?"

Gemma threw back another shot as soon as the bartender placed it in front of her, then turned her attention to Brandt. "I think I'm up for a ride."

He chuckled around the woman trying to suck his face off. "Suit yourself, Gems."

She pinned me with her brilliant blue eyes, one eyebrow lifting toward her hairline. "What about you?"

I clenched my molars together, barely managing to rein in my irritation. "No."

One corner of her mouth kicked up. "What? Don't think you can last eight seconds?"

I stared down at her, unwilling to rise to the bait. A couple silence-filled seconds later, she let out an irritated little huff and spun on her heel, then stomped toward the mechanical bull in the corner. Great. This night just kept getting better and better.

Beside me, Brandt shoved the brunette's head away from

his face and glanced at me. "You can take off, Ink. We're all headed back to my place after this."

Oh, hell no. Bad shit seemed to follow Brandt wherever he went, and the trouble that didn't follow him he brought on himself. He was a borderline alcoholic, and I didn't trust the kid as far as I could throw him. The last time they'd hung out at his place, he decided it was a good idea to pull out a pistol indoors.

One of the other morons in the band had dared him to pull the trigger, and he either hadn't checked to see if it was loaded or he hadn't given a shit. The bullet had passed through two walls before lodging in the drywall of the bedroom where one of his drunken trysts was passed out. There wasn't a snowball's chance in hell that I was letting Gemma hang out with that stupid fuck.

"She's gotta be up early," I said by way of response. "We're taking off as soon as she's done here."

I closed my eyes and released a long exhalation through my nostrils as a loud—and very familiar—"Hey, y'all, watch this!" split the air. Turning toward the small padded arena, I watched with dismay as Gemma lifted one arm high over her head, the other hand fisted around the reins of the fake bull as it began to rock back and forth. I had to give the girl credit. She was actually pretty coordinated, even half-intoxicated.

A small crowd gathered around, and hoots and hollers filled the air as the bull bucked wildly and Gemma did her best to hold on. Her tiny denim cutoffs bunched up around her hips with each rocking motion, exposing the curve of her ass cheeks. Resigned to let this play out, I folded my arms over my chest. If she wanted to make a spectacle of herself, that was her choice. Her PR person made way more money to put up with her shit than I did.

Almost as soon as the thought crossed my mind, Gemma was thrown off the bull's back and landed with a giggle on the inflatable floor surrounding the contraption. I pushed off the bar and strode toward her, then hooked one hand around her elbow as she stumbled to her feet. "Fun's over, trouble."

Snatching up the fringed cowgirl boots on the floor, I hauled Gemma across the bar and out the door.

"Hey!" Gemma dug in her heels, trying to pull me to a stop, but I paid her no attention as I pushed out the front door. "What are you doing?"

She pulled against me again, and I ran my tongue over my teeth. Releasing her elbow, I wrapped my arm around her waist and lifted her to my hip like a toddler. My other arm slid under her ass, and I sucked in a breath as my fingers skated over miles of perfectly toned flesh. She seemed too stunned to speak as I stormed toward my truck, and I was grateful for the temporary reprieve. We crossed the parking lot, and I opened the passenger door, then plunked her ass down on the seat and tossed her boots on the floorboard.

"Hey, asshole, that's—" She abruptly cut off and gave me a funny look.

I settled one hand on her shoulder and dipped my head to look into her eyes. "You good?" She pressed her lips together and nodded slightly. "You sure? Because if you feel—Fuck!"

I tried to jump backward as that last shot of whiskey and everything that had preceded it throughout the course of the day splattered across my boots. Keeping one hand on her shoulder to steady her, I closed my eyes and counted to ten. I ground my molars together and glanced up at Gemma's pale face. Perspiration dotted her forehead, and I lightly tapped her cheek to get her attention. "You with me?"

Her eyes opened slowly, sluggishly, and met mine. She gave a listless nod.

"Come on. May as well get the rest of it out." As if my words triggered another bout, she leaned forward and heaved again. This time, I was quick enough to move out of the line of fire. Avoiding the pile of vomit on the pavement, I maneuvered myself between the open door of the cab in an attempt to keep anyone from seeing her.

I was grateful that the parking lot had been packed when we arrived and we'd had to park all the way off to the side. I glanced around but saw nothing, and I prayed that no one had seen. We'd made something of a spectacle leaving the bar, and it wouldn't surprise me in the least if someone tried to capture our little scene on camera.

Turning my attention back to Gemma, I ran my hand in light circles over her back. When she was done, she leaned back against the seat, panting heavily. I opened the back door and hunted around for a bottle of water, then passed it to her. "Drink." She did as she was told, then moved to hand it back to me. "Keep it. You need to rehydrate." I curled her fingers around it and set it in her lap so she'd have it when she needed it.

Pulling the seatbelt across her torso, I snapped it into place then slammed the door. For the first time ever, I cursed the fact that we weren't at one of her tour stops with a hotel nearby. I could get us a place for the night, but I was already tired as shit, and all I wanted to do was get her ass home then do the same.

I headed around to the driver side, then cranked the engine and pulled out of the lot. On the radio, one song was ending, bleeding right into another, and Gemma roused enough to reach over and crank up the volume. Before I had the chance to brace myself, she belted out the lyrics, and I cringed as her high soprano bounced off my eardrums. "Jesus, woman!"

Gemma took the volume down a couple notches but continued to sing along with Reba enthusiastically. A few minutes later, she grew quieter and quieter, then finally— blessedly—completely silent. Thank fuck. Forty-five minutes later, I pulled up in front of her house and cut the engine, then pocketed my keys. "Let's go, sleeping beauty."

Next to me, Gemma snored softly in her seat. I rolled my eyes, then made my way around and pulled her out. Her head lolled back as I lifted her in my arms, and I awkwardly maneuvered her dead weight toward the front door. I punched in the code to the electronic keypad above the door handle that she'd opted to use instead of a physical key. The security system beeped a warning as I stepped inside, and I juggled Gemma as I closed the door and disengaged the alarm.

Gemma blinked up at me as I made my way through the living room and down the hall. "What are you doing?"

"Putting you to bed." I used my elbow to flick on the light as I carried her into her bedroom. She swayed as I stood her on her feet next to the bed. "Your boots are still in my truck. Do you want me to get them?"

She waved my offer away. "No. I need to use the bathroom."

She stumbled in that direction, and I waited awkwardly in the bedroom, trying to ignore the sound of her using the toilet. Water flushed, and I breathed a sigh of relief. Thank Jesus. Now she could go to bed, and I could go home. My hopes went up in smoke when I heard the shower come on.

"Goddamn it, Gemma." Growling in frustration, I stormed toward the bathroom. I stopped dead in my tracks in the doorway, stunned, as I took in Gemma standing under the spray of the shower, fully clothed. Jesus Christ. "What the hell are you doing?"

She turned those giant blue eyes on me. "Washing off. What does it look like?"

I stared at her for a long moment, barely fighting back the urge to tell her exactly what I thought. "Come on, let's just get you to bed."

"Hold on," she complained. "I'm almost done."

I waited for about half a second before I stomped across the room and flicked off the water with a quick turn of my wrist. "Now."

"All right, all right. Jeez." But instead of climbing from the shower, her hands moved toward the button of her shorts, and she shimmied the soaked denim over her hips and down her legs, taking a pair of skimpy pale pink panties with them. I quickly averted my eyes and grabbed a towel from the rack, holding it in front of me like a shield.

God give me strength. I wasn't gonna lie—Gemma without clothes was something else. Not that she'd ever know it, but I'd lusted over her hard for the past twelve days, ever since I'd been hired on. It was my first job since my honorable discharge from the Marines, and I was nervous as hell. I didn't want to screw up. She'd flirted with me a bit over the first couple of days, but hard as it was, I refused to give in to her charm. I wasn't about to risk my job for a pretty face.

Good thing I hadn't tried anything either, because her true colors revealed themselves soon after. For the past week and a half or so, she'd acted like an absolute spoiled little brat who treated me like a servant instead of the man hired to protect her. It irked the hell out of me, but I'd be damned if I let her know she'd gotten under my skin.

I watched over the edge of the towel as her hands moved to the pearl buttons of her pink and blue plaid shirt, and it seemed to take an eternity for her to get them all unsnapped. She pushed the fabric off her shoulders, then let out a little grunt of distress as her arms got trapped inside the sleeves.

"Stupid thing..." She shook one arm, succeeding only in making it worse as the wet fabric clung and tangled together.

"For fuck's sake." I dropped the towel and reached for her. "Turn around."

She wobbled on her feet but managed to turn her back to

me, and I peeled the sodden material down her arms and dropped it in the tub.

She gathered her hair, and dragged the damp locks over one shoulder as she glanced back at me. "My bra?"

Jesus. Who had I killed in a past life to deserve this? Clenching my teeth, I released the clasp in the middle of her back and yanked the straps down. As soon as it hit the ground, Gemma let out a little sigh and fell back against me. I caught her around her waist to keep her from falling, and she grasped my arm where it banded just beneath her breasts. I forced myself to stare straight ahead and not give in to the temptation to look at those gorgeous tits spilling over my forearm. Gemma tipped her head back against my shoulder and wiggled her bottom against me as if trying to get closer.

"Gemma..."

My dick obviously didn't give a shit that she was drunk—maybe even drugged, considering her erratic behavior—and stratospherically out of my league. It thickened at the feel of her and pressed against the front of my jeans, instinctively seeking out her heat.

Gemma reached behind me and grasped the back of my thigh, arching her back like a kitten as she rubbed against me. That in itself told me how out of her mind she was. The girl never looked at me with anything other than complete and utter disdain. For her to touch me, let alone intimately like this, was completely out of character.

I peeled her hand away and spun her in my arms. "Look at me." Her glassy eyes flitted around for a moment before locking on mine. "You good?"

"I could be better." She lifted her hand and cupped my erection tenting the front of my jeans, then smiled, slow and sultry. "I could make you feel better, too."

I snatched her hand away. "Gemma, stop."

She leaned forward, pressing her breasts against my chest and pouted up at me. "Why don't you like me?"

I swallowed down the urge to comfort her. It was just the alcohol talking. "Let's just get you to bed. You've had too much to drink."

"Whatever." She rolled her eyes and pulled away from me, her lips turning down in a frown. "I don't know why you hate me so much."

The way she said it sent a little pang of unease through me. "I don't hate you."

"Right." She threw a sad look my way before leaving the bathroom.

I propped my hands on my hips and tipped my head back, drawing in a deep breath. I didn't hate her—I didn't. She was just... young and immature and frustrating as hell. My cock throbbed in my jeans, reminding me once again how long it'd been since I'd had a gorgeous woman throw herself at me.

I adjusted myself, thanking God that I'd had the presence of mind to turn her down. My dick wasn't happy about it, but I liked my job, and I wouldn't jeopardize it, even for her. My only consolation was that Gemma was almost completely inebriated, and with luck, she would forget all about this by the time she woke up tomorrow.

I glanced at my watch. Just after three. Goddamn it. By the time I got home it would be almost four, and I'd have to be up in a couple hours anyway. Resigning myself to staying here for the night, I grimaced as I glanced down at my boots and puke-splattered jeans. I'd definitely experienced worse, but I sure as hell couldn't sleep like that on Gemma's couch.

I peeked out of the bathroom, relieved that she'd crawled into bed. Turning off the light, I cut across the house to the laundry room and toed out of my boots—no saving those suckers—then tossed my shirt and jeans in the washing machine. I'd crash out for a while then dry them in the morning.

Moving through the dark house, I reset the house alarm, used the key fob to lock my truck, then headed back to Gemma's room to check on her. A soft snuffling sound greeted me, and I approached the side of the bed, listening intently to her breathing. By the time she'd left the bathroom, she'd seemed, if not fully coherent, at least slightly less drunk than when we'd left the bar. She made the soft gurgling sound again, and I rolled my eyes. Just what I needed, for her to choke on her own vomit and die in her sleep.

She let out a grumble as I rolled her to her side, then she snuggled back into her pillow and dropped off again with a little snore. I scrubbed one hand over my face before I reluctantly strode around the bed and climbed in the other side. At least this close, I'd be able to know if something was wrong.

I tucked my arms behind my head and closed my eyes, already dreading the morning to come.

ALSO BY MORGAN JAMES

QUENTIN SECURITY SERIES

Twisted Devil – Jason and Chloe

The Devil You Know – Blake and Victoria

Devil in the Details – Xander and Lydia

Devil in Disguise – Gavin and Kate

Heart of a Devil – Vince and Jana

Tempting the Devil – Clay and Abby

Devilish Intent – Con and Grace

Quentin Security Box Set One (Books 1-3)

Quentin Security Box Set Two (Books 4-6)

*Each book is a standalone within the series

RESCUE & REDEMPTION SERIES

Friendly Fire – Grayson and Claire

Cruel Vendetta – Drew and Emery

Silent Treatment – Finn and Harper

Reckless Pursuit – Aiden and Izzy

Dangerous Desires – Vaughn and Sienna

Rescue & Redemption Box Set One (books 1-3)

RETRIBUTION SERIES

Unrequited Love – Jack and Mia, Book One

Undeniable Love – Jack and Mia, Book Two

Unbreakable Love – Jack and Mia, Book Three

Pretty Little Lies – Eric and Jules, Book One

Beautiful Deception – Eric and Jules, Book Two

Sinful Illusions – Fox and Eva, Book One

Sinful Sacrament – Fox and Eva, Book Two

Retribution Series Box Set 1

Retribution Series Box Set 2

Retribution Series Box Set 3

The Complete Retribution Series

STANDALONES

Death Do Us Part

Escape

BAD BILLIONAIRES

(Radish Exclusive)

Depraved

Ravished

Consumed

ABOUT THE AUTHOR

Morgan James is a USA Today bestselling author of contemporary and romantic suspense novels. She spent most of her childhood with her nose buried in a book, and she loves all things romantic, dark, and dirty. She currently resides in Ohio and is living happily ever after with her own alpha hero and their two kids.

www.ingramcontent.com/pod-product-compliance
Lightning Source LLC
Chambersburg PA
CBHW050825190726
48286CB00007B/1990